CW00799125

The Cornish Vintage Jewellery Shop

Copyright © 2024 Elizabeth Holland

All rights reserved

The characters and events portrayed in this book are fictitious. Any similarity to real persons, living or dead, is coincidental and not intended by the author.

No part of this book may be reproduced, or stored in a retrieval system, or transmitted in any form or by any means, electronic, mechanical, photocopying, recording, or otherwise, without express written permission of the publisher.

Cover design: Elizabeth Holland in collaboration with Dawn Cox Photography

Elizabeth Holland is a writer of romance novels. She enjoys the escapism of picking up a book and losing herself in a new world. Elizabeth is a keen advocate for mental health and often speaks out about her own struggles. She writes to escape her own thoughts. When Elizabeth isn't writing, she's usually outside walking the dog. Her favourite walks are when it's cold and rainy, so she can work on her next plot.

Dear reader,

Thank you for picking up The Cornish
Vintage Jewellery Shop.

Padstow-on-Sea is my fictional version of Padstow.
It's just how you might imagine it with little
shops around the harbour, boats bobbing on
the water, and seagulls squawking above.

If you haven't already read The Cornish
Vintage Dress Shop then I'd recommend
picking it up once you're finished.

I hope you enjoy your visit.

Content Warning
I want you to enjoy this book and lose
yourself in the escapism. However, there
is mention of losing a family member to
suicide. If you feel this could be triggering, I'd
recommend trying another of my books.

Lots of love, Elizabeth xxx

CHAPTER ONE

The door wouldn't open. Belle braced her shoulder against it and pushed with all her strength. Hinges groaned, and the door inched open. The bottom scraped against the floor and a high-pitched screech resounded around the shop. Belle breathed in and a musty smell assaulted her senses. She screwed up her nose and left the door ajar to allow the salty sea air to filter in. She took another step into the shop, ignoring the echoes of memories surrounding her.

"How does it look?" her father, Louis, asked.

"It looks like nobody's stepped inside for ten years," Belle replied. She flipped the camera on her phone so Louis could see for himself.

"It's how we left it," Louis said. His French accent thickened, and he cleared his throat.

"Just with a few inches of dust," Belle said, trying to lighten the mood.

"Yes, well, that can be cleaned. When's the builder coming?"

Belle checked her watch. "He's late. Should have been here five minutes ago."

"That's Cornish time for you."

"It's like that in France, too."

Louis let out a harrumph. "I have to leave for an auction. I'll speak to you tonight about what the builder says. Au revoir, ma chérie."

Belle said her goodbyes and hung up. The shop was eerily quiet. Outside, the sun shone brightly in the sky as eager tourists milled around with cups of takeaway coffee. Seagulls lurked at every corner, waiting to swoop down and steal flaky pasties from unsuspecting hands. The water was a hive of activity as skippers bustled around on boats, readying them for their daily outings. It was like the calm before the storm as the little harbour prepared for the daily influx of visitors.

The builder was now ten minutes late and the stuffy air inside the shop felt as though it was becoming thicker with every breath. Belle opened the windows and winced as a chunk of paint came away. It had been ten years since she was last inside the shop. She'd been fourteen years old and life had looked very different. Then everything changed after that phone call. Belle could remember the day as though it were yesterday. She'd finished school and walked to her father's antique shop on the harbour. It was a dismal November day, and the weather was horrendous. Belle was soaked through from the rain and windswept from the gale-force winds. Her father had ushered her into the backroom before she could drip on any of his priceless antiques.

She had sat in his office, warming her hands by the electric heater, when the phone trilled. She knew better than to answer and waited for him. Belle had watched his face turn ashen as he listened.

"Hello?" a male voice with a Cornish twang called from the doorway, pulling Belle from her memories.

Belle jumped and turned to see a pair of green eyes staring at her. The light caught them as they glistened a deep Colombian emerald shade of green.

"Can I help you?" she asked. Her mouth was dry, and it was an effort to get the words out. His sandy hair stuck out in all directions from underneath his baseball cap. He wore a tatty t-shirt which was almost see-through in the bright sunlight and highlighted his toned body. Belle tore her gaze away.

"I'm Nick, your builder," he introduced himself and pointed to the door in an unsaid question.

"You're late," Belle said, motioning for him to come in.

"Sorry. My alarm didn't go off. You know how it is."

Belle frowned. She didn't know. "Does it happen often?"

"More than it should." He winked.

"Brilliant," she sarcastically bit back. "I'm Belle." She held out her hand.

"I was expecting you to be more French," he said and shook her hand. His grasp was firm.

"French?" She glanced down at their hands. He still had her hand clasped in his. At her look, he let go, and Belle took a step back.

"Your email address was French."

"Oh, of course. I've just moved back from France."

"That's a relief. I was worried you'd only speak French."

"My emails were in English." Belle's thoughts were becoming muddled and with it, she was moving away from the tangled emotions that had crept up on her.

"You could have been using a translator." Nick shrugged and looked around the shop.

"I don't speak French."

"Really?"

"Really."

"Nor do I. All I know is Voulez-vous coucher —"

"I think we all know that one," Belle interrupted. A blush rose on her cheeks and she cleared her throat. "Shall we have a look around? I'm only looking for a quote at the moment."

"You won't get anyone else. It's the busiest time of the year. Everyone's getting their building work finished before the season starts. Lucky for you, I'm free."

"Why are you free when everyone else is busy?" Belle raised her eyebrow. His business card had been pinned to the Padstow-on-Sea's community noticeboard. She'd expected a middle-aged man with experience to turn up, not a muscular, Cornish, Ken doll.

"I've just started. You're my first customer. Congratulations." He smiled. His face lit up and a cheeky glint danced in his eyes.

"You've just started?" she enunciated each word. However good-looking he was, it was his experience she was interested in.

"Yep. Lucky you, eh? Right, let's have a look around." He rubbed his hands together before he pulled a pencil from behind his ear and a tatty notepad from the back pocket of his jeans. It was falling apart. "I'll take some notes on my phone instead."

Belle went to take a deep breath but stopped as she saw the dust particles floating through the air. "There's nobody else available," she muttered under her breath and followed him through to the office.

Nick wandered around and made notes.

"So, what's the verdict?" she asked.

"It's structurally sound," he said, nodding as he looked up towards the ceiling.

"I know that. I had a survey." Belle's father had insisted on having a structural survey before he signed the shop over to her.

"What do you want doing?" His gaze bore into hers and a flush rushed across Belle's cheeks.

"The place needs re-plastering and then decorating. The kitchen and bathroom look as though they'd be fine after a good scrub. I'll need some new shelves and cabinets. The office needs painting. It's got all the safes in there and I want to keep them."

Nick raised his eyebrows at her. "What kind of shop are you opening?"

"Vintage jewellery."

He let out a low whistle. "You should probably get those safes serviced."

"Is that a thing?" Belle's brow furrowed. Something else to add to her endless list of things to do.

"No idea. Should be though. Maybe it's a service I should offer." He winked at her again, and Belle ignored the way it made her stomach flutter.

She decided not to point out the pitfalls in his plan. "The shop needs a complete refit," she said, drawing his attention back to the matter at hand. "The shelving is all dated and damp. I think it's best if we rip it out and replace it."

"Sounds good. What did you want to replace it with?"

Belle pulled out her phone and brought up her *Pinterest* app, which was filled with interior inspiration. She didn't know exactly what she wanted, although she had gathered a handful of pictures.

"I could use reclaimed wood to make the shelving units and whitewash them to give them the shabby-chic-meets-nautical style you're going for," Nick said. He held Belle's phone and was studying the picture.

Belle blinked. "You can do that?"

"Woodwork is my speciality. There's not enough demand for it around here, so I've diversified into building work." He handed her back the phone.

"Sounds smart," Belle commented.

"What about security?" asked Nick.

"I've got the safes out the back and I'll look into some CCTV."

"I've got a friend who can do that and he can install a panic button under the till. I'll give him a call."

"Nick, I'm not sure I can afford it."

"He owes me a favour."

"I couldn't ask that."

"I'll sort it," he promised. "So, when do you want me to start?"

"Shouldn't you send me a quote first?" Belle raised her brows.

"I can, but you want to snap me up before someone else does." He smirked, and the edges of Belle's lips quirked upwards. She stifled the smile before he could see it.

"I suppose you've got me backed into a corner, but I expect a first-customer discount."

"Sounds fair."

"So, when can you start?"

"Tomorrow?"

"Don't you need to get permits for skip hire

and stuff like that?" Belle didn't know much about building work, but she suspected the quaint town of Padstow-on-Sea wouldn't appreciate a skip filled with rotting wood on their picturesque seafront.

"I'll fill my van and take it to the skip at the yard."

"Tomorrow sounds good," Belle agreed.

"Perfect. We'll get you open before the end of the season. The winter months can be tough."

"Thanks."

"See you tomorrow, Belle." He waved and Belle's stare fixed on him as he left, already missing how he made her smile.

Alone, Belle glanced around the shop. She should start clearing things to make it easier for Nick in the morning, but being here sent a chill down her spine. It was an empty shell of the once bustling *Louis's Emporium*. Her father's antiques had left Cornwall with them, packed into the back of a hire van. After the death of Belle's mother, Cornwall lost its charm and Louis took Belle home to France. They hadn't been back since.

The shop's beating heart had stopped that day and never started again. Once settled in France, Louis started buying and selling antiques, and Belle spent her spare time working with him. She'd never really settled into their new life. Her poor grasp of the language kept her on the outskirts of the community and her father's successful business afforded a tutor for her, which meant outside of their bubble she had very little contact with children her age. Despite it all, Belle was never lonely. How could she be when she was always surrounded by antiques and the memories they held?

Unable to bear the emptiness any longer, Belle grabbed her keys and locked up. Outside, the sun was high in the sky and the sound of chatter drowned out the gentle crashing of the sea. Belle wound her way through the crowds of tourists to The Little Coffee Shop by the Sea on the opposite side of the harbour. The exterior was painted black with its name in gold swirls above the door. A little brass bell rang out as the door opened. Inside, the dark interior was complemented by the big windows and their sea view. Rich coffee beans and sweet cakes filled the air, and Belle's stomach rumbled. She'd been too nervous to have any breakfast.

"Can I help you?" asked the woman behind the counter. Her hair framed her face in an explosion of corkscrew curls as dark as a starless night in winter. She wore silver rings on both hands, each with intricate detailing on the bands.

"Could I have a cappuccino and a slice of that chocolate cake, please? To take away." Belle pointed to the decadent dark chocolate sponge cake, covered in a tempered ganache with fresh, vibrant berries piled atop. She deserved an indulgent treat after stepping back into the shop after ten years.

"Good choice. I'm Jada, by the way. Owner of this delightful coffee shop and baker of these delicious desserts."

"Lovely to meet you, Jada." Belle smiled

timidly at the woman.

"This is usually the part where you'd introduce yourself." Jada shot her a wink.

"Sorry, I'm out of practice meeting new people." Not that she'd ever been in practice. Her experience with meeting new people was limited to auctions where they all had a passion in common. "I'm Belle. I've taken over the old antique shop." She glossed over the fact it had once been her father's.

"Lovely to meet you, Belle. It'll be nice to have another young female business owner around. Give me a shout if you need anything."

"Thanks, Jada. I doubt I'll be able to stay away from your café for very long." Belle's eyes lingered on the other goodies on display as Jada made her cappuccino.

"I've recently bought a recipe book from an amazing patisserie chef, Carrie Mackenzie, and I need someone to try my creations."

"I'm your girl." Belle relaxed in the woman's presence.

"Perfect. See you soon, Belle." Jada handed her the coffee and a large slice of cake nestled inside a takeaway box.

"Bye," Belle called. "I'm sure you'll be seeing a lot of me."

It was a short walk home, although it was made longer by the tourists milling around and stopping to take pictures down the quaint cobbled streets. Belle had to move someone off her doorstep. Her little cottage had no front garden and tourists could come straight up to her door. She breathed a sigh of relief once she'd closed the door behind her. The cottage was the one place Belle truly felt at home. She'd grown up there with her parents, and it was where her happiest memories lived. Belle set her coffee down on the worktop and got some cutlery for her cake. The forks were all small and Belle suspected they were meant for children. Over the last ten years, Louis had rented out the cottage and an array of other people's belongings had been left behind. Belle was thankful for it since her budget hadn't stretched to furnishing somewhere. She'd made a few changes to make it feel like home. Belle had found a nautical blue and white striped rug in a charity shop, which she'd put down on the bare wood floors in her bedroom. The existing furniture was sparse, so she'd ended up with a jumble of cheap charity shop finds and expensive antiques. As a moving-in gift, her father had sent her a catalogue for an auction and told her to let him know what she needed. Belle had wanted to circle everything but had settled for an antique oak console table, a Georgian writing bureau, and an antique Rococo walnut bed frame. Her father had bought it all and had it shipped straight to her. He'd also picked up an old chair with worn blue upholstery, a collection of mismatched plant pots, and a hatstand. It was an odd collection, yet somehow, Belle had thrown it all together, and it worked.

At the back of the cottage was a small courtyard. It was a combination of weed-choked flower beds around the perimeter and an overgrown hedge. With a little time and effort, it could be pretty. For now, Belle was happy to have some outside space to herself. She sat on the bench and put her coffee beside her. The cake was rich and delicious as she sat with the sun shining on her. In the silence, she allowed her mind to wander over the day. Going into the shop had stirred up a plethora of emotions and memories that Belle would rather have forgotten about. Nick's appearance had silenced her mind and she couldn't help the way he'd made her smile. She was looking forward to working with him. Despite his infuriating cheeky charm, he would be the perfect distraction to her past.

Belle pulled her phone out to find an email from Nick. She was pleasantly surprised by his quote. He'd included a five per cent discount for being his first customer. The email ended with a jaunty 'see you tomorrow' followed by a thumbs-up emoji. She smiled and emailed back, reminding him to be on time.

CHAPTER TWO

Belle had tossed and turned all night. Eventually, she gave up on sleep and padded downstairs to make a cup of tea. She grabbed the powder blue enamel biscuit tin and lit a fire in the living room. The past had been stirred up, and she didn't know how to move on. Over the last few weeks, Belle's energy had been focused on making the cottage home. If she was honest, she'd been using the cottage to distract herself from the task of setting up the shop. Yesterday was the first time she'd stepped inside. Before that, she'd peered through the window until the memories overwhelmed her. Belle wished her father was with her, but he hadn't been able to face the memories and she could understand that. The kettle whistled furiously as it boiled and pulled Belle from her thoughts. She swooped down to take it off the hob and stop the piercing noise. The sun hadn't risen yet, and she had neighbours on either side.

The fire crackled in the hearth as she curled up on the sofa and dipped a biscuit in the tea. Her phone buzzed. It was an email from Nick. She opened it and chuckled. It simply read, 'Don't worry. I'm already awake. See you soon.'

As the sun peeked above the horizon and the final flickers of flames extinguished, Belle went to get ready. She pulled on a pair of leggings and an old oversized t-shirt she'd picked up from a market in France. It had a cartoon croissant on the front. She secured her hair in a bun and grabbed her backpack before heading out into the morning. It was early enough for there to still be a chill in the air. Seagulls squawked and circled as she walked down the cobbled path to the harbour. The sun rose above the sea, and Belle paused to take it in. A golden glow filled the sky. There wasn't a cloud in sight. She closed her eyes, took a deep breath, and smiled. This was why she was back in Cornwall. She was home.

"Morning, Frenchie!" Nick's voice shattered the moment.

"Call me Frenchie again and I'll need a nickname discount on your bill." Belle put her hands on her hips.

Nick chuckled and held up his hands. "Sorry, French—Belle." He smirked, and the corners of her mouth tugged upward, although she quickly smothered it.

She tilted her head and looked at him. He wore jeans and a t-shirt with a Bob the Builder cartoon across it. She raised an eyebrow and continued her assessment. His hair was pushed back under a cap and his tired eyes glimmered in the early morning sunlight. Belle realised she could happily lose herself in them.

She cleared her throat. "Come on, Bob the Builder." She turned and walked towards the shop.

"My mum got me it," he said, following her.

"I'm not sure that makes it any better." Belle chuckled as she unlocked the door. It was stuck again. She pushed against it, but it wouldn't budge.

"Shall I?" Nick offered.

Belle stood aside and watched as Nick tensed. The muscles in his arms rose as he pushed against the door. Belle swallowed and turned her gaze towards the sea.

Within a couple of seconds, she heard the scuff of the door opening, followed by a curse from Nick as he fell in.

"Are you okay?" asked Belle.

Nick had stumbled into the shop and fallen into a shelving unit, which had collapsed beneath him. He groaned but nodded. "I'll look at the door first."

"Perfect. What shall I get started on?" Belle glanced around and blew out a long, slow breath. Everything needed to be dismantled and taken out of the shop.

"You don't have to help, Belle. That wasn't why I gave you a discount."

"I know, but surely between the two of us we can get it finished quicker."

"Why don't you start picking all the debris off the floor? I've got a skip bag in the boot. Don't fill it so much I can't lift it. Let me grab you some gloves."

With her instructions, Belle set about picking the debris up off the floor and throwing it into the big yellow bag Nick had brought in. He was humming to himself as he sanded the door frame.

Outside, the harbour was growing busy with the day's tourists.

"You should get a sign printed to let people know you're opening a jewellery shop," Nick said.

"That's a good idea. I'll have a look online tonight. Thanks."

They lapsed back into silence. When Belle had finished her task, Nick showed her how to unscrew the shelving units, and she dismantled the smaller ones near the old counter.

"Do you want to keep the current layout with the till towards the back of the shop?" Nick asked. He was taking down the old counter. Belle's heart lurched as he used a hammer to break the wood apart. Although it had long faded, there was once a floral mural painted by her mother on the front. Blooming lilacs and roses had wound around the burr walnut, with the shop's name painted in the centre. As the damp inside the shop had grown, it had feasted on the wood and there was no longer a trace of her mother's artwork. The ghost of it was still there and a tiny piece of Belle's heart broke away as she said goodbye.

"I think so. I know Dad put a lot of thought

into the shop's layout so I'll trust his judgement." Her voice was strained as she swallowed back a wave of emotion.

"Your dad used to own this shop?" Nick dropped the piece of wood he was holding.

"Yeah. Didn't you realise?"

"No. I thought you'd bought it. A few years back there was talk of the shop going to auction and we all assumed it had gone ahead."

"We couldn't part with it in the end. My mother grew up here and inherited the shop from her grandfather. It didn't feel right for it to leave the family." Belle and her father had spent many late nights sitting out on their terrace discussing what to do with the shop. Eventually, Belle decided it was time she went home and faced her past.

"Right." Nick's voice wobbled.

Belle turned to look at him. His tanned face had turned ashen. "Nick, what's wrong?" she asked.

"You're Belle Roux, aren't you?"

"Yes," she answered. "It's on my email signature. Didn't you see it?"

"I should pay more attention."

"What's wrong?"

"You look different," he finally said. He studied her, and her face stiffened as she forced a neutral expression.

"What do you mean, I look different?"

"I remember you from school."

"We went to school together?" Belle's voice shook. She turned and loaded the shelves into the skip bag. Her memories were threatening to come flooding back and she couldn't allow it.

"You don't remember me?"

Belle dropped a heavy piece of wood into the bag, and the thump echoed throughout the shop.

"I don't remember much about my time at school. I've blocked it out."

"That's understandable."

Belle felt as though the walls were closing in on her. She shut her eyes with her back towards Nick and dug her fingernails into the palm of her hands. The pain kept her in the moment and stopped her mind from dredging up memories she had buried.

"I think we could both do with a break," Nick said. He was strolling towards the door. "Why don't I get us lunch from The Little Coffee Shop by the Sea?" He left without waiting for her reply.

"Lucky I don't have any food allergies," Belle muttered to herself.

Alone in the shop, Belle pushed aside the rubble and stumbled through to the office. Her father's wooden chair still sat in the middle, but she didn't dare sit on it. With the rotted wood, she'd fall right through. This office had once been her haven. She'd get off the school bus, come into her father's shop and shut herself away in the office while he worked. Inside these walls, she'd read countless books ranging from fantasy to how to spot a genuine 18th-century antique. She would escape to new worlds or revel in the memories of the past to keep herself from going over the horrid words other children had thrown at her in school.

"Here." Nick handed her a receipt.

"Oh. Do you want cash, or I can transfer it straight into your account?"

"Belle, no. Sorry, that's not why I gave you it." He put the brown paper bag with their sandwiches on the only clear surface. "Jada wrote her number on the back for you. She asked if you wanted to pop around to the café tonight for a drink."

Belle turned the receipt over to see Jada's number scribbled. "Thank you." She took out her phone and sent a message to Jada, thanking her and asking what time she should arrive.

"Lunch is my treat," Nick said. He'd moved to sit on the window ledge at the front of the shop. He'd taken his cap off and his blonde hair stuck out in every direction.

"Thanks. I'll get lunch tomorrow, or maybe I'll bring some sandwiches in. This could get expensive."

"You don't have to be here every day. Believe it or not, I know what I'm doing." His tone was clipped.

"I'm not checking up on you, I promise. I need to be here to keep myself busy." She also needed to get used to being in the shop without opening a vortex of emotions.

Belle took her sandwich and sat beside him. It wasn't very comfortable, but it was nice to rest her feet.

"So, how do you go about setting up a vintage jewellery shop? It must be expensive."

"It can be."

"How have you financed it?" Nick took a bite of his sandwich. He was sitting with one ankle resting on his knee.

"Why?" Belle asked, picking at her sandwich. It made her uncomfortable when people asked questions about money.

"Sorry, I didn't mean to offend you. I'm curious. It was expensive to set myself up. I've hired most of my tools to keep the cost low. I was just wondering how you've done it, as you obviously can't hire jewellery."

"Actually, you can," Belle muttered. The moment she said it she regretted letting the words escape, knowing Nick would ask more questions.

"How?" he asked.

"My father has a large inventory of jewellery. He's loaning me some pieces. I'll sell them and then we'll split the profit. I'll then reinvest the profit in more jewellery. I also have my own collection of antique and vintage jewellery that I've gathered over the last ten years."

"Wow, you're super organised," he said before taking a sip of his takeaway coffee.

"You think?" Belle asked, glancing at him. He looked lost in thought, yet there was no hint of judgment on his face. She'd worried people would think she'd chosen the easy option by taking over her father's shop.

"Of course. I might ask my dad if he'll rent me some of his tools when he's not using them. Could be cheaper for me and Dad would benefit, too." Nick was talking to himself.

"You don't think I'm a spoilt nepo baby?" Belle's voice sounded small and weak.

"You're here helping me clear out the mouldy, rotten wood. I saw you picking a splinter out of your hand earlier. Actually, are you up to date with a tetanus?" Nick didn't wait for a reply. "You're obviously here to make this work. I wouldn't have my own building business without the help of my father. Most of the shops on the harbour have been passed down through generations. We look out for each other around here. That's not necessarily a bad thing."

Belle mulled over Nick's words as she sipped her coffee. Nobody had looked out for her at school.

"I have savings, too. I've been trading antiques with my father since I could speak. He'd always take me to auctions, even when we moved to France, as he had nobody to look after me. The first few times, my dad gave me a twenty euro budget but I soon made enough profit that I didn't need any pocket money from him." Belle smiled as she remembered her first big sale. She'd picked up a pair of pearl earrings from a flea market in a small village they'd driven through. The woman selling them had assumed they were costume jewellery. She'd bought them for fifty cents and sold them for one hundred euros. From that moment, Belle had invested all her time and money into jewellery. Her father's friends had called her The Magpie.

"You've done well for yourself, Belle."

"Thanks, Nick." She smiled at him and he returned it. Belle ignored the feelings that rushed through her at the sight of his smile.

CHAPTER THREE

It had been a long day, and they'd made real progress. The door no longer stuck, and the debris had been cleared. They'd agreed that tomorrow they would dismantle the rest of the shelving units and begin the tedious task of driving the debris to Nick's yard. Belle was glad to be home. She jumped in the shower to wash off the day's dirt. She had an hour until she was due to meet Jada at The Little Coffee Shop by the Sea. Belle took her time drying her hair in a sleek style. It was naturally wavy, and she rarely did anything to it. She pulled on a beige jumper with flowers embroidered on it and matched it with a pair of white wide-leg trousers. The trousers had a thick belt which cinched in her waist. It was rare Belle had the chance to dress up. In France, most of her time was spent in auction houses, making her way through mountains of dusty furniture to find hidden gems. However, that hadn't stopped her father's friend, Estelle, from treating her to various outfits whenever she saw them. Belle was looking forward to working in the shop and having the opportunity to show off her pretty clothes. Tonight's jumper was one she'd inherited from her mother. There was a seamstress in their village who had altered and embroidered some of Belle's mother's clothes. Her father had cried when she'd brought them home.

Belle opened her jewellery box and turned her attention to her favourite part of getting ready. Louis had commissioned the box as a present for her eighteenth birthday to keep everyday jewellery inside. It was in the shape of a heart and covered in pink velvet with a lace trim. Belle kept her more expensive pieces in a safe at the bottom of her wardrobe. Glancing at the jewellery in front of her, Belle picked out her favourite ring. It was a plain gold band with a pattern around it. The ring itself was nothing special. It was from the 1930s and had belonged to a woman named Juliane. Belle had seen the ring at an auction house outside of Paris. It had been nestled in a leather box and an elegant-looking lady had been peering down at it. Belle had sidled up to her and commented on how beautiful the ring was. The woman introduced herself as Véronique, Juliane's granddaughter. Véronique was auctioning off countless lots to facilitate a move overseas. She'd told Belle how Juliane's father had bought her the ring for her thirteenth birthday shortly before he passed away. Belle had immediately felt a connection to the young girl who had lost a parent. The ring had cost Belle her entire budget for the day, but she'd walked away with it proudly on her finger.

With the ring chosen, Belle pulled out a gold necklace to match it. She didn't know the history of this piece. It had a gold heart locket on a delicate yellow gold chain. Inside the locket was a faded picture of a little girl. It was still there, hidden beneath a picture of her mother. Belle hadn't been able to take it out, knowing that many years ago, someone had lovingly placed it inside. That little girl meant something to someone and Belle would honour that.

A glance at her phone told Belle she had twenty minutes. She gathered her bag and shoes and left. At twenty-four years old, Belle had no experience with being invited around to a friend's for the evening. From the networking events she'd attended, she knew it was always polite to bring something.

The harbour was still busy with people out for dinner or getting last-minute ice cream before the shops shut. Next to the pub, there was a newsagent. She'd made a few trips down for milk and the odd packet of biscuits but mostly avoided it since the prices were inflated for tourists.

Tonight, the newsagent was quiet. It was small yet well-stocked with every sweet or chocolate bar you could ask for. Belle breezed past them, reminding herself that Jada would no doubt have something sweet for them. The alcohol was at the back of the shop. Belle instinctively picked up a bottle of Rioja and went to walk to the till when she realised she didn't know if Jada drank red.

"Belle?" someone called. She looked up from the bottle and turned to see Nick beside her.

"Hi, Nick," she said distractedly.

"Almost didn't notice you without a layer of dust," he teased.

Belle laughed and diverted her attention from the wine. She focused on Nick and noticed he was staring at her. His gaze roamed across her, and the familiar sparkle was in his eyes.

"I didn't think Jada would be so welcoming if I turned up in today's outfit." Belle's gaze looked back towards the shelf. It was a warm night and Nick's look had heated her to the core.

"Good point."

"You off out?" Belle asked. Nick was also looking a lot smarter than when she'd last seen him. He was in a fresh pair of jeans and a white Oxford shirt with the sleeves rolled up, showing off his tanned forearms. His hair was styled back from his face. He was very attractive and Belle's body recognised it as a fizz of attraction flew through her.

"Yes. This girl I'm...um...seeing, it's her sister's birthday. They're having a barbecue." He stepped forward and picked up a few bottles of Prosecco.

"Have fun," Belle said. Even to her own ears, her voice sounded overly chirpy. It was the first time he'd mentioned a girlfriend.

"You okay? You looked confused when I walked over."

"I popped in to pick up a bottle of wine to take to Jada's, but I don't know what she drinks." Belle held up the bottle of red.

"She'll drink that," Nick said, nodding.

"Really?"

"I used to work at the pub and I've served her many times."

"A barman. You certainly get around." Belle's eyes widened as she realised what she'd said. "Sorry, I didn't mean it like that."

Nick chuckled. "I'll let it slide this time." He winked and Belle's grip on the wine tightened. "Go on, you go first or else you'll be late." He inclined his head towards the till.

"Are you sure? You've got your hands full. I don't mind waiting."

"Go on, Belle."

Belle could feel him behind her as she walked to the till and paid.

"See you tomorrow," she said.

"See you tomorrow, Frenchie!" he called back.

Without turning around, Belle stuck her middle finger up at him. His chuckle followed her out of the newsagent. Once outside, Belle sucked in a deep breath of fresh sea air.

Jada was waiting for her outside the coffee shop. "Hi." She waved.

"Hi, Jada. Thank you for inviting me." Belle held up the bottle of wine. "I got this for you. Nick said you drank red."

"Nick, hey?" Jada laughed and took the bottle. "Come in."

Belle followed Jada into the shop and through a door at the back, which led to a flight of stairs. "Welcome to my humble abode," Jada said, opening the front door to her flat.

"I didn't realise you lived above. What an amazing view." Belle kicked off her pumps and walked across the room to the windows, which looked out over the harbour.

"It's stunning. If you stay long enough, you'll see the sunset," Jada said from the kitchen.

The living area and kitchen were open plan and Jada's walls were covered in pictures of her family and friends. Bags of flour and icing sugar littered her kitchen counters, and a stack of recipe books covered the breakfast bar. On the opposite side of the room was a black velvet sofa covered in blood-red scatter cushions.

"Sorry about the mess. I've been experimenting with new recipes. Make yourself at home. What can I get you to drink?"

"I'll have whatever you're having," Belle said. She sat on one of the wooden stools at the breakfast bar.

"Let's open this red. It's my favourite." Jada pulled out two black wine glasses and poured them a generous measure. "Cheers." She handed Belle her glass and held hers up to clink.

"Cheers," Belle echoed.

"What brings you to Padstow-on-Sea?" Jada gestured towards the sofa, and Belle followed.

"I grew up here. My mum, Kerenza, was Cornish, and my dad, Louis, is French."

"Was?" Jada slapped a hand over her mouth. "Sorry, I didn't mean to say that out loud."

"It's okay. My mum died ten years ago. That's when we left Cornwall. My dad couldn't cope with all the memories of my mother."

"Moving must have been tough."

"Not really. I loved Cornwall, but it was hardly the happiest of childhoods here."

Jada stared at Belle and chewed her lip.

"You can ask," prompted Belle.

"Why didn't you have a happy childhood here?" she asked, hesitation filling her voice.

"I was the odd one out at school. There was a lot of bullying. There was this one girl, Tegen, who despised me. Ironically, her name means pretty, as does mine in French. That's where the similarities between us began and ended." Belle let out a sharp laugh.

"You don't have to tell me this," Jada reassured her.

"Sorry, I shouldn't have. I've no idea if Tegen still lives here. Do you know her? Have I put you in an awkward position? Shall I leave?" Belle was rambling, and she couldn't stop the words from spilling out.

"Take a breath." Jada took the wineglass from her hand and placed it on the floor.

"I'm sorry," Belle muttered. She took a deep breath and pinched the bridge of her nose. "I'm not very good at the whole people thing."

Jada laughed. "What would a girly evening with wine be without some oversharing?"

"I've never really had a girly evening." Belle's attention had wandered to the window. The sky was slowly darkening as the sun slipped below the horizon.

"Well, here's to many more." Jada handed her the wineglass. "Maybe you didn't overshare. Perhaps you saw yourself in me. I was bullied too. Mostly for my skin colour, although sometimes it was because of the food in my lunch box or the way my hair was different. My mum's Nigerian, but my dad's Cornish."

"Oh, Jada. I'm sorry."

"Let's not allow those bullies to ruin our Cornwall."

"No. This is our home and we have a right to be happy here," agreed Belle.

Jada nodded. "So, you don't know if she still lives here?"

"I'm not sure. It's been ten years. I don't even know if I'd recognise her."

"I don't think I'd recognise any of my bullies either. I grew up on the Cornwall-Devon border, so I don't have to worry about walking down the street and bumping into them."

"Is that why you moved here?"

"That and a bad break-up." Jada's stare was

fixed on the wineglass in her hand. "Anyway, enough about me. Tell me about your shop."

They chatted as the sun set and Belle watched in awe as the sky lit up in a beautiful muddle of blue, gold, and soft pink. A timer rang, signalling that their dinner was ready.

Jada had set the breakfast bar for them to sit and eat at.

"It's nothing fancy, just a lasagna."

"It smells amazing," Belle said. It had been a while since she'd had a home-cooked meal.

"How's the work going at the shop?" Jada asked.

"We started clearing it today. Do you know much about Nick's experience?"

"As a builder or in bed?" Jada raised her eyebrows and giggled.

"I think you've had too much wine. As a builder, obviously." Belle rolled her eyes.

"Obviously. His dad did the building work on the coffee shop, and Nick made most of the fittings. I don't know him well, but I've seen him around and everyone seems to love him."

"He's been great. It worries me that I'm his first customer."

"Are you overthinking it?"

"Most likely. This lasagna is amazing, by the way. I might have to ask you for some cooking lessons. On a good day, I can boil pasta, but that's the extent of my culinary expertise."

"Maybe I could pop over to yours at the

weekend and we could cook something?" Jada suggested.

"I'd love that." Belle was dreading the weekend. Without the distraction of clearing the shop, she'd be forced to confront everything she'd been feeling.

"Perfect. And you can update me on how things are going with Nick."

"They're not going anywhere. He has a girlfriend."

"That's disappointing. So, what's your dating history look like?" asked Jada.

"There's not much to say. I've dated a few men I've met at auctions. We had our love for antiques in common, but nothing beyond that. It made for some very awkward morning after conversations." Belle giggled.

"Belle, that's tragic." Jada laughed with her.

"I know. I'm happy on my own, though."

"Cheers to that," Jada said and refilled their glasses.

CHAPTER FOUR

Belle winced as she pulled her sunglasses off and rooted around inside her bag for the shop's keys. The bag was overflowing with letters she needed to catch up on, lunch for herself and Nick, and colour swatches that had arrived yesterday.

"I take it the wine was a hit," Nick called from behind.

Belle groaned and turned to face him, wincing as the sun shone on her. "Wine and lack of sleep. I didn't leave Jada's until the early hours of the morning."

"You didn't have to turn up. You've employed me to do this for you."

"I want to. Hold on, I need to find the keys." She knelt on the floor and emptied out the bag's contents. The last thing to fall out was the single key for the shop. She kept it apart from her bunch of keys to stop the powder blue silk ribbon attached to it from getting damaged. It was the one Kerenza had always worn in her hair.

Nick knelt and helped her pick up everything. She glanced at him and caught the hint of a smirk on his face. Belle scowled and grabbed the last letter from his hands.

"I've got a kettle and other bits in my van. I'll get them while you open up and then I can make you a coffee. Looks like you might need it."

"Thanks," Belle said. She unlocked the door, and it opened with ease. Using a heavy piece of wood, Belle propped it open to let some air in.

"Do you mind if I use the office?" Nick asked, carrying a kettle, a mini fridge, and a shopping bag. "The kitchenette needs a good scrub before we prepare anything in there."

Belle was standing in the doorway, taking big gulps of the fresh air.

"I'll take that as a yes." He chuckled.

Belle took a final deep breath, and the wave of nausea subsided. She needed to eat something. "Do you have biscuits?" she asked, following Nick into the office.

"I don't usually share my biscuits."

"What if I promise to bring some custard creams tomorrow?"

Nick's brow furrowed. Belle could see him weighing the pros and cons. "Fine, but they have to be a whole unopened packet."

Belle nodded and made a mental note to pop into the newsagent later. Nick set up the mini fridge and kettle and unpacked the contents of the shopping bag. He'd thought of everything from milk to spoons for their drinks.

"We'll have this then start clearing the rubble and taking down the remaining shelving. I need to start thinking about ordering flooring, paint, and all that fancy interior stuff at some point. We'll have a sit down with the brochure and you can let me know exactly what you want."

Belle hummed her agreement and took a tentative bite from the digestive. Despite the packet already being opened, it was fresh.

"Don't look so worried. My mum packed all this for me."

"Now that makes a lot more sense." Belle laughed and wandered back into the shop. As hard as she tried, she couldn't visualise her plans for the interior. Despite the endless *Pinterest* boards, she couldn't make a decision. All she could see was her father's shop.

"How was your evening with Jada?" Nick asked.

"It was lovely. I should make more of an effort to get to know the other business owners." She sighed.

"There's a monthly meeting for business owners. They all get together and meet for a coffee. You could come along and meet everyone at once. You'll already know me and Jada."

"I'd like that. Thanks, Nick." Belle smiled at how thoughtful he could be.

"If you want to meet more people, then come to the pub tonight. I'll be there with some friends."

Belle quickly swallowed her mouthful of coffee. "That's not really my kind of thing," she said. "I'm not very good with groups of people."

"It's alcohol and chatting. Like you did with Jada yesterday. What's not to like?"

"I'll think about it," Belle lied. She'd already made up her mind. There was no way she was going to the pub tonight. Even if she wanted to, she'd made a promise to herself when she woke that morning that she'd never touch another drop of alcohol.

It was another long day and Belle's muscles ached from all the lifting. She'd often helped her father rearrange his antique furniture in the barn at their home, but it didn't compare to the physical toll of stripping the shop. Belle soaked her sore muscles in the bath when she got home. After jerking herself awake, she got out and pulled on her pyjamas.

"What's for dinner?" she muttered to herself. Unaccustomed to living alone, Belle had noticed she'd often speak to herself in the evenings. Earlier, she'd left the shop and gone to the newsagents to buy some custard creams for tomorrow, but she'd forgotten to see if they had anything for dinner. Her fridge was empty, but there was a frozen microwave meal at the bottom of her freezer. Belle stabbed the plastic and put it in the microwave. It would take a few minutes, so she phoned her dad. She wouldn't be long. He wasn't very good on the phone.

"Hello, Louis Roux," he answered on the second ring.

"Dad, your mobile shows you who's calling," Belle reminded him for what felt like the hundredth time.

"Belle, you know I don't understand this modern technology."

"How are you?" Belle sat on the sofa and tucked her legs underneath her. She missed her father. After her mother died and they moved to France, he'd been all she had. Together, they'd thrown themselves into their shared passion for antiques and muddled through the heart-wrenching grief.

"It's quiet around here. I went to an auction today. There was lots of costume jewellery. You would have loved it."

"I wish I'd been with you." Belle took a deep breath to collect herself.

"There'll be plenty of auctions in the future. I ordered a few bits for you. They should be delivered in the next week or two."

"Thanks, Dad."

Her father cleared his throat. "How's the shop refit?" Belle knew from his tone that he was struggling, too.

"We've almost gutted the place. I still need to make some final decisions on the interior."

"That's unlike you, Belle. You normally have a

vision for these things."

"I know. For some reason, I'm finding it difficult to know what I want."

The microwave pinged, but Belle ignored it.

"Whatever you choose will look lovely. Keep me updated on how it's going so I can book a ferry in time to get there for your opening."

"You're coming over?" Belle's voice caught in her throat.

"Of course. I wouldn't miss your grand opening. Besides, I don't trust some of the pieces with a courier. I'd rather deliver them to you myself."

Belle nodded, even though her father couldn't see her. She knew he was lying. They often used the same courier to take things between France and England, and Louis had trusted him with high-value items before.

"I can't wait to see you," Belle admitted. For the first time in her life, she was truly alone, and it was leaving her vulnerable to her thoughts and emotions. Things she'd buried ten years ago were creeping back into her consciousness.

"I can't wait to see you either. Belle, are you happy?" her father's voice was quiet.

"Honestly, Dad? I'm not sure. France never felt like home, but I had you and our life. Now, it feels like home, but I don't have you and I've lost everything I'd grown to know." She let out a sigh and massaged her temple.

"You'll settle in. Push yourself to go out and meet people. I know everywhere is filled with memories of your mother, but don't lose yourself in her shadow, Belle. You're as beautiful, funny, and amazing as she was. You don't have to hide behind her memory."

Belle couldn't speak without a sob escaping her. "I love you, Dad," she whispered.

"Love you. I'll see you soon."

Belle clutched her phone and stared at the empty fireplace. Was she hiding in her mother's shadow? Belle had always been timid because of how others had treated her. With the right support, she didn't know who she could be. Maybe it was time she found out. Padstow-on-Sea would never be home if she didn't make the effort.

With a groan, Belle went to get her dinner from the microwave. If she was going to make an effort, she should go to the pub. She carried her dinner upstairs and took a mouthful before she went to her wardrobe. She'd moved into her childhood bedroom. The two bedrooms were much the same size, and she'd opted to leave her parents' bedroom as the spare room. It looked nothing like it had when they'd lived there ten years ago, however, it was a step too far for Belle.

Deciding to keep it casual, Belle pulled out a fresh pair of black leggings, a navy striped jumper, and a pair of knee-high, flat, black boots. She dressed quickly and took another bite of her dinner, careful not to drop it down herself. With a quick burst of the hairdryer and some hair oil, her hair was ready. She put some light makeup on and finished her dinner as she contemplated what jewellery to wear. Some women chose clothes or makeup to boost their confidence, but Belle wore jewellery. She pulled out her favourite gold ring and spotted the gold Tiffany necklace below. It was eighteen-carat yellow gold. The pendant was a small heart with a keyhole lock in the centre. It was much smaller and more delicate than its modern counterparts. Belle fumbled with the clasp as her hands shook. The clasp snapped shut, and Belle glanced at her reflection in the mirror. Her mother's pale green eyes stared back at her. She bit back the tears and squared her shoulders, remembering her father's warning not to live in her mother's shadow. Cornwall was her home too, and she would make this work.

It was a warm evening and by the time Belle reached the pub, she regretted wearing a jumper and boots. The Cornish Arms was on the edge of the harbour and boasted an undisturbed view towards the sea. In recent years, it had undergone a facelift to fit the trendy image of the harbour. However, Belle still remembered The Cornish Arms of her childhood where the garish carpet clashed with the green walls. Now, the outside had been stripped back to the brickwork and huge hanging baskets hung, blooming with an array of brightly coloured flowers. Wooden tables and chairs filled the front terrace, each one occupied with people laughing, chatting, and drinking. Belle squeezed past everyone to the doorway. She pushed her way inside and immediately regretted her decision to come. Inside was hot and stuffy, and the noise of people was overwhelming. Her instincts urged her to turn around and walk out. Nobody would ever have to know about this. Belle sighed; she couldn't turn around and leave because she would know. She drew her shoulders down and held her head up as she pushed her way to the bar.

There was no sign of Nick, so Belle ordered an alcohol-free beer and stood by the bar, surveying her surroundings. All the tables were full and there was a crush of people standing drinking and talking. The pub looked nothing like the one she remembered from her childhood. A flagstone floor replaced the sticky red carpet, and the walls were a fresh white. Layers of thick white paint had been sanded off the beams, leaving them exposed.

"I didn't think you'd come!" Nick said as he pushed past a group of men to greet her.

"No, I hadn't planned to, then I realised I need to integrate myself."

People around them had turned to look and were paying attention to their conversation.

"We don't bite, I promise." Nick beamed and Belle fought to extinguish the sparks he lit inside her. The smouldering embers glowed as he slung an arm around her shoulders.

"Sorry, I'm not very good at meeting new people." That was a lie. Belle was great at meeting new people at auction houses. She only struggled when she had nothing in common with them.

"Come on, let me introduce you to everyone."

He guided her through the crowd of curious locals.

Nick led Belle to the back of the pub where a conservatory had been added, with extra seating. Fairy lights were strung from the ceiling and a cosy atmosphere filled the room. The chatter was quieter and the open windows let in a soft breeze. For the first time since she'd stepped inside The Cornish Arms, Belle felt as though she could breathe.

"We're sat over the back." Nick pulled back his arm and walked ahead. Belle followed, his tall frame blocking the view. She allowed her nerves to simmer away as a distraction from the loss of his touch. Her reaction to him was unnerving, and she was sure it was simply because it was a novelty to be working with a man around her age who was objectively speaking, handsome.

"Everyone, this is Belle," announced Nick.

Belle had lost herself in her thoughts and hadn't realised they'd come to a halt by a table. There were six seats, with five occupied. She plastered a smile on her face as she readied herself to meet everyone.

"Belle Roux," a nasally voice filled her ears, and Belle recoiled at the memories it stirred.

"Belle, this is Tegen. I'm guessing you remember Belle from school, T?" Nick took the seat beside Tegen, leaving Belle standing alone in front of a table of her childhood bullies. The blood drained from Belle's face as she realised Tegen was Nick's girlfriend.

"Oh, I remember Belle," Tegen said with a

sneer across her face. She looked the same as she had at fourteen. Her blonde hair fell, framing her heart-shaped face, and her piercing blue eyes still sparkled underneath long lashes. The girl next to Tegen giggled.

Belle felt her teenage self cowering inside. She picked up her feet and pushed her way back through the crowds. Nick shouted after her, but Belle didn't look back. Outside in the harbour, Belle fought to steady her breath. She wandered over to the barrier and leant against it. Going to the pub had been a stupid idea.

Belle could hear their footsteps coming closer. She squeezed her eyes shut and pressed herself against the locker, hoping they wouldn't see her.

"Can anyone else smell that?" Tegen's voice filled the school hallway, and the footsteps stopped.

Belle held her breath.

"I smell it. It smells like second hand clothes," Tegen's sidekick said and the group of girls dissolved into giggles.

Belle balled her fists at her sides and took a deep breath. "What do you want?" she shouted at the girls and stepped away from the lockers.

"She's getting angry," Tegen teased.

"What's your problem?" Belle growled back. Her insides were doing somersaults, but she'd promised her

dad she would stand up for herself the next time the girls said something.

"You're my problem." Tegen stepped closer to her and crossed her arms as she stared straight at Belle.

Belle forced her legs to step forward and met Tegen's gaze. She had to crane her neck up since Tegen was the tallest in the year, but Belle squared her shoulders and held her ground.

"Leave me alone," Belle shouted at the top of her lungs. Her face turned bright red with exertion and tears threatened to fall.

"She's mad, like her mum," one of Tegen's friends shouted from behind.

"My mum says hers has to take tablets just to get out of bed every morning," Tegen added.

"You're a nasty piece of work, Tegen Thomas," Belle echoed her mother's words.

"Girls, what's going on here?" A teacher had walked out of a classroom at the sound of shouting.

"Belle's upset and we were checking on her," Tegen's face morphed into one of innocence as she swivelled on her heel to look at the teacher.

"What's wrong, Belle?" asked the teacher.

There was no point in telling the teacher about the way Tegen and her friends had treated her. She'd tried before and somehow they always spun the story in their favour, leaving Belle in trouble. At eight years old, Belle had already learned to keep her head down.

"I'm not feeling very well, Miss," she stuttered, staring at a mark on the floor.

"Oh, dear. Perhaps Miss Thomas could take you

to the nurse?" suggested the teacher.

"I can make my own way there, Miss. Thank you." Belle picked up her feet and trudged down the hallway before anyone could insist on Tegen accompanying her. She could hear the girls being praised for how thoughtful they'd been.

As Belle sat on the edge of the nurse's bed, her feet swung beneath her and she replayed Tegen's words. She'd known her mother took tablets every morning. When Belle was little, she'd asked what they were, and Kerenza had simply told her they were to help her feel happy. She hadn't thought about them again and had accepted her mother's explanation.

"Your dad's here," the nurse announced from the hallway.

Belle picked up her schoolbag and hopped down from the bed. Her dad glanced at her and took her hand without speaking.

"I'm sorry, Dad," Belle said once they were in the car on their way back to the harbour. "I tried to stand up to them, but it didn't work."

"Let's go home for a sandwich, then we can open the shop for the afternoon," Louis said and shot her a sad smile.

"Dad?" Belle asked as they turned the corner into the harbour.

"Yes, Belle?"

"I think I'd like to try some of Mummy's happy pills."

Louis made a strange noise and pulled the car over. "What do you mean, Belle?" He turned to face her.

"I'd like to wake up feeling happy every day."

"There's more to your mother's pills than feeling happy, Belle."

"But Mummy said she takes them every morning to feel happy."

"She does, but it's because she's not very well and the tablets fix the problem."

"So they wouldn't work on me?" Belle sagged against the chair.

"I'm afraid not."

"The girls at school were talking about Mum's pills."

Louis scrubbed a hand across his face before he spoke. "I'm sorry, Belle. I didn't realise they knew. We can keep this a secret between us? Oui? Sorry." He gripped the steering wheel. "I don't want to upset your mother."

Belle's heart lurched at the idea of making her mother sad. "Of course. I won't tell her."

"Come on. Let's go get some lunch, then you can help me unpack a delivery of antique vases."

Belle gasped. She'd suppressed that memory, but seeing Tegen must have unlocked something in her brain and allowed the memory to spring free of its trappings.

"Belle." Nick jogged across the road and leaned against the barrier beside her.

"What do you want?" she asked, her voice weak.

"What was that about?" He put his hand on her shoulder, but Belle shook it off.

"You should speak to your girlfriend about it."

"She's not—"

Blood rushed through Belle's ears and drowned out Nick's voice. She sucked in a deep breath to calm herself before she continued.

"You remembered me from school, right?" Belle swiped at the tear rolling down her cheek. She needed to know how much he remembered.

"Yeah," he confirmed.

"I saw how your face paled when you realised who I was. You remember what I went through, don't you? The bullying?"

"It was rubbish, Belle, but that doesn't mean you have to blame everyone in your year."

"You were the year above, right?"

He nodded.

"It wasn't the entire year bullying me, Nick. There was one bully and a few of her friends."

She watched as his face shifted, and it dawned on him. "No. You must not remember it properly. Time does that, especially if you went through something traumatic." He reached for her again, but Belle stepped back.

"Don't you dare!" She pointed at him, feeling the anger inside her rally.

"I'm sorry, Belle. I didn't mean to upset

you. It's just I know Tegen. She would never hurt anyone."

Belle let out a bitter scoff. "She enjoyed every second of it."

"Maybe it was her friend, Morwenna? They look very similar."

"You can deny it as much as you want, Nick, but the truth is, it was Tegen. Yes, her friends went along with it, but she was the leader."

He shook his head and turned his back on her to look out towards the sea. "I'm sorry for inviting you tonight," his voice was barely a whisper.

"I should go," Belle said, but she made no move to leave. Her focus was on his crestfallen expression. "Are you going to be okay?" she asked him.

"Belle, you've just come face-to-face with the girl you said made your childhood a living hell and you're asking me if I'm okay?" His hands gripped the railing, but his face was impassive as he turned to her.

"Don't get me wrong, it was horrible, but it wasn't a big shock. I've been half expecting it. Every time I walk around a corner, I'm terrified of bumping into her. At least now it's over with. You're the one that's had a shock tonight."

Nick laughed. "I still don't know who you are, Belle Roux. Every time I see you, I meet a different side."

"I'm not sure even I know who I am."

His gaze fell on her, and Belle felt a jolt as she

raised her eyes to meet his. "Anyway, I should go. See you tomorrow." This time, she started moving before she'd even finished speaking. "Bye Nick," she said without looking back.

"See you tomorrow, Belle," he called after her.

CHAPTER FIVE

Belle woke to a knocking on her front door. She groaned and pulled herself out of bed, grabbing her vintage silk dressing gown from the back of the door.

"Coming," she shouted as another knock echoed through the cottage. Belle glanced down to check she'd done the dressing gown up before she opened the door.

"Morning," Nick said cheerily, holding a takeaway cup of coffee out for her.

"Nick, what are you doing here?" Belle squinted at the clock on the far wall.

"I was worried about you after last night."

"How did you know where I live?"

"It's a small place." He shrugged.

Belle sighed. "Why don't you come in?"

The cottage shrank as Nick entered, his head a mere couple of inches from the ceiling beams. "Do you have any sugar? I forgot to add some to my coffee," Nick said, glancing towards the kitchen.

"Of course, come through. What are you doing here at seven in the morning?" she asked.

"I hardly slept last night. I feel awful about inviting you."

"Nick, I don't blame you." She handed him the pot of sugar and a spoon.

He added two heaped spoons of sugar into his coffee and stirred.

Belle grabbed the packet of custard creams from the side and offered him one. "Shall we sit down in the living room? We might as well be comfortable for this conversation."

Nick followed her into the living room and sat in the armchair. "Don't mind me, you can go get dressed if you want. I'll keep myself entertained."

Belle glanced down. She'd forgotten she was in her dressing gown. It was a stunning piece she'd picked up a couple of weeks ago. Belle had discovered *The Cornish Vintage Dress Shop* while exploring one of the local villages and had left with a few treasures and a promise to return. The sleeves, collar, and bottom seam were trimmed with white feathers. It ended above her ankles and swished with her body as she walked.

"I'll get dressed in a minute. Are you sure you're okay?" she asked. Nick still wore the same jeans and shirt from last night and had dark circles under his eyes.

"I went back to a friend's last night," he said,

noticing her looking at his clothes. "Then I came here this morning rather than going home to get dressed." His brow knitted.

"Well, thank you for the coffee."

"You're welcome. Do you fancy having a day away from the shop? We need to order the flooring, paint, and wood for the shelving units. I know you've been having trouble finding inspiration, so I thought we could go for a day trip to St Ives. We can wander around all the shops and see how they're decorated. I'd also like to see how the shelving units are made."

"Sounds like an excellent plan." A heaviness lifted from her chest at the thought of getting away from Padstow-on-Sea for the day. "I'll get ready. Help yourself to anything you need." She took her coffee upstairs with her.

Belle stared at the clothes in her wardrobe, not knowing what to wear.

"It's only Nick," she muttered and grabbed the first pair of jeans she could reach. They were a white pair of 80s Levi wide-leg jeans which were cut above her ankles. Belle pulled them on and folded the bottoms of the legs. She'd found the jeans in *The Cornish Vintage Dress Shop*. The owner, Rosie, had offered to alter them for her, but Belle was too impatient and wanted to take them home. It was forecast to be a nice day, and Belle pulled out a pale green blouse with bell sleeves and tucked it into her jeans. She'd found the shirt in a charity shop and it had come with a matching silk scarf. Belle pulled back the front of her hair and tied the silk scarf into a bow. She finished the dregs of her coffee, brushed her teeth, and chose her jewellery for the day.

"Sorry, took me longer than I expected," Belle said as she went downstairs.

"That was quick. I'm barely halfway through the biscuits." Nick held the half-empty packet up.

"Bring them with us. I could do with some breakfast." Belle opened the cupboard under the stairs and rifled through the pile of shoes to find her white trainers.

"I could make you some shelves for your shoes if you'd like," Nick said. He'd wandered up and was peering over her shoulder.

"Maybe," she said, pushing the door shut before he could inspect the chaos.

"You ready to go?" he asked, putting the biscuits in his jacket pocket.

"Did you want to get changed?" she asked, remembering he was still wearing last night's clothes.

"I probably should. Sorry, I could have run home while you were getting ready."

"No worries. Why don't you head home now and I'll meet you at the harbour in thirty minutes?" Belle suggested, ignoring the truth that she'd enjoyed getting ready, knowing he was sitting downstairs.

"See you in thirty," he said, already at the door.

"Leave the bisc—" The door slammed shut.

Belle went to the bread bin and pulled out a mass-produced brioche. She winced as she bit into it. If her father saw her eating this, she'd be in trouble. Back home in France, every other day they would walk to the boulangerie in the village for fresh bread, croissants, and brioches. She remembered the first time she'd gone with her father. After weeks of shutting herself away in her new bedroom, he'd coaxed her out. She'd cried every second of the journey from Cornwall to France and as soon as they'd arrived, she'd slammed her bedroom door and wouldn't come out.

"Come with me, Belle. There's an antique shop in the village, we can have a look. Please," he'd said through her door. There was no lock on it, but Louis respected her privacy and didn't try to open it. Instead, he spoke to her through the door and left her meals for her to collect.

"I can't go." She'd sobbed and for the first time in two weeks, she opened the door to see her father.

"Why not?" He'd blinked at the sight of her.

"Because if I go out there and accept this new life, then I'll be saying goodbye to Mum."

"Oh, Belle." Her father wrapped his arms around her and pulled her tight. "No matter where you are in the world, you'll always have your memories."

Belle had sobbed into her father's shoulder. Two weeks of pent-up grief spilling from her.

"Cornwall wasn't the only place Kerenza made memories, you know? We used to come here on holidays when you were young. Then I took over the antiques shop and couldn't take the time off to visit."

"Mum's been here before?"

"We spent a long time here after we married. The yellow walls are thanks to your mother. She got bored one day and made me drive out to the closest paint shop. This house has been in my family for a very long time. Passed down to each generation. I inherited it at twenty when my parents died."

"I didn't realise." Belle glanced at her surroundings. Everything looked different, knowing her mother had once been there. "Let's go and explore." Belle took her father's arm and allowed him to lead them out of the house and into the bright sunshine.

They followed the winding road into the village. In the centre was a square with a linden tree in the middle. Benches were dotted around with a handful of people sitting on them.

"There's the antique shop." Her father pointed to the first shop on their right. It took up the entire three-story building and from peering through the window, Belle could tell it was a treasure trove inside.

She pushed the door, but it wouldn't open. "It's closed," she commented.

"They don't have enough staff to open it full time, but I've been speaking to the owner, and she's offered me half of the top floor if I would be willing to work in the shop two days a week." Her father watched her as he waited for a response.

Belle gulped. "We're staying here for good, then?" She'd hoped her father would see sense, and they'd re-pack the car and go home.

"We need a fresh start, Belle. Everything in Cornwall is shrouded in memories of your mother."

Belle nodded as the ache in her chest grew. Despite the way her heart felt as though it was breaking all over again, she knew her father was right. Moving here meant they could escape the memories and the pity glances from their community. It also meant she wouldn't have to see her bullies again.

"Okay."

"Come on, let's look at the fresh bread. We can pick some to have with soup for dinner."

"Dad, we've not even eaten breakfast and you're thinking of dinner!" Belle let out a hollow laugh. It sounded strange. It had been a long time since she'd laughed.

"It's never too early to think about dinner, Belle."

The boulangerie was on the other side of the square, set into a grand white building. A sign above the door read 'boulangerie' in fancy gold writing against a black marble backdrop. Outside, white wrought iron tables and chairs were filled with customers drinking coffee and eating a selection of pastries.

"Wait until you see inside," Louis said, watching Belle take in the sight.

They stepped inside, and Belle inhaled the sweet scent. Behind the till were loaves of crusty bread stacked almost to the ceiling. Displayed in the glass counters were croissants, almond croissants, pain au chocolats, *pain au raisins, and brioches.*

Everything looked and smelt divine. Louis had allowed Belle to pick one of each pastry, and they'd bought a couple of loaves of bread. On the walk back, Louis pulled a paper bag from his pocket.

"What's that?" asked Belle.

"I got an extra brioche for the road. It's chocolate." He tore it in two and handed Belle the larger half.

"I wish I'd learned French," Belle mumbled around a mouthful of brioche.

"It's my fault, Belle. I should have pushed you when you were younger, but we always got distracted with auction brochures or television programs about antiques."

"Are there many auction houses nearby?"

"There's one half an hour away."

"When's the next auction?" Belle knew her father would know.

"Tomorrow."

Belle chewed her mouthful. The brioche was delicious and melted in her mouth. "Let's go."

"Okay. We can stop for more brioches before we leave."

Belle tried to smile, but her mouth wouldn't move. It would be their first auction since her mother's death. She sucked in a deep breath, knowing there would be many more firsts in the coming weeks.

CHAPTER SIX

Belle was five minutes late once she untangled herself from her memories. She then lost her handbag and spent ten minutes searching for it, only to find it hidden in a pile of washing, waiting to go into the machine. Belle had half walked, half jogged to the harbour and was out of breath by the time she came to a halt outside her shop. She realised they hadn't agreed on a specific meeting place and everywhere was busy.

"You're late," Nick said. Belle spun on her heel to see him leaning against the wall. He'd showered and changed. His hair was still damp, and he wore dark blue jeans that fitted his sculpted legs and a plain white t-shirt.

"Sorry, I got distracted." She was still distracted.

"You're here now. Come on, my van's parked on one of the streets outside the harbour." He pushed off from the wall and walked next to her.

"I'm picking up a sign for outside the shop next week," she said.

"Brilliant. It'll be good for people to know what we're doing."

"It will. I found a local artist to paint it. She's also designing some leaflets for me."

"Where are you picking them up from?"

"Port Isaac."

"I'll come with you if you want."

"I appreciate the offer, but one of us should probably be doing some work on the shop if I ever want to open." She glanced sideways at him.

"Fair point." He laughed.

They walked in the road, going against the people heading towards the harbour. Nick led them down a side street and took another turn. His van was parked halfway down the road.

"I moved some furniture for a friend last night and left my van outside his," Nick explained.

Belle went to climb in and winced at the state of the seat. It was covered in brick dust and she was wearing white jeans.

"Sorry, let me get that." Nick pulled a small handheld hoover from the glove compartment and cleared the seat for her. "T got me this last week. She was sick of getting covered in all sorts." As the words left Nick's mouth, his face fell. He met Belle's eyes and she could see the regret on his face. "Sorry," he muttered and closed the glove compartment harder than necessary.

"It's okay. You can't pretend she doesn't exist for my sake. We'll be seeing each other a lot over the next couple of months. I don't want things to be awkward." Belle put on her seatbelt.

Nick pulled away from the curb and wound his way out of the village to the main road. "I am really sorry for inviting you."

"Stop apologising. Why don't we agree not to talk about her today? I think we could both use the distraction."

"Okay." Nick glanced over at her as she played with the ring she wore. "Is that a vintage piece of jewellery?"

"This is the most special piece of vintage jewellery I own. It was my mother's engagement ring." Belle's father had given it to her shortly after their first trip to the French auction house. He'd watched her face light up at the sight of the sparkling jewels. Louis had kept her mother's wedding ring and wore it around his neck, but he'd gifted her the sapphire engagement ring. The centre stone was an oval cut, deep blue sapphire with a halo of white diamonds surrounding it on a platinum band. Her mother had never been one for yellow gold.

"It's beautiful." He shot her a smile before turning his attention back to the road. "What about the other pieces you're wearing? Are they all your mother's?"

Belle thought about the pieces she wore. She was wearing a small pair of aquamarine stud earrings and a ring. It was a greenish-blue to match the earrings, but it was coloured glass. Belle had bought it from a charity shop because she loved the floral shape. It was fun and a change from her serious purchases, where she had to consider the price and the profit margin.

Belle recalled the stories of purchasing both the earrings and the ring, and Nick had asked lots of questions about her life in France.

It was an hour to St Ives, but it passed quickly as conversation flowed effortlessly between them.

"Do you think you'll go back?" he asked, swinging the van into an empty parking space.

"To where?" Belle asked. The golden sand and bright blue sea ahead had stolen away her attention.

"France," Nick said.

"I don't plan to, but it's nice to know I have somewhere to go if things fail here."

They climbed out of the van, and Nick led the way into the town. Winding streets made their way down to the sea. The little shops were bustling with people, each one selling something different and unique.

"I loved France, but I could never get my head around the language," Belle continued.

"Really? Isn't your father French?"

"He is, but we always spoke English at home. If you heard him speak, you wouldn't know he was French. He's worked hard to lose his accent, so the French auction houses assume he can't speak the language." Belle chuckled as she remembered how excited her father had been when the idea had come to him. "When we moved, he tried to teach me, but after my mother's death, my mind shut down. After a few months, we gave up."

They wandered further into the town and the atmosphere almost hummed with excitement. Belle looked from one side of the road to the other as she took in all the different shops.

"Where shall we start?" she asked.

"What about this one?" Nick pointed to a jewellery shop.

"The Jewel of St Ives," Belle said, reading the name above the door. "Come on," she called and pushed the door open.

Inside, the walls and floor were white, with spotlights above that bounced off every surface. It was a bright day outside, but Belle could tell that even on the darkest of days, the shop would glow. Mirrored stands and cabinets were dotted around, drawing attention to the jewellery. It was all very modern for Belle's taste, but it had shown her how important lighting was.

She wandered around the displays. The shop sold bespoke silver pieces, each one delicate and beautiful. Belle peered through a glass cabinet at a pair of silver earrings which had been crafted in the shape of a starfish. She could feel Nick's presence behind her as she moved on to look at the silver bracelet with detailed charms attached to it. There was a fish, a Cornish pasty, and a sailing boat. The work that had gone into these pieces was stunning.

"These are nice, but they're not your vibe, are they?"

"They're not. I'm impressed you could tell." Belle kept her voice low, not wanting to upset the owner.

"Shall we move on to somewhere else?" He offered his arm and Belle took it, a smile playing at her lips at the thought of people thinking they were a couple as they meandered down the pretty streets.

"Can we pop in there?" Belle asked, pointing to a bookshop.

Nick agreed, and they crossed the road. Inside, the shop was silent, with the odd rustling of pages heard now and again.

"Look at the colour of the bookshelves," Belle said. She tried to keep her voice low, but she could feel herself being swept away by the tide of excitement.

"They're pretty," Nick commented, his brow furrowed.

"Look, they're almost the same as this." Belle pulled the shop's key from her handbag and showed the ribbon to Nick.

"You want the shop to be this colour?" he asked, taking the key from her and threading the soft silk through his fingers.

"It was my mothers," Belle said, her voice choking up at the words.

"Belle, most DIY stores will colour-match this. You could have this exact colour on your walls." He'd stepped closer to her so she could hear without him having to raise his voice and disturb the other customers. Nick handed the key back and his fingers brushed against the palm of her hand. A spark of energy surged through her. Her heart stuttered as her stare lowered to his lips. She wanted to reach up on her tiptoes and wrap her arms around his neck.

"Are you looking for anything in particular?" somebody asked, breaking the odd spell that had fallen over them.

Belle shook her head both in answer and to shake the daze she was in. "No," she said, her voice wobbled. She cleared her throat. "Sorry, no, we were just browsing."

"Very well. Let me know if you need anything," the woman said before moving to the next aisle.

"That's the paint sorted," Nick said.

Belle glanced up at him and noticed his eyes had glazed over. "Yes," she agreed. "Shall we get some lunch?"

They wandered a few doors up to a bakery and each got a Cornish pasty and a coffee. With their lunch in a takeaway bag, they walked to the beach. Belle pulled off her shoes and socks and sank her toes into the cool sand.

"Watch out for the seagulls," Nick said, tipping his head up towards an angry flock that circled above them.

"They're not getting their hands on this." Belle laughed and took a small bite from the edge of the pasty, just big enough to let the heat escape.

Steam poured out and floated away with the sea breeze.

"Thanks for today," Belle said after she finished her last bite of pasty. The flaky pastry melted in her mouth as the rich flavour of the filling assaulted her taste buds. "I needed it."

"It's been nice. I can't remember the last time I had a day like this." He smiled and leaned back on his forearms, turning his face towards the sun.

Belle blinked a few times before she tore her gaze from him. She wanted to ask why he didn't enjoy days out like this with Tegen, but instead, she moved the conversation back to the shop. "We've even decided on the wall colour. I need to decide on the flooring and shelves now."

"Think about it over the weekend." Nick screwed up their empty paper bags, stood and held a hand out to help her up. Belle wanted to refuse, unsure how her body would react to his touch, but she couldn't think of a way to politely decline. She took his hand and pushed back against the way his skin felt against hers.

"Come on, there's a bakery a few streets down," Nick said, throwing an arm around her shoulders.

"You've just had lunch!"

"And now I want dessert." He winked, and Belle felt her face flush. She pushed at his chest and laughed to cover the desire that flooded her as her hand made contact with his tight abs underneath the t-shirt.

Sugary treats filled the bakery window. Belle's mouth watered at the sight of the huge meringues. The cracks in them looked like invitations to break them apart and devour them. Nick pulled Belle inside. It was busy, and she found herself pressed up against him. Her heart thundered in her ears and she tried to reason with her body's response to him. She hadn't been this close to a man in a while. That was why her body was reacting like this.

"What do you want? My treat," he said.

Belle realised her attention had been focused on him and she hadn't glanced towards the goods on display beneath the glass counters.

"I'll have what you're having," she said, unable to pull her thoughts back to make a decision.

"I was going to have a sausage roll," he said, his voice deadpan.

"You've just had a Cornish pasty!"

"I'm winding you up." He laughed, and his face lit up. She turned her back on him to look at the selection.

"I'll have a croissant, please."

"Are you sure? Aren't you something of a croissant connoisseur?"

"Is this your way of telling me they're not very good?" Belle raised her eyebrows.

"I couldn't comment. I've never had one." He shrugged as if he'd told her it was going to rain tomorrow.

"You've never had a croissant?" Belle screeched, causing a few heads to turn in her direction. "Sorry." Her cheeks flushed.

"Never."

"You have to get one."

Nick rolled his eyes, but as he took his turn at the counter, he ordered one sausage roll, two croissants, and coffee. They wandered back to the beach and found a bench to sit on. Belle sipped her coffee and hummed her approval at the rich, smooth blend as the sun warmed her skin. When she turned to Nick, she saw he was watching her.

"Good?" he asked her.

"So good. Let's hope their pastries are the same standard." She took a croissant from the bag and handed it to Nick before she pulled out the second one for herself. Belle could feel how flaky they were underneath her fingers.

"On three?" Nick asked.

Belle laughed and took a bite, leaving him to follow her lead.

"That's delicious," he mumbled around a mouthful.

Belle chewed and swallowed before she answered. "It's not bad. A little soft, but the taste is there."

"You'll have to bring me some back from France next time you go," Nick said around another bite.

"I'll bring you back one of everything." Belle giggled.

She took another sip of her coffee and soaked in her surroundings. The blue sky above was reflected in the sparkling sea. Seagulls flew above them, poised to swoop down if they dropped a single crumb. Children played on the sand, laughing and squealing as the waves came in. There was a gentle hum of conversation. Despite the crowds, Belle was at peace for the first time in a long while. A break from her to-do list at home was what she needed, and Nick's company had only improved the day.

CHAPTER SEVEN

Belle's phone vibrated with a text from Jada, reminding her of their evening cooking class. Belle texted back to ask if she should buy the ingredients, but Jada promised she'd bring everything they needed. With that sorted, Belle opened all the windows, put on an audiobook and cleaned the cottage from top to bottom. She remembered how her mother would wrap a scarf around her unruly hair, turn the radio on, and dance around the cottage as she hoovered and dusted. Belle turned up the volume on her audiobook to drown out the memories.

The sunlight poured in, and the freshly polished surfaces gleamed. Belle popped the kettle on and made a coffee. She'd bought an electric kettle after a few early mornings when the high-pitched whistle was too noisy. Belle took her coffee into the courtyard and allowed her mind to wander over yesterday's trip with Nick. Her memories kept shifting to the way his lips had moved as he spoke, or how his face softened when he smiled. "This is no good," Belle grumbled. She was a grown woman. She couldn't develop a crush, especially not on someone whose girlfriend was her childhood bully.

Deciding she needed something more consuming to distract her, Belle opened her emails and found an auction brochure sent to her from her father. She scrolled through, but even the lots of Edwardian jewels couldn't keep Belle's thoughts from straying to Nick. It would be a while until Jada arrived, so she pulled on a pair of denim shorts and a white vest and threw a grey cardigan around her shoulders. She got some cash from her purse and took the door key, but left everything else behind.

The harbour was busy, but Belle navigated her way through the cobbled streets to The Flower Shop opposite Jada's café. She bought two bunches. One was a selection of beautiful wildflowers for Jada. Belle had recognised the white daisies, purple chicory, and heather. It was a beautiful selection that reminded her of Jada's zest for life. The second bunch was twelve white lilies wrapped in brown paper. The silky white petals stood out against the vibrant green leaves. They were beautiful, and they were her mother's favourite.

"Thank you," she said to the florist and rejoined the hustle and bustle of the harbour. Belle kept the flowers close to her chest to stop them from being crushed in the crowd. She nipped down a side street and wound her way through the maze of side roads back to her cottage. Belle walked past her home and carried on to the church at the end of the road. The graveyard was almost empty besides a few stray tourists wandering around. Belle took the right fork in the path towards the back of the church. When she'd come back to Padstow-on-Sea, she'd been surprised to find her father had employed someone to keep her mother's grave presentable, and he had the florist deliver flowers every couple of weeks. It had been Kerenza's wish to be buried there beside her parents. Belle's grandparents had died when she was a baby. In the early days, Belle had found some comfort in knowing that her mother wasn't alone.

"Hi, Mum," Belle said softly as she approached the marble headstone. She placed the lilies on the ground and crouched down. "I miss you."

A flock of birds took flight, stealing Belle's attention. She watched as they flew across the sky, heading towards the harbour, no doubt in search of a few stray crumbs.

"It's strange being back here without you. Dad told me to be careful not to lose myself in your shadow, but I don't know how to avoid it." She passed a blade of grass through her fingers. "I saw Tegen the other day, and I wanted nothing more than to come home and feel your arms around me. Do you remember when she threw my lunchbox into the sea and I came home hungry? Despite the awful day I'd had, that's one of my favourite memories.

You took me down to the bakery and bought some scones, raspberry jam, and clotted cream. Then we came back and had a living room picnic.

"I wish we could have done that on Thursday. Although maybe now we could have got some chips and a bottle of wine. Red, of course. Your favourite. We'll never get to sit and share a bottle of wine." Belle took a deep breath to steady herself and to stop her overwhelming emotions.

"I brought you lilies. They smell lovely. I also bought a bunch of wildflowers for my friend who's coming around tonight. She's going to teach me how to cook. I know you were never very good. Dad was worse. We lived on pasta and croissants in France." Belle had always spoken to her mother, but now it was nice to have somewhere to go where she could let in her memories.

"The shop is coming on well. I've found a lovely local builder who is helping me. He took me out to St Ives yesterday and it was just the break I needed. I'm going to make Padstow-on-Sea my home, Mum. I promise." A soft breeze blew leaves on the tree above and caressed her cheek.

Belle had told her mother about Nick, but she hadn't mentioned how he made her feel. It felt like a secret that would shatter into a million pieces if she said it aloud. Her heart stuttered every time she saw him and sped up when he smiled at her. She hated to admit it, but she'd missed him today. After spending the week with him, it was odd to be on her own. Belle kept having to remind herself that he had a girlfriend. He was just being friendly with her.

Jada would be there soon, so Belle ignored her jumbled thoughts and focused on getting ready. She pulled on black leggings and an old navy jumper, which she didn't mind cooking in. She tied her hair back into a bun and slid a pair of ruby studs into her ears. They'd been a twenty-first birthday present from the lady who her father rented his antique shop from. Estelle had taken Louis under her wing and introduced him to the local antique dealers. After a reluctant first meeting, Belle had grown close to Estelle. She'd become the closest thing Belle had to a living female relative. Estelle still checked in from time to time and texted Belle to see how she was getting on.

There was a knock on the front door as Belle pulled on some fluffy socks. It might be spring, but the kitchen's flagstone floor was cold. "Coming," she called.

Belle opened the door to Jada. "Hello," she said, throwing her arms around her.

"It's lovely to see you," Jada said, awkwardly wrapping an arm around Belle. She clutched a heavy shopping bag in her left hand.

"Come straight through," Belle took the bag from Jada and stepped aside to let her in.

"This cottage is lovely. Is it yours?" Jada asked. She removed her shoes and left them on the mat in the little alcove by the door.

"It belongs to my father. He's letting me live here rent-free until the shop picks up," Belle explained.

"That's nice of him. It can be difficult to open a new business. My landlord gave me the first two months at half price while I found my feet. Come on, let's open the bottle of wine. It's non-alcoholic since I have an early morning. Is that okay?"

"That's perfect."

Belle led Jada to the kitchen and put the bag on the worktop. Jada unpacked while Belle went in search of two wine glasses.

"Sorry, they're not matching," Belle apologised. She made a mental note to pop into the charity shop in the harbour and pick some more glasses up. So far, it wasn't something she'd thought about as she'd had no company.

"As long as it doesn't leak, it'll be fine." Jada smiled and unscrewed the bottle. "I purposely chose one without a cork, as I didn't know if you'd have a corkscrew."

"Good idea. I probably haven't got one. I'll make a list and I'll be better prepared next time you come over." Belle opened a new note on her phone and jotted down 'wine glasses and corkscrew'.

"What are we cooking?" Belle asked, staring at the array of ingredients. There was one red onion, garlic-infused olive oil, a jar of what looked like spices, a sandwich bag filled with half-defrosted peas, a packet of halloumi, and some potatoes.

"I'm going to teach you how to make a roast potato and halloumi curry," Jada said, opening the bag of potatoes. "Do you have a knife?"

"A what curry?" Belle asked and pulled out two knives. She followed Jada's lead and started peeling potatoes.

"Trust me."

Belle did everything Jada told her to as she boiled and roasted potatoes. Then she measured out the spices before toasting them in a dry pan.

"Now add the garlic oil and fry your onion," Jada instructed.

"It smells amazing already." Belle sighed and her mouth watered.

"You should take some notes, then you can recreate this when you ask Nick over for dinner," Jada teased as she handed her the chopping board so she could scrape the onion into the frying pan.

"I won't be inviting him round," Belle muttered, concentrating on avoiding the oil which spat as the cold onion hit it.

"Why not? You like him, don't you?"

"Am I that obvious?"

Jada handed Belle the halloumi. "Cut that into cubes a couple of centimetres big. I wouldn't say you're that obvious, but I have noticed how you light up at the mention of him."

"I'll work on dimming that light."

"What's wrong about liking him? You can put the halloumi in. Let it brown on all sides." Jada topped up their glasses.

"He has a girlfriend, Jada."

"Okay, but that doesn't mean you can't have a crush on him. You don't have to act on your feelings. Enjoy being young and being attracted to someone."

"His girlfriend was one of my biggest bullies in school." Belle watched each cube of halloumi, waiting to turn it.

"Really?"

"Tegen Thomas. She made my life a living hell."

"You could steal her boy—"

"Don't even finish that sentence!" Belle pointed the spatula at Jada. A smile threatened to ruin her stern expression.

"It would be the ultimate revenge," Jada argued, holding her hands up.

"Not happening. I intend to do everything I can to stay away from Tegen. Besides, it's a silly crush. I hardly know Nick."

They stayed away from the topic of Nick as they finished the cooking lesson. Belle was surprised to discover how simple and quick the curry was to cook. She set the small table in the kitchen and lit a pillar candle to put in the centre.

"This is the most romantic meal I've had in a long time," Jada commented as she laid the cutlery down.

"I'm not sure I've ever had a romantic meal." Belle saw Jada's look of horror and quickly moved the attention off of her. "When was your last date?"

Jada told her how the pub's landlord had

taken her to a fancy restaurant. Belle listened as she
ate.

CHAPTER EIGHT

"Do you want coffee?" Belle called, hearing Jada moving around upstairs. They'd stayed up talking last night and Jada had slept in the spare room, so she didn't have to walk home in the dark.

"Better not," Jada said, coming down the stairs. "I have someone opening the coffee shop today, but I need to be in for the mid-morning rush. I'll make a coffee when I get there."

"Of course. Don't let me hold you up."

Belle waved goodbye to Jada before she turned back to the empty living room. It had been lovely lying in bed, knowing someone was next door. Belle hadn't realised how much she craved company. With Jada gone, the cottage felt empty again. She pulled her dressing gown tighter and went to make a drink. It was Sunday, so Nick wouldn't be working, but she was considering going down to the shop and seeing if there was anything she could do. She needed to get used to being there alone.

Belle rolled her shoulders. She had to find something to do today to rid herself of this pent-up energy. She added milk, stirred her coffee and decided to go to the shop and inspect the safes. Her dad would be around today if she needed to video call him for advice.

The sky was cloudy, and there was a chill, reminding Belle that it was still only spring. She'd wrapped up in a pair of jeans and a jumper that had been a moving present from Estelle, who insisted she needed warmer clothes for her move back to Cornwall. Belle hoped she wouldn't stumble upon any messy jobs while she was wearing it.

The shop was different this time. Instead of memories of her mother, she thought of Nick and his smile. It was as though the place was coming to life around her. Belle wandered across the shop floor and imagined what it might look like when finished. She would put diamonds near the window and they could shine in the natural light. Followed by a selection of rubies and sapphires to allow the rich colours to glow. Belle stood in the middle of the shop and let out a squeal of joy.

The mood shifted as Belle's hand lingered on the office door. She couldn't help but wonder if she would ever walk into this room without the agonising memories hitting her like a punch to the stomach. Focused on the task at hand, Belle pushed back against the pain that tried to invade her peace.

Checking the safes was easier than she thought it would be. As a child, her father had always allowed her the job of unlocking and locking them.

"Belle, we have to go home soon. Your mother will be waiting for us and dinner will be ruined," Louis called through to the office from the shop floor.

"Okay, Dad," Ten-year-old Belle shouted back. She was sitting at her father's desk, sorting through a box of beads from an auction delivery. Her school bag rested against the desk where she'd discarded it.

Louis walked into the room holding a vase. He had gloves on to protect the antique. Belle didn't know much about vases, but she knew this one was worth a lot of money.

"Can I open the safe?" Belle asked, dropping a handful of beads back into the box.

"Go on then, but be quick. I don't want to hold this vase for too long."

Belle jumped up from the leather chair and ran to the floor-to-ceiling safe. Although they called them safes, they were more like vaults. The heavy iron doors opened to small cupboards, filled with shelves to hold the precious goods. Young Belle twisted the dial on the front of the door to unlock it. With both hands, she grabbed the handle and yanked. It took all of her weight to heave the door open.

While Louis filled the vault with the precious

antiques, Belle gathered the smaller ones. When she was little, her father described the process of putting the items to sleep, and they still referred to it as that.

"Is that everyone put to bed?" Belle asked, stifling a yawn.

"Everyone's sleeping tightly. Can you close and lock the door while I turn off the lights in the shop?"

Belle nodded and went through the process of closing and locking the safes. Once they were locked, she pulled on her coat and picked up her school bag.

Louis took her hand as they walked out of the shop and up the road towards home. It was a blustery October evening. Lights glowed from inside the houses they passed and smoke billowed from the chimneys.

They walked into the cottage to a fire roaring in the hearth and Belle's mother, Kerenza, in the kitchen, cooking dinner.

"Belle, run upstairs, wash your hands, and get changed out of your uniform," her mother called.

"Okay, Mum." Belle did as she was told.

Downstairs, the kitchen table was set for dinner. Her mother stood at the stove stirring a pot. Her long red hair was pulled back into a ponytail and she wore pyjamas that matched Belle's.

"How was school?" Kerenza asked. She put a plate of buttered bread on the table. Belle and her father took a slice and devoured it.

"It was okay," Belle mumbled around her mouthful.

"Did you have any more problems with those girls?"

"No," Belle lied, stuffing more bread into her mouth.

"How was work?" asked Louis, changing the subject.

"Busy," Kerenza said, pouring soup into three bowls. She worked down at the harbour selling tickets for boat tours. "You'd think people would avoid going out in this weather. The waves are all over the place and that wind is bitter."

"Everyone wants to go home and say they had the full Cornish experience."

Belle zoned out of the conversation as her mother placed a bowl of tomato soup in front of her. It was tinned, but it was delicious. She was starving after the girls at school had stolen her lunch again.

"What would you like to do tomorrow, Belle?" her mother asked, pushing the last slice of bread towards her.

"Can I go to the shop with Dad?" she asked, glancing towards her father.

"Are you sure? It's Saturday, you don't have to," Louis said, putting down his spoon.

"I like being in the shop."

"Why don't you spend the morning in the shop? I'm working until lunchtime. I'll pick you up on my way home and we can make some sandwiches and watch a film. How does that sound?"

Belle shook her head to rid herself of the memories

that consumed her. A sadness lodged in her heart. She'd felt as though she were back in the same room as her parents. Belle swiped at a stray tear and walked out of the office. It was lunchtime, so she decided to wander down to the bakery and buy a loaf of fresh bread. She'd go home, make some lunch, and put her favourite film on.

The bakery was busy, and the shelves were almost empty. It was a typical Cornish bakery, selling loaves of bread, Cornish pasties, and the odd jam doughnut.

"What can I get you, my love?" asked the woman behind the counter. She wore a blue apron and had her hair pulled back into a hairnet.

"A loaf of your crusty white and a jam doughnut, please."

"Here you go, my love. I've popped in an extra one. We close in five minutes and I don't want them going to waste." The woman shot her a kind smile.

"Thank you." Belle paid and left with two paper bags.

The overcast weather meant there were fewer tourists around today, which made walking home much easier. She was only stopped by one person who asked her to take a photograph of them standing in front of a blue cottage. Belle quickly snapped a few shots and speedily walked away before someone else asked anything of her.

Once back in the cottage, she set about lighting a fire. It was cold and gloomy inside, but as the little flickers sparked, it transformed the room.

Warmth wrapped around her, and Belle went to change into some jogging bottoms. She flicked the light switch in her bedroom, but nothing happened.

"That's odd," she murmured and wandered to the bathroom to try the light in there. Each time she flicked the switch, nothing happened. Belle pulled her phone from her pocket and dialled her dad's number. It rang, but there was no answer. "Brilliant," she muttered to herself.

Downstairs, none of the lights were working. The kettle wouldn't switch on and the fridge was off. Belle drummed her fingers on the worktop, staring out at the courtyard where a bird perched on the edge of the table, pecking at invisible crumbs. "What should I do?" She hoped the sound of her voice would help ease the growing loneliness. Her words echoed around the kitchen. She tried her dad again, but it went to voicemail. Her signal wasn't strong enough to Google a local electrician, and the WiFi was off along with everything else. She could knock on one of the cottages next door, but both sides were holiday lets. Belle wondered how much Jada knew about electrics, but a glance at the time told her she'd be busy with the lunchtime rush. There was one other person she knew in Padstow-on-Sea. Belle groaned as she scrolled through her contacts. Her fingers hovered over Nick's name. It was no good. She had to call him.

"Hello, Nick speaking," he answered on the third ring.

"Nick, it's Belle. I hope you don't mind me

calling. I have a bit of a situation at the cottage and don't know what to do," she rambled.

There was the sound of a door closing before his soft, calm voice filled Belle's ears. "Belle, calm down. What's wrong?"

"I went out this morning and came back to find I've got no electricity. My lights won't switch on, and the fridge and freezer are off. I can't even make myself a coffee." Tears brimmed in Belle's eyes. "I hate feeling this out of control." She fought against the sob rising in her chest.

"Take a deep breath. I can be with you in ten minutes, okay?"

"Thank you." A whoosh of relief flooded through her.

She put her phone down on the worktop. Her hands shook and her insides churned. She turned to the fireplace and added another log.

As the fire flickered, there was a knock at the front door. It was Nick. He stood there in jeans and a white shirt, and his hair styled. The toolbox in his hand looked out of place.

"Thank you for coming," Belle said, forcing her gaze to move from him.

"No worries." He stepped into the cottage. "Where's your fuse box?"

Belle blinked. "My what?"

Nick let out a low chuckle. "Oh, Belle," he said, shaking his head.

"Should I know what that is?" Belle's voice wobbled and she could feel the day's emotions gathering.

"Yes, but it's okay. Everyone has to find it at some point. Better now than in the middle of winter when it's dark and freezing cold. Why do you have the fire on? Were you planning on cooking sausages on it if the electricity didn't come back on?" he teased.

"I'm cold," she said, turning her back on him to collect herself.

"I'm sorry. I didn't mean to…" he trailed off. "Actually, I'm not really sure what I've done."

Belle chuckled. "Sorry, it's me. I've had a tough day, and the electricity has sent me over the edge."

"Let's see. I worked with my dad when he did a kitchen refit in one of the cottages along here. I'm sure the fuse boxes will all be in the same place. They're usually by the front door."

They both searched the tiny porch area and living room for the fuse box, although, if Belle was honest, she didn't know what she was looking for.

"Got it," Nick called. He'd opened the cupboard above the front door. The one Belle had never been able to reach. "Do you have a stepladder?"

"No, sorry."

"It's fine. I've got some in the back of my van, but I'd already had a drink so couldn't drive over."

"I'll get you a chair from the kitchen," Belle said.

She came back with a wooden chair. "I'm sorry I interrupted your afternoon. Were you up to much?"

"Just Sunday dinner at the pub with Tegen and some friends," Nick said absentmindedly as he tested the chair to check it would hold his weight.

Belle's jaw dropped, and she let out a groan. "I interrupted your day with Tegen."

"Don't worry about it. I didn't tell her it was you."

"Nick, that's even worse. You can't lie to her about who you're visiting." Belle held her head in her hands.

"Honestly, Belle, you're worrying about nothing. She won't mind who I'm with. I was grateful for the excuse to leave." Nick flicked a switch on the box and the lights clicked on. "All done."

"It was that easy?" Belle slowly looked up from her hands.

"Yeah. Something must have tripped. Now, can I get a coffee for all my hard work?" He stepped down from the chair and carried it back into the kitchen, leaving Belle staring after him.

"Don't you want to get back to the pub?" She caught up with him and switched on the kettle.

"Not really. I doubt they've even noticed I'm gone. I'll text them to say it's going to take me a while." He winked at her before he tapped out a message on his phone.

Belle turned back to the kettle and got out two mugs. One was a garish green, the other had the estate agent's logo printed on the front. She really ought to buy some matching ones.

"Can I help with anything?" He stood beside her, his arm brushing hers, and a frisson of excitement charged through her. She stepped aside to get the jar of coffee and to put space between them.

"Can you finish the drinks? I've not had lunch, so I was going to make a sandwich."

Belle got some butter, cheese, and salad from the fridge and set about making some lunch with the loaf of bread she'd bought earlier, although it seemed like a lifetime ago now.

"Did you go to the bakery?" Nick asked, looking towards the other brown paper bag.

"Yeah. I was lucky and got there minutes before they closed."

"Does that mean they gave you an extra doughnut?"

"How do you know?"

"My mum runs the bakery, and she always gives the stock away before closing."

"Your mum runs the bakery? You lucky thing. There are two jam doughnuts, you can have one."

"Thanks. She gives the stock away to avoid bringing any home," he huffed.

"Uh oh.' Belle chuckled and cut her sandwich in half. "Come on, let's sit down in the living room."

They wandered back through, and Nick threw an extra log on the dwindling fire.

"There's no coffee table. You can pop your mug on the floor," Belle said. She curled up in the armchair by the window, leaving the two-seater sofa for Nick.

"I'm not overstaying my welcome, am I? I don't want to intrude on your afternoon plans," Nick said as he pulled the doughnut from the bag. He held it over the opening as he took a bite so it caught the sugar.

"Of course not. I was planning an afternoon on the sofa watching a film."

"Don't let me stop you."

"Are you sure?" Belle asked, reaching for the remote control.

"What were you going to watch?"

Belle fidgeted with the remote, avoiding his gaze.

"Belle," he prompted.

"I was going to watch Beauty and the Beast." She picked at the crumbs on her now empty plate.

Nick let out a snort of laughter that caused sugar to spray across the living room. "Sorry," he wheezed out between laughs.

Belle pressed her lips into a straight line and stared at him. She didn't last long and was soon laughing until her sides ached.

The afternoon passed them by as they watched the film. Nick kept the fire alight, and Belle joined him on the sofa. As it grew dark outside, she closed the curtains and snuggled underneath a blanket. She offered the other half of the throw to Nick, but he declined, saying the fire was enough.

"That wasn't as bad as I thought it would be,"

Nick commented as the end credits rolled. "Is it my turn to choose a film?"

Nick's choice wasn't as bad as Belle had feared, although there were a handful too many bloody scenes for her taste.

"What are your plans for dinner?" he asked, standing to stretch.

"A sandwich?" Belle rubbed her eyes.

"You had a sandwich for lunch," he pointed out.

Belle was taken aback. "I didn't realise you were monitoring my meals." She raised her brows at him.

"Shall I go down to the harbour and get a takeaway?" he asked.

Belle's stomach rumbled. "Shouldn't you go back to Tegen and your friends?"

"They'll have gone home by now," he said, pulling on his trainers. "You get some plates warming in the oven. See you soon." He left before she could argue.

With the blanket wrapped around her shoulders, Belle switched the oven on. She noticed her phone still on the side where she'd left it earlier. She had a missed phone call from her dad.

Louis answered the call on the first ring. "Belle, is everything okay?" he asked, his voice holding an edge of concern.

"All good. Sorry, Dad. I didn't mean to worry you."

"As long as everything's okay. I went for lunch

with Estelle at the vineyard and forgot my phone."

"That sounds lovely," Belle said, her heart constricting at the thought. Now and then, Estelle would treat them to lunch there. The food had been delicious and her father enjoyed the red wine. They even took Belle there for her eighteenth. By then, everyone recognised them and some of the staff joined in with their celebrations.

"Belle?" her father asked and pulled her from her thoughts.

"Sorry. All's fine here. The fuse tripped, but I phoned a local builder." She didn't mention that it was Nick or that he had spent the rest of the day watching films with her.

"Glad you've got it sorted. I'm leaving early tomorrow for an auction. If I see anything you might like, I'll send you pictures. Keep your phone to hand."

"No, Dad. Don't send me any more. I can't afford anything until the shop is open." She knew it was pointless, her father would send the pictures.

"I'll lend you anything you need," he promised her.

"Dad, you can't keep doing this. At some point, I have to stand on my own two feet."

"Belle, I won't be around forever. While I'm here, I'll do everything I can to help you."

A lump formed in Belle's throat. "Thank you."

Once she put the phone down, Belle pulled on a thick jumper. She couldn't shake the chill that had seeped into her bones when she realised how alone she would be if anything happened to her father.

The kettle clicked off as Nick walked back into the cottage, not bothering to knock.

"Tea?" Belle asked as he walked in with a carrier bag.

"Yes, please. I can't believe it's June out there. It's freezing," he complained, pulling out the portions of fish and chips wrapped in paper.

Belle used a tea towel to pull the warm plates out of the oven, and Nick dished their food up as she made the drinks. It was as if they'd done it a thousand times over and moved in sync.

The smell of vinegar filled the small kitchen, and they sat at the kitchen table. Belle had left a plate of buttered bread in the middle of the table, and Nick was making a chip sandwich with it. It was with a jolt that Belle realised this was what she wanted. She wanted to come home from a long day at the shop and have someone to eat dinner with. Someone who took note of when she hadn't eaten. Someone to curl up on the sofa with and watch a film, however rubbish that film might be. She wanted to share her life with someone. With a sharp intake of breath, Belle realised it wasn't just anyone she wanted to spend her life with. It was Nick. As the thought hit her, she coughed, choking on her dinner. It was a stupid thought. He had a girlfriend.

"You okay?" Nick asked. He put down his fork and flailed his hands around as if he wanted to help, but didn't know what to do.

"Fine," Belle gasped. "Just too much vinegar,"

she lied, as her eyes watered.

"I told you it was too much when you poured it on." He chuckled and dug back into his food.

They finished eating and Belle suggested another film. She didn't want him to leave.

"I should probably go." He glanced at the clock above the kitchen doorway. It was almost nine.

"No worries," Belle said, keeping her voice bright.

"I need to pack the van for tomorrow. We'll measure up for the shelving units and you can tell me where you want everything. I also need to sketch some ideas for your new counter. Think about what you want. Once we've got the shop completely cleared, I can give it a clean and plaster the walls."

Belle nodded. She didn't want to talk about the shop, but she couldn't tell him that.

"See you bright and early. I'll bring biscuits." He smiled at her before he swooped down and pressed a chaste kiss to her cheek. "Sleep well, Belle," he said as he picked up his toolbox and left.

Belle felt a cool rush of air whip around her as the door opened and closed. Her cheek burned from where his lips had been pressed moments ago. She sighed, knowing she needed to get her feelings in check. Nick was a friendly person, and he was treating her how he would anyone else. There was nothing more to it. They'd laid on the sofa watching films all afternoon, that was all. If anything, it showed he only saw her as a friend.

Needing to calm her racing mind, Belle ran

herself a bath and used the French lavender bubble bath her father had bought her last Christmas. She hoped it would be as relaxing as the bottle claimed.

CHAPTER NINE

Belle had just closed her eyes when her alarm blasted through the room. She groaned and turned it off as quickly as her sleepy joints would allow. Her mind had raced all night with thoughts of Nick and the idea of coming home each day to him. At some point in the endless darkness, Belle had buried her head in her pillow and screamed in frustration. It was all too much. She couldn't have a crush on Nick. He had a girlfriend and was only being friendly towards her. If he felt anything for her, it was probably pity. Her attraction to him and her loneliness was spinning it into something more. In those dark early hours of the morning where everything and nothing was possible all at once, she decided to simply ignore her feelings.

Knowing it would be another day of building work, Belle dressed in an old pair of striped dungarees with a white vest underneath. The dungarees were already splattered with paint from when she'd helped her father redecorate the antique shop. They'd painted it a bright white instead of the nicotine-stained yellow it had previously been. Estelle had been so grateful for Belle's help that she gifted her a butterfly brooch she'd been pining over.

With no time for breakfast, Belle filled a mug with coffee and threw her handbag over her shoulder. Yesterday's weather had passed, and the sky was blue again. Belle received a few odd glances as she wandered down to the harbour, sipping her coffee from a fish-shaped mug. She really needed to buy some and donate the ones in her cupboard - not that anyone would buy them.

"What on earth is that?" Nick asked, arriving at the shop at the same time as her. Despite her resolution to ignore her attraction towards him, she couldn't stop the butterflies that awoke in her stomach.

"I was running late and grabbed the first mug I could reach. Here, hold it while I find the keys." She thrust the mug into his hands before he could argue. Belle dived into her handbag in search of the key while Nick glanced around and used his hands to shield the offensive mug.

"Belle, will you get me a key cut so we don't have to go through this every morning?"

"You say this as if it happens all the time. You've only done a few day's work in the shop. Ah, got it!" She unlocked the door as Nick said something under his breath.

The shop looked as it had when she walked out yesterday, but she felt like a different person.

"Here's your mug." Nick handed it back to her as soon as her hands were free.

She took it from it, careful not to let their fingers touch. "Thanks. What shall I get on with?"

"Belle, you don't need to do anything. You're paying me to do it."

"I know, but what else am I supposed to do?"

Nick stared at her for a moment. His gaze bore into her as though he were peeling away her layers. "Why don't you make another drink? Then you can get started cleaning. I'll clean the office, then I can plaster in there. Probably best to start with the kitchenette, since we won't be able to use the office anymore."

Belle groaned. The kitchenette was in an awful state and she'd been putting off cleaning it. She made herself another coffee in the fish mug, not wanting to wash up an extra one.

It was a relief to get some space from Nick, even if he was in the other room. She might have decided to ignore her crush, but she couldn't stop her physical reaction. Belle gathered the cleaning products she'd used to clean the bathroom and began scrubbing the grime from the kitchen.

She lost herself in the task until there was a knock at the door. Belle stuck her head around the corner and spotted Tegen standing on the other side.

"Nick! Door for you," she shouted, but there

was no response from him. "Nick," she said again, but there was still nothing. Belle groaned as she heaved herself off of the cold floor. Every part of her ached, and she'd lost track of how much time had passed while she'd been scrubbing the cupboards.

"Hi, can I help you?" Belle said as she opened the door to Tegen.

"I'd like to speak to Nick," she said, her voice cold. Tegen looked her up and down, but didn't acknowledge their past.

"I called to him, but he must be busy," Belle said. She squinted as the sun shone in her eyes. Tegen wore a short denim skirt and an oversized white shirt tucked into it with the sleeves rolled up. Come to think of it, it was probably one of Nick's shirts. Belle swallowed against a wave of nausea.

"He'll want to talk to me," Tegen insisted, shooting Belle a condescending smile with her perfectly straight, bright-white teeth. She flicked back a strand of curled hair.

"He's through there plastering. Be careful." Belle gave her a sickly sweet smile as Tegen crossed the threshold and teetered towards the office in her far-too-high wedges.

Belle considered stepping outside for some fresh air and to allow Nick some privacy, but she couldn't resist eavesdropping, so she returned to her scrubbing.

"Nicky, baby," Tegen's high-pitched voice called. Belle screwed up her face and tightened her grip on the sponge.

"Tegen, what are you doing here?" Nick said. Belle could hear the surprise in his voice. Her hands stilled as she waited to see what he would say next.

"I came to see you. I missed you last night. Why didn't you pop over once you finished the job?"

"It was late by the time I finished. Besides, we don't stay over at each other's. That's one of our rules."

Belle forced her hands to move again in case either of them came out and saw her listening. At the very least, she could pretend she was working.

"You left the pub around two, Nick. Surely you weren't working for that long." Tegen's tone had hardened from the flirty, high-pitched one.

"I was tired, Tegen. I left the job and went straight home to bed." That wasn't exactly a lie.

"Yesterday's meal came under our agreement," Tegen said, and Belle frowned, wondering what the agreement was.

"I'm starting a new business. Surely you understand that I'm busy. I don't moan when you cancel because your friends need emergency nail appointments." Nick's sigh carried through to the shop.

"I don't like you working here with her. People will talk."

Belle shrunk against the cupboards and wished she'd gone outside for some fresh air.

"Don't bring Belle into this, Tegen." Nick's voice was hard and Belle could imagine him standing there with his arms across his chest and a stony expression on his face.

"You could have the pick of customers around here. I don't understand why you'd choose someone like her."

"I think it's best we continue this conversation another time."

Belle stared resolutely at the sponge in her hand as Nick led Tegen back into the shop and over to the door. Neither of them said goodbye to each other. Nick opened the door for Tegen and closed it behind her.

"I'm sorry, Belle," Nick said, wandering to where she was hunched over.

"It's fine," she mumbled. "Do you want a pasty for lunch? I might run out." Belle pushed past him. He called after her, but she didn't turn around.

The harbour was busy, but nobody noticed Belle stumbling through the crowds. She walked to the other side and made her way up the hill. It was quieter here, with fewer tourists milling around. Belle climbed up to the back of the hill and sat down on the grass. The sea was calm and the odd sailboat bobbed past. She wiped her eyes and was grateful she hadn't had time to put any makeup on that morning. She couldn't help but let Tegen's words get to her. Even as an adult, she didn't feel like she was enough, and Tegen's presence reinforced it. Anyone who saw Nick leaving her cottage last night wouldn't have worried about what he was up to. Why would they when he had a gorgeous girlfriend to go back to?

Belle took a deep breath and stopped her thoughts in their track. She needed to get a grip. Being back in Cornwall and then meeting Nick had churned up her emotions. She had to pull herself back and regain control. If she hadn't left her phone at the shop, Belle might have texted Jada to see if she wanted to get a coffee. Instead, she stood up and brushed any grass from her.

The bakery was busy, but Belle didn't mind queueing. People came and went as she waited. A couple of women stood side-by-side in the queue, each holding a toddler's hand. Belle watched as they reached the front. The women swung the toddlers into their arms to pick out their sugary treat. They left with them clasped in their hands, with huge smiles, and a smudge of jam across their mouths.

As Belle reached the front of the queue, she realised it was the same woman who had served her yesterday. "Belle, why didn't you introduce yourself yesterday?" The woman smiled.

"Sorry, Nick didn't tell me you ran the bakery," Belle said. She needed to find out the woman's name without pointing out that Nick hadn't told her that either.

"I'm sorry. That son of mine can be useless. I'm Jenny Penhale. I would shake your hand, but then I'd have to wash mine." She smiled and Belle immediately recognised it as Nick's.

"Lovely to meet you, Jenny. Nick's doing a wonderful job at the shop."

"Thank you, my love. It's nice to hear. Now,

what can I get you?"

"Two pasties, please."

"Is one of these for my son, by any chance?" asked Jenny, as she pulled two of the steak pasties from the industrial oven.

"It is."

"Nick came home last night complaining about how I never bring doughnuts home. Did he manage to fix your electricity?"

Belle took a moment to reply, shocked that his mother knew the truth about where he was. "He did, thank you. A doughnut was a small price to pay."

"Have a lovely afternoon." Jenny waved her off before turning to the next customer.

Belle wandered back across the harbour to the shop in a daze, wondering why he had told his mother the truth. Wasn't he worried she would say something to Tegen?

Nick was waiting for her when she returned. "I saw you crossing the harbour," he said as he held the door open.

"I've got lunch. Shall I put the kettle on?" She avoided his searching eyes.

"You sit down. I'll put the kettle on." They'd moved the drink-making items into the shop until the kitchenette was cleaned.

"How's the plastering coming along?" asked Belle.

"It was going really well before I was interrupted. No worries, I should have the office finished by the end of the day."

Belle nodded.

"Listen, Belle, I am sorry about Tegen. She shouldn't have come into your shop and spoken like that."

"It's not your fault. I let her in." Belle took a bite from her pasty. It was blistering hot.

"Well, I'm sorry."

Belle chewed the molten hot food and winced as she swallowed. "Why are you dating her, Nick?" she asked.

"I'm not." His brow furrowed, and he looked at her. "Wait, you think Tegen's my girlfriend?"

"Isn't she?"

"No! She's not my girlfriend, but I am seeing her." He plonked a mug of tea down beside her.

"Is there a difference?" Belle asked, picking at the pastry around the edge.

"Yes. We're not exclusive. I know she sees other men."

"I'm confused," Belle admitted. She put her pasty to the side and blew on the tea before she took a sip.

"About six months ago, we were both at the pub, surrounded by all our friends in relationships. We were the odd ones out and we made a pact to be each other's dates. Everyone else in the pub was in a relationship or babysat me growing up so it felt like a good idea. We go on dates, and I guess people think we're dating, but we're not exclusive. I don't see a future with Tegen and I'm sure she doesn't see one with me."

"I thought you were childhood sweethearts." Belle was horrified that she'd jumped to such a conclusion.

"Childhood sweethearts?" Nick laughed. "She's not my type."

"What is your type?" the question left Belle's lips before she could stop it.

"Brunette women with a soft spot for vintage jewellery." He winked at her.

Belle blushed and turned her gaze to look out the window as she processed the conversation. Tegen wasn't Nick's girlfriend, but they still had an agreement between them.

After lunch, Belle brushed the sugar from her fingers and finished cleaning. Her phone beeped, and she almost ignored it. Louis had been sending her pictures of jewellery all afternoon. However, this message was from the woman who was designing her advertisement board to say it was ready and she could collect it tomorrow.

"Nick, where can I get another shop key cut?" Belle asked, leaning against the doorway. Nick had taken his shirt off and was plastering in a thin t-shirt that was completely see-through. Belle sucked in a breath and forced her attention back to the freshly plastered walls.

"The DIY Shop by the Sea cuts keys," Nick said. He was reaching up to plaster a bit of the ceiling, and his top rose to reveal his taut stomach.

"Thanks," Belle gulped. "See you soon." She pushed herself to walk away.

Getting a key cut was easier than Belle had anticipated. Jago did it while she waited. She wandered the aisles for a few minutes while the key was cut. Once done, Belle shoved the original one in her pocket and held onto the new one to give to Nick.

By the time she returned, Nick had finished plastering. He was washing his hands in a bucket of water, which had turned murky from the plaster.

"That was quick," he commented as she walked in.

"Jago did it straight away. Here you go. Here's your very own key." Belle put it down beside his phone since he couldn't take it from her.

"Finally," Nick teased.

"I might not make it into the shop tomorrow. I need to pick up the advertisement board from Port Isaac. Will you be okay without me here?" she asked.

"Of course. I'll fit the spotlights this afternoon and my friend's popping in to install the CCTV and panic button this evening. The shop should be ready to plaster tomorrow, so it'll probably be easier without you here."

"Cheers!" Belle laughed.

"I didn't mean it like that," he stuttered.

"I know. I'm winding you up. See you soon." Belle collected the mugs and made to leave.

"When will I see you next?" Nick called after her.

"I'm not sure. Probably on Wednesday." Belle didn't linger to see Nick's reaction.

CHAPTER TEN

Belle walked the long way to her car to avoid passing the shop and bumping into Nick. He'd texted earlier, letting her know the key had worked fine, and he was planning to plaster the walls in the main shop. Belle had agonised over whether to add a kiss to the end of her reply. Eventually, she settled on one, not wanting to be rude. Her mind was still reeling from Nick's revelation yesterday. Was an agreement between Nick and Tegen any better than them being in a relationship? And then he'd admitted that she was his type. Her mind was a muddle and Belle needed to escape the harbour to put some distance between herself and Nick.

She dressed in a white A-line skirt that ended mid-thigh, with a white vest, and wrapped a blue and navy striped cardigan around her shoulders. Belle opted for a blue topaz ring, which was a simple solitaire on a silver band, and paired it with the matching earrings. They were simple pieces that would glisten in today's sunlight. Finally, Belle pulled on a pair of white trainers and grabbed her bag, making sure she had her car keys in there.

The garage was on the other side of the harbour, and Belle wove her way through the residential streets. With a deafening squeak, the garage door opened and Belle gingerly stepped inside. Her red Peugeot had a manual key. She reached the driver's door and unlocked it, careful not to brush her white outfit against the dirty car. A few flakes of paint floated to the ground as she opened the door. On the second try, the engine spluttered to life. Belle let out the breath she'd been holding and slowly reversed out of the garage.

It was a beautiful day. Belle unwound her window to allow the warm air to flow into the stuffy car. The drive to Port Isaac was half an hour, and she pootled along the country lanes.

"Come on, Marie," Belle encouraged the car along. She'd bought the car at eighteen after earning a profit on a first edition of Lewis Carrol's Through the Looking-Glass. Belle had discovered the book in a flea market and had been sure it was an original printed in 1871. Her father had thought she was wrong but suggested she buy it anyway since it was only fifty cents. In the car on the way home, Belle had spotted the telltale misprint of 'Wade'. The following day, they'd brought the book to an auction house where they confirmed it was a first edition. It sold the following weekend for one thousand euros.

The next weekend, Belle and her father bought the red Peugeot from an elderly man in their village who had been forced to stop driving due to his deteriorating eyesight. André had owned the car from new and had looked after it. He hadn't driven it much over the years, so it had travelled very few miles. Although the car meant a lot to her, Belle knew she would have to get a new one soon. The left-hand drive on the Peugeot made the winding country lanes difficult to navigate.

As Belle turned a corner, the sea came into view. She parked in the visitor's car park at the top of the hill. Zoe, the woman who was designing the board, told Belle to park there and had offered to drive her back to save her from carrying the board.

On the walk down to the sheltered harbour, Belle was grateful she'd opted for trainers. Although it was all downhill, the roads were steep. She wound her way through the streets, past the fishermen's cottages and an ice cream shop; Belle made a mental note to visit in the future. She followed the directions Zoe had texted her and took a left turn. She wanted to look out towards the vibrant sea and watch the world pass her by, but she didn't have enough time. Zoe was expecting her in five minutes.

Zoe's studio was housed in one of the old fishermen's cottages. Belle knocked and waited for an answer. Zoe had explained that she was closed to the public today.

"Belle." Zoe threw open the door. She wore a pair of green linen dungarees and her black hair was thrown up in a messy bun with a paintbrush speared through the middle.

"Zoe, lovely to meet you." Belle smiled as she noticed a smudge of white paint across the woman's cheek.

"Come in. Sorry, I lost track of time."

The studio was bright inside, with white walls. House plants covered every spare surface. There were even a few hanging from the ceiling. Zoe's painting equipment was strewn across the room. An easel stood by the window, positioned towards the harbour. A canvas was propped up on it with a half-finished painting of a fishing boat. Pots of paint lined the back wall. There must have been at least fifty different pots.

"Please excuse the mess," Zoe said. She'd picked up a cloth from the back of a chair and wiped her hands and face with it.

"You should see the state of my shop."

"I can't wait to visit when you're open. I've got the board out back. I didn't want it to be splattered with paint. Let me go fetch it."

Zoe returned with an A-frame board wrapped in bubble wrap. "Here it is," she announced as she set it in the middle of the room. Zoe gently peeled the tape off and unwound the protective wrap.

Belle gasped as she saw the design. At the top, '*The Cornish Vintage Jewellery Shop*' was painted in beautiful calligraphy. Below was a woman wearing a white 1950s dress. The skirt flared out and fell in beautiful layers, all of which had been shaded perfectly to show the fabric's movement. The woman wore a stunning ruby necklace which drew the eye. A halo of diamonds surrounded the dazzling jewel and a delicate gold chain wound around the model's neck. Zoe had used flecks of white paint and shading to show the light dancing off the fiery ruby. It was stunning. A pair of diamonds sat in the woman's ears and a gold watch wrapped around her wrist.

"Zoe, this is truly beautiful."

"Thank you. It's the same on the opposite side but different colours." She turned the board around. The woman wore a red dress and the red ruby had been swapped for a deep blue sapphire.

"I'm speechless. This is beyond anything I could have hoped for." Belle grasped for words to tell Zoe how wonderful her art was, but none were coming to her.

"It's got a protective clear coat, so you don't have to worry about the salty air damaging it. I've also popped a strip of chalkboard at the bottom." Zoe pointed to the part which read 'coming soon'. "Once you're open, you can rub that off. It could be left blank or you can pop your opening times on it."

"You've thought of everything."

"I've made one or two of these." Zoe chuckled. "Belle, do you have a website? I tried searching for you when I was looking for some inspiration for the jewellery, but couldn't find an online presence."

"No, I haven't. It's on my very long list of things to do."

"Feel free to say no, but I freelance as a web designer. I can help you out if you need one."

"That would be wonderful." Belle's gaze fell back on the advertisement board. If Zoe was half as good at designing websites, then she'd be lucky to have her.

"Do you have time this morning?" Zoe asked. She looked hopeful as she bounced from one foot to the other.

"I have no plans for the rest of the day."

Zoe clapped her hands and pulled Belle over to the corner of the room, which housed a huge desk with a computer and laptop set up.

Hours passed as Zoe and Belle chatted and designed the website. They settled on a colour scheme similar to the interior of the shop. Belle had shown Zoe the ribbon, and she'd been able to match the colour. The website was aesthetically pleasing and easy to navigate. It just needed pictures of the jewellery now. Zoe taught her how to upload the pictures and set the pieces up on the website. Belle promised to get started tomorrow.

"Gosh, it's past lunchtime. Do you fancy popping out for a bite to eat? My treat," Zoe said, stretching as she stepped away from the desk.

"That would be lovely. I forgot to eat breakfast this morning. I'm starving." Belle had been too busy fretting over her reply to Nick's text.

"Come on, there's a little café at the top of the hill that overlooks the harbour. Hopefully, we can nab a seat outside." Zoe ushered her out the door and locked it behind them.

They took a slow walk up the hill towards the café. Below, the sea glittered underneath the afternoon sun. Children ran in and out of the waves, giggling as the water splashed their toes. Dogs jumped through the shallow waters, barking with excitement. The people below became smaller with every step they took. Soon, they stopped outside the café. The outdoor seating was scattered across the pathway, with one spare table with an unspoilt view of the harbour. The two women strolled towards it and sighed as they sank into their seats.

"This is stunning," Belle commented. She picked up the menu and fanned herself with it.

"Isn't it? I must have the willpower of a saint not to wander up here every day. The scones are delicious."

Belle glanced down at the menu, but it was futile. The mention of scones had already swayed her decision. A waitress wandered over, and Zoe and Belle ordered scones with pots of tea.

"Did you grow up in Port Isaac?" Belle asked, unable to tear her gaze away from the view.

"No. Camden, actually. My parents retired to Cornwall and as soon as I visited them, I fell in love with the area. I only had enough to buy the studio, so I live in my parents' converted garage. It's not ideal, but it's much better than London. I get to look at this view every day and do what I enjoy for work." Zoe smiled and leaned back in her chair.

"It's hard to escape Cornwall once it touches your heart."

"What about you? Did you grow up here?"

As they waited for their lunch, Belle told Zoe the brief version.

"Are you glad to be back?" Zoe asked.

There was a pause as the waitress came over with their order. Belle used the interruption to consider her answer.

"I am glad to be back. It's been tough and I don't think it's going to be plain sailing. There's a lot of trauma connected with Cornwall, but I'm working through it."

Zoe nodded but didn't question Belle further.

The plain scones were served on blue and white plates, decorated with little pictures of willow trees. Belle remembered her parents had a similar set when she was little. A white ramekin was filled with luscious clotted cream and they each had two little pots of jam; one raspberry and one blackberry. Belle opted for blackberry jam and smothered half of a scone with it, then she added a thick layer of the cream, watching as it bled into the jam and created a beautiful swirl.

Zoe groaned around her mouthful. "This is amazing," she said, her eyes fluttering closed. Belle hummed her agreement as she sat back in her seat and ate the delicious treat.

Time slowed as they ate and drank. The world

around them seemed to float by, but it didn't touch them. Perched at the top of the harbour, it was as though they were caught up in a bubble.

As promised, Zoe drove Belle and her new advertisement board back to the car park.

"Thank you for this," Belle said and gave the woman a timid hug.

"You're most welcome. I cannot wait to see it outside your newly opened shop!"

"I'll send you an invite to my opening party. Will I see you before then?"

"Of course. Why don't we have dinner one evening?" suggested Zoe.

"How's Friday night? I'll invite Jada who runs the coffee shop. We can have some dinner and a chat."

"That sounds perfect. See you Friday."

Zoe waved Belle off as she navigated the roads back to Padstow-on-Sea, careful not to swing around the bends for fear of the board moving in the boot.

By the time Belle parked in the garage, it was almost five o'clock. The day had whizzed past in a blur of website designs and cream teas. Not wanting to leave the board in the boot, Belle carried it back to the cottage. She considered taking it to the shop but didn't know if Nick would still be there. Even if he wasn't, she didn't want to risk brushing against the wet plaster.

The walk back to the cottage felt five times longer than this morning. Belle took the back roads to avoid the crowds. She unlocked the cottage and left the board in the living room, still safely wrapped for when she carried it down to the shop.

It was a warm evening, and Belle didn't light a fire. She boiled the kettle and put some pasta on for dinner. While it boiled, Belle checked her phone and saw a text from Nick. He'd sent a picture of the plastered shop and told her it would need a week to dry out before they could start decorating. There was no kiss at the end of the text. Belle's heart dropped at the thought of not seeing him all week, but she sent him back a cheery message telling him to enjoy his week and that she would speak soon. She didn't put a kiss.

CHAPTER ELEVEN

Belle woke before sunrise the following morning. Her list of things to do churned in her head, and she couldn't delay it any longer. Still in her pyjamas, and with a coffee resting on the hallway floor, Belle unlocked the hatch to the loft and pulled down the metal stairs. She shivered as her foot touched the first rung of the ladder. As a child, the loft had terrified her, and as an adult, she wasn't feeling very brave. However, with nobody else to do it for her, Belle took another step towards the opening. A part of her wanted to jump off the ladder and text Nick to see if he was busy, but the sensible side of her brain warned her against it. She needed to stand on her own feet. She couldn't rely on him to bail her out again. With a deep breath, Belle ascended the ladder and pulled herself through the opening. She flicked on the switch and the small space lit up. At the back of the loft was a large safe, which contained all of

Belle's stock for the shop. These were pieces she'd spent years collecting. She crossed the boards in the loft, careful not to step in between them for fear of falling through. When her parents bought the cottage, her father had the loft reinforced, but Belle still hated going up there.

The safe was filled with jewellery. Belle picked out two of her favourite items. One was an Edwardian Aquamarine necklace. Oval Aquamarine stones were set in an elaborate nine carat gold pendant with seed pearls scattered amongst the pattern. The second piece was a Victorian eighteen carat gold ring with a cabochon amethyst in the centre. It was stunning, and when the light caught it, the amethyst glowed. The ring was in its original leather box, but the necklace hadn't come with one. Instead, Belle had sourced a pretty blue box that matched the colour of the aquamarine. She clutched the boxes tightly to her chest, locked the safe, and climbed back down the steps.

Belle placed the boxes on the kitchen table as she surveyed the cottage. Everywhere was too dark to show the gems off. She made a mental note to talk to Nick about having somewhere in the shop where she could photograph items. For now, she'd have to make do with the courtyard. Belle tidied up as much as possible. She'd take the pictures close-up to not include much of the surroundings. The outside table was rusting, so Belle used rattan placemats as a backdrop. By now, the sun was high in the sky and the jewels glistened beneath it.

The aquamarine shimmered as the light danced off it. It was the colour of a tropical sea and beckoned you closer with every sparkle. Belle had discovered the necklace as part of a larger lot. It wasn't uncommon to find people selling off the family heirlooms to finance estates. This necklace had been a part of a lot with an eye-watering reserve price. Belle had longingly stared at it through the glass and watched as the light reflected off the stones. The colour reminded her of the shallow Cornish rock pools that her mother would take her to. They'd spend hours watching the little fish swim and navigate the rocky waters.

"It's beautiful, non?" Estelle joined Belle.

"It's part of a bigger lot." Belle sighed and her shoulders sank.

"What a shame." Estelle wandered on to the next piece, leaving Belle behind.

"That's my favourite piece, too," a woman said. She reached out towards the glass case but pulled her hand back before she touched it. "It was my great-great-grandmother's."

Belle's attention switched from the necklace to the woman. She was at least a foot taller than Belle, with a blunt black bob and a tear-stained face.

"It's beautiful." Belle smiled. "The colour reminds me of the rock pools in Cornwall. My mum

would take me in the summer and we'd watch the small fish darting in and out of the shade." Belle sniffed. "Sorry."

"Nothing wrong with losing yourself in your memories." The woman's accent was surprisingly British, considering they were at an auction house in Paris.

"You'd get more money for the set," Belle automatically replied. She winced. "Sorry."

"No, you're right. My mother loved the earrings, so I had to keep them." The woman's stare was far away. Belle recognised the look.

Belle's heart ached for the woman. "Can't you keep the necklace?"

"No. I've inherited a chateau with half a roof." She huffed out a hollow chuckle. "Also, the necklace doesn't hold any memories for me."

"Oh." Belle had met many people in similar situations where families hadn't looked after their fortune and eventually it had all fallen on some poor soul's shoulders.

"Sorry. It's been a long few weeks."

"I can't speak for the chateau, but the loss gets easier." Belle reached out and placed a hand on the woman's arm. "The pain never goes, but it gets easier to live with." She shot the woman a sad smile and wandered after Estelle.

The auction had whizzed past in a frenzy of French that Belle couldn't understand. Estelle had helped her buy a couple of small lots, but for the most of it, her head had whirled at the chaos surrounding her.

Once it was over, Belle stood at the entrance, waiting for Estelle to finish the paperwork. The fresh air had been welcome after the stuffiness of the auction house.

"Let's go," Estelle said and ushered Belle towards the car.

"Can we get some lunch?" asked Belle. Her stomach had been rumbling for the last hour.

"I have something for you. Hold out your hand," Estelle instructed.

Belle raised an eyebrow and held her hands out. She jumped as the cool feeling of jewellery hit her hands and pooled in the middle. It felt like a necklace chain with a heavy pendant.

"I thought we were having everything shipped to us?" asked Belle, her brow furrowed.

"This was a gift."

Belle gasped as she spotted the aquamarine necklace nestled in her palms. "Estelle, it's too expensive. You can't gift me this."

"It's not from me. The woman said it was a gift for you. She said you're the only one who had shown her kindness." Estelle shrugged.

Belle's heart hurt for the woman. "I should go back inside and find her."

"She went out the back. Poor girl, tears were falling down her face."

"I shouldn't accept this, Estelle. It's too much."

"Keep it, Belle. Its value is nothing compared to what the woman's lots have sold for. Use it for your future."

It was two o'clock by the time Belle sat down with a sandwich. Having made several trips back up to the loft, she'd photographed twenty pieces of jewellery from the safe upstairs. While she ate, she uploaded them to her new website and typed out extensive descriptions for each piece. Once that was finished, Belle pulled a suitcase from underneath her bed where she kept the less expensive jewellery. These pieces were costume jewellery. The jewels were either of a lesser value or were coloured glass. Belle was adamant that she wanted the shop to be for all budgets, which was why she'd been collecting these pieces for a while now. Her plan for the afternoon was to shoot some of the cheaper pieces and upload them on the website.

Belle let out a yawn as she snapped the final picture. Her phone pinged with a notification, and Belle clicked on it. She'd sold the aquamarine necklace. Unable to contain her excitement, Belle went to her phonebook and called Jada.

"Hello?" she answered straight away.

"Jada, do you have any plans for this evening?"

"Not really, unless you count bingeing Netflix. Why?"

Belle explained how she'd spent the day setting up her website and had sold her first piece of jewellery. "I want to do something to celebrate. Shall we go for dinner? My treat," Belle said. She crossed her fingers as she waited for Jada's reply.

"I'd love to. Where were you thinking?"

"What about the new restaurant at the top of the harbour?" Belle suggested.

"I've been wanting to try it. Shall we meet there at seven? I'll call them and see if we need to book a table."

"Perfect. See you soon."

Belle put the phone down and made a coffee as she sat to upload the costume jewellery to the website. She also ordered some packaging to send the necklace off in the next couple of days. Belle made a mental note to look into personalised packaging once the shop was established.

"There you are." Jada waved as Belle walked up the final few stairs. She was out of breath and regretted her outfit for the warm spring evening. "You look amazing!"

"Thank you, so do you. I love this dress." Belle embraced Jada, who wore a beautiful green dress with a corset top and an A-line skirt. Her dark skin glowed against the colour of the dress and her hair was pulled back with a matching green silk scarf.

"I bought it ages ago, but haven't had the chance to wear it and tonight seemed perfect. You must be hot in those. They look amazing, though,"

Jada said, glancing down at Belle's leather trousers.

"Thanks. It was chilly inside the cottage. I didn't realise how lovely the evening was." Belle had chosen the straight-leg trousers with a matching black vest and a belt that cinched her in at the waist. Truthfully, the outfit was simply a backdrop for the jewellery she'd chosen. The necklace was a chunky cluster of faux pearls and white glossy shells. She'd paired it with pearl stud earrings and put her hair up in a claw clip to stop it tangling in the necklace.

"I'm sure you'll be okay. I love this necklace. Are they real pearls?"

"Unfortunately not. I found this in a house clearance on the outskirts of Toulouse. My dad took me with him to view some of the furniture and I spotted this at the back of a cupboard. The woman's daughter hadn't realised it was there and gave it to me." Belle had been ecstatic with her find. Her father had pointed out that it didn't hold much value, but Belle didn't mind, since selling it had never crossed her mind.

"Shall we head in?" Jada asked, tilting her head towards the restaurant behind them.

The Seaside Cauldron was at the top of the harbour and boasted the best views in town. Blooming wisteria covered the front of the building and filled the air with the gentle hum of bees. In the middle was an arched doorway with a pale blue door, which they walked through. They were greeted by a waiter and shown to the outside terrace, which overlooked the sea. Sailing boats bobbed up and down on the harbour below. Beyond, Belle could see Padstow Bay enveloped in the evening's golden glow. The sand was like shimmering honey and the deep blue sea lured swimmers to the shore.

"This is stunning," Belle said, settling into her chair. Despite being at the top of the harbour, the air still had a salty tang to it.

They ordered their meals, both sticking to soft drinks as Jada had to be up early to bake for the coffee shop and Belle wanted to get an early start photographing more stock.

"I think I met Zoe briefly at a Cornish networking event about a year ago," Jada said as her finger traced the rim of her glass.

"That's cool. She was lovely and really helpful. If you ever need a website for the coffee shop, then she's your girl."

Jada hummed in response, but she looked far away.

"Are you okay?" asked Belle.

"Yes, sorry." Jada shook her head and focused her eyes on Belle. "Can I tell you something, Belle?"

Belle nodded.

"Zoe is just my type," Jada whispered. Her eyes flickered back to her glass.

"Oh!" Belle let out a chuckle of relief and reached out to squeeze Jada's hand. "You have good taste. I think."

Jada laughed.

"If we're being open here, then I guess I

should tell you that Nick is just my type." It was Belle's turn to glance down at her glass.

"I think everyone in Padstow-on-Sea knows that." Jada laughed, and Belle joined in. "Speaking of Nick, I saw him having dinner at the pub with Tegen last night. The atmosphere was tense, and she stormed off halfway through the meal."

"Oh, no. I think it might be my fault." Belle sighed before she told Jada about Tegen's visit. "Then Nick told me they're not actually dating. They have this agreement. Reading between the lines, it sounds like a friends-with-benefits kind of situation."

"So he's not actually off the market?"

"Is an agreement any better than a relationship?" Belle's shoulders sagged as she finally voiced her thoughts. Girlfriend or fake girlfriend, Tegen was still a part of Nick's life.

"If they're seeing other people, then it makes a big difference. It means his flirting with you means something."

Belle fiddled with the edge of her napkin. "He said I'm his type."

Jada's jaw dropped and their food arrived. Jada had opted for the Lobster salad and Belle had chosen the battered cod, triple-cooked chunky chips, and minted peas.

"Belle, this is huge. He likes you!" Jada said as she loaded her fork with a mouthful of salad.

"I'm not looking for a relationship." Belle picked up a chip and nibbled it. It was delicious with a crunchy shell and a fluffy inside, but she was no longer hungry.

"Who says it has to be something serious?"

"I'm so confused. I have all these thoughts and feelings and I don't know what to do with any of them."

"Nick's not going anywhere, Belle. You have time to work through everything."

As they ate, Belle moved the conversation onto their businesses.

By the time they left The Seaside Cauldron, the sun was dropping below the horizon. They linked arms and wandered back down to the harbour. It was a barmy evening and people spilled out of the restaurants as they passed by.

"Belle!" The shout came from a pizzeria on their right. Belle turned her head and searched the people for someone she recognised. It was Nick. He was sitting in the middle of a table with six other men surrounding him. From the way he was slouched in his seat, Belle guessed the bottle of beer in front of him wasn't his first.

"Evening, Nick," she called back to him, pulling Jada to a halt beside her.

"Join us for a drink?" he slurred.

"No, thanks. We've got an early morning," Belle said, cringing as everyone turned to watch their conversation.

"We could stop for one," Jada said quietly in her ear, but Belle shook her head.

"Your loss," Nick shouted back.

Belle rolled her eyes and waved. "See you

soon," she said, which earned some raucous hoots from his friends.

Belle and Jada walked to the middle point of the harbour, where they then split off in different directions.

"Pop in one day for a coffee," Jada said, throwing her arms around Belle.

"I will. Zoe's coming round for dinner on Friday. Why don't you join us?" Belle suggested.

"I wish I'd never told you," groaned Jada.

"When you stop teasing me about Nick, I'll stop teasing you about Zoe."

"You don't play fair, Belle Roux."

"Goodnight, Jada." Belle waved as she took the lefthand fork in the path and made her way up the cobbled street to her little cottage.

Inside, Belle changed and took off her makeup. She made herself a cup of tea and brought it up to bed with her. Belle was tempted to light the lavender-scented candle her father had bought her on a trip to the vineyard but decided against it. At home in France, she had no worries about lighting candles, knowing her father would be up late and would put it out if she fell asleep. She slid under her covers and pulled them around herself. Despite the warm evening, the draughty cottage was cold.

She sent a text to Jada, thanking her for a lovely evening. As she was about to put it down on her bedside table, a text from Nick came through. Belle opened it and chuckled as she read it. He apologised for being drunk and told her he'd speak to her soon. At the end, he'd added 'You looked hot in those trousers.' With nobody around to see, Belle let a huge smile spread across her face. Perhaps embracing his flirting would help her work through the jumble.

CHAPTER TWELVE

Belle gathered the packages and slid them into a tote bag to carry down to the post office. After the first sale on her website, Belle uploaded more stock and things were selling fast. Her father had shared the site with his network and from there, her audience had grown. She had a delivery of jewellery from her father coming that afternoon, and she'd decided to put most of it away to stock the shop. With the success of the website, she needed to open the shop soon, or else she'd run out of stock.

The walk into the harbour was busy. It was almost July and school holidays would begin soon. For now, Padstow-on-Sea was filled with childless couples enjoying the last few days before families descended. The post office was nestled at the back of the newsagent and was surprisingly quiet. Belle sent the packages off and hoped their new owners would love them. These were all costume jewellery purchases. The courier that was delivering her jewellery was also picking up the more expensive pieces she'd sold.

With her errand complete, Belle popped over to Jada's coffee shop. It was busy inside. Jada spotted her and waved, pointing her towards an empty table by the till. "I'll be over in a bit," she mouthed. Belle nodded and took a seat, watching the customers come and go. It was a treat to be able to people-watch. Lately, Belle had too many things running around her mind that she couldn't sit still.

Nick walked through the door and goosebumps broke out across Belle's body. She shivered at the feeling and moved her attention to the sticky tabletop. They hadn't spoken since his drunken text, and while Belle knew they needed to, she was keen to put it off for as long as possible.

"Hi, Nick," Jada called across the café. Belle kept her head low. "Let me serve these customers, then I'll be with you. Take a seat over there with Belle and I'll bring you both a coffee in a minute." Belle could hear the smile in Jada's voice.

"Morning, Belle," Nick said, taking the seat opposite her.

"Morning," she replied, lifting her head to meet his gaze. His eyes captured hers, and Belle couldn't stop her smile. She felt shy around him. Nick didn't have a girlfriend, but what did that mean for her crush on him? He still had an agreement with Tegen.

"How are you?" he asked as he put down a

notepad, pencil, and tape measure.

"I've been busy setting up the website for the shop. How're you?"

"I still have a headache from the other night, to be honest with you." He chuckled and winced.

"You seemed very merry. Were you celebrating?"

"Something like that." He nodded.

"Do you know how well the plaster is drying?" Belle asked, steering the conversation onto a safer topic.

"It should be ready for us to decorate next week. I've been making the display cabinets and counter. If it all goes to plan, we'll have you open in two weeks at the latest."

Belle blinked and swallowed the emotions building inside of her at how he kept saying 'we'. "Sounds great."

"Here's your coffee. Sorry, we've been super busy and someone phoned in sick." Jada put down two cappuccinos and took the third seat.

"I can help out if you want?" Belle offered.

"No, you've got your own things to do. I've got someone coming in for the lunchtime rush. I'll be fine."

"If you talk me through your plans, then I'll measure up. I can come back tomorrow when you're not as busy to talk through quotes," Nick said.

Belle sipped her coffee and listened to Jada and Nick. She gathered that Jada was looking to turn the courtyard into a decked outside seating area.

"I need to go. There's a customer. I'll see you Friday, Belle?" Jada said, standing up and waving to the customer.

"Yes. Let's meet by my shop and I'll drive us to the bay," Belle said. She'd spoken to Zoe and arranged for the three of them to have a beach picnic on Friday evening.

"Text me what food you want me to bring." Jada blew her a kiss and disappeared behind the counter.

"Is business—" Belle began, but was interrupted by Nick.

"We should go for a drink sometime," he said. "Sorry, what were you going to say?"

Belle opened and closed her mouth, but nothing came out. She cleared her throat. "I was, um, going to ask if your business is picking up?"

His eyes darkened. "Yes, it is." He swirled the coffee in his cup.

"Anyway, I should be getting off. I'm expecting a courier this afternoon." Her chair scraped against the floor as she stood.

"Yes, I should start measuring up for Jada." He drained his cup. "See you soon, Belle," he said before he picked up their empty cups and took them to the counter.

Belle's legs shook as she walked to the door and out into the bright day. A seagull flew above her head and startled her. She picked up her feet and walked back to the cottage in a daze. Had he really asked her out for a drink? She'd acted as if she hadn't heard him, but she'd seen the way his eyes had changed.

The courier arrived at midday and unloaded wooden crates into Belle's living room. She could just about squeeze around them to get to the kitchen. Belle's fingers itched to undo the delivery, but she slowed herself and made a cup of tea first, knowing that she'd be unboxing items for the next few hours. She chose a packet of malted milks and settled on the floor of the living room, ignoring the niggling memories of Nick and his love for biscuits.

Belle undid the first crate and unpacked a few of the items. Her father had wrapped them in old newspaper, followed by a layer of bubble wrap, and old sheets between each piece. The first item Belle picked was a large square leather box, which looked as though it would hold a necklace. Belle held her breath as she opened it, but was surprised to find it held four vintage gold chain link watches. There were many of these around, but most weren't real gold. Belle noticed a small note attached to the box. It was from her father telling her he'd found them at a bargain price and that they had all been certified as nine carat gold. The watches were pretty, each one had a different clock face, one was round, while another was rectangular. Eager to discover more, Belle put the leather case on the sofa to organise later.

The next items she pulled out were vintage cuff links, followed by a pretty brooch from the sixties, a handful of signet rings, and a vintage gold bangle with a floral design engraved on it. There was a stunning garnet dress ring set on a white gold band. The stone was eye-catching and Belle wished she'd known its history, who had worn it, and what parties it had attended.

By the time Belle had gone through the contents of the first crate, she'd finished her cup of tea and was halfway through the packet of biscuits which were doubling as her lunch. On the sofa, which she rested her back against, was a pile of jewellery in various boxes. Some original, and others makeshift ones to transport them. The box had been filled with costume and vintage jewellery, most of which retailed at a lower price, but was still integral to the shop's success. Belle was excited to open the second box since her father had notified her of a handful of antiques that he'd picked up on his travels.

Belle opened the second one and found a parcel wrapped in pink tissue paper at the top with a card stuck to it. She undid the card and immediately recognised the handwriting as her father's.

Dear Belle,

I saw this piece and instantly thought of you and your mother.

Keep this one as a gift.

Lots of love,
Dad xxx

With shaking hands, Belle undid the tissue paper to discover a small black ring box inside. She took a deep breath, unsure if she was ready for whatever feelings were about to hit her. With a jaunty click, it opened to reveal a beautiful Art Deco ring nestled against the cream velvet. The ring's silver band was in a chevron and was set with small round cut, black spinels. In the centre was a pearl cut in a kite shape with a halo of black spinel. It was identical to the one her mother had once owned. They'd lost it during the move to France, and despite emptying every box and turfing through its contents, they'd never found it. Belle remembered the day her mother had bought the ring.

"Why can't I go with Daddy?" Eight-year-old Belle wailed as she watched her father climb into the taxi outside their cottage.

"He's going to be gone for a few days, Belle, and you have school on Monday," her mother reminded her. She was standing behind Belle with a hand on her back. Louis turned and gave them a wave, which only caused Belle to sob. "Why don't we do something fun together?" her

mother suggested.

"Can we go to your favourite antique shop?" Belle stuttered out.

"Of course we can. You run up to the bathroom and dry your eyes and I'll make us some sandwiches for the journey."

Belle did as she was told. While she was upstairs, she went to her bedroom and put on the necklace her father had bought her on his last trip. It was a simple silver chain with a heart pendant hanging from it made from coloured glass. Belle had loved it and had begged to wear it to school, but both of her parents had said she couldn't.

"There you are. Your necklace looks beautiful," Kerenza said as she wrapped their sandwiches in foil and placed them in the cool bag.

"Thank you, Mummy," Belle said. "I like your necklace."

Kerenza wore denim shorts with a blue flowery blouse, with a simple silver chain around her neck. It was the first day of July and it was the hottest day of the year.

They got into the family car, and it took all of Belle's strength to unwind her window. The car was stifling hot, but her mother promised they would cool down once the car moved and the breeze flowed through the windows.

Kerenza opted to take the longer route, taking them along the coastal road. They passed beaches with golden soft sand and bright blue sea. On their other side were meadows filled with wildflowers. The air was sweet as the breeze filled the car and the sound of 80s hits came out of the CD player. Kerenza parked on a grass verge and helped Belle out of the car. They carefully climbed down the steps that led to a secluded bay occupied by a handful of people.

Belle sat on the sand and looked out towards the sea as her mother unpacked the picnic. She wondered where her father was right now.

"Here you go. It's cheese and salad. There's crisps and a couple of cans of lemonade."

They ate as they watched a spaniel run in and out of the waves. Now and then he would run back to his owners and bark as he shook water onto them. Belle laughed.

"Where do you think Dad is right now?" Belle asked as she unwrapped the chocolate bar.

"He'll be on the train to London. I'm sure he'll call us tonight once he's settled."

They'd sat in companionable silence for a while longer before her mother asked her how she was getting on at school.

"It's okay." Belle stared out to sea as she balled up the empty chocolate wrapper in her fist.

"Just okay? I saw you talking to those girls in the playground when I picked you up yesterday."

Belle dug her toes into the sand. "I wasn't talking to them."

"Well, they were talking to you."

"They said I smelt funny," Belle admitted. Her voice was small against the crashing of the waves, the bark of the dog, and the squeals of young children.

"Oh, Belle." Her mother wrapped her arms around her hugged her tightly. "They're silly, mean girls."

"I know," sniffed Belle. They'd had this conversation many times.

"Do you want me to have a word with your teacher?"

"No, thanks, Mum. It didn't help last time." Last time, Mr Knowles had made her sit and eat lunch with them. Once the teachers had left them to it, Tegen made fun of her lunchbox and asked if everything inside was also second hand.

"Okay. Well, let's forget about those girls. It's Saturday, and it's our treat day. Come on, let's head back to the car and drive on to the antiques shop."

The shop in question was located in a small village just twenty minutes away. It was housed in an old Tudor cottage where the floors sloped and the ceilings were so low Belle could almost touch the dark wooden beams.

Glass cabinets were filled with an assortment of antiques, from teddy bears to diamond rings. Belle wandered over to a box filled with beads. They were the cheapest thing in the shop, but she loved the colours and how they would look in the sunshine lined up by her bedroom window.

"Belle, what do you think of this?" Kerenza beckoned Belle over to a cabinet filled with Art Deco jewellery. Belle clasped the four beads she'd chosen in her hand and went to see what her mother was looking at. It was a beautiful iridescent pearl cut into a kite shape with tiny black round gems surrounding it, which continued onto the band of the ring.

"I love it, Mum," Belle said, staring at the jewellery. "It would look lovely with your favourite red nail varnish."

"It would, wouldn't it? I know what your father would say about the price." Kerenza slid the ring onto her finger and admired it.

"I've seen similar sell for the same price," Belle said, her eyes transfixed on the ring.

"Have you now?" Kerenza chuckled.

"Dad sometimes reads me the auction brochure before bed."

"I'll be having words with him about that. Children your age should be reading something exciting, not guideline prices for Art Deco jewellery." Kerenza rolled her eyes but smiled.

"I don't mind," Belle said, her attention moving to the shelf below where there were more beads.

"I'll get it. Have you found anything?"

Belle held out her closed hand and opened it to reveal the four beads she'd picked up. She'd chosen four different colours, a vibrant orange, a dusky pink, a lavender, and a silver one.

"They're beautiful. Come on, let's see what else the shop has. Although I think we've both already blown our budgets!"

It took them an hour to walk around the two floors of antiques. Neither Belle nor Kerenza picked up anything more to buy. They enjoyed walking around and looking at everything. Belle spotted a vase similar *to one her father had recently purchased and took out the small notebook and pen that she kept in her back pocket. She jotted down the price to tell Louis. Once they'd paid for their items, they declined a bag. Belle put the beads in her pocket and Kerenza wore the ring.*

"Shall we get milkshakes from the cafe next door for the drive home?" suggested Belle.

Belle blinked as she focused on the ring still clasped in her hands. It was truly identical to the one her mother had found that day. She slid it on her finger and was surprised to find it fit. Belle shook her head. She should have known her father would think of something like that. The day out had been one of Belle's favourite memories with her mother. They'd bought milkshakes and driven home. Louis had phoned before bedtime and Belle had told him all about their day out and the vase she'd spotted.

CHAPTER THIRTEEN

"Did you get the parcel?" Louis asked as soon as Belle answered the phone.

"Morning, Dad," Belle yawned. She sat up in bed and picked up the watch on her bedside table. It was six in the morning.

"Sorry, did I wake you?"

"Yes, but it's fine. I should be up now, anyway. I've got a few more pieces I want to photograph and upload to the website."

"Did you find the ring?"

"I did. Thank you. I tried calling you last night, but your phone went straight to voicemail."

"The battery died, and I lost my charger," he explained. His voice shook, and Belle knew he was lying. Louis didn't lose anything. He could find a pin amongst his hoards of antiques.

"No worries," Belle said. She wasn't sure she was ready to question him about where he'd been lately, or who he'd been with. Ten years might have passed since her mother's death, but she couldn't imagine him with anybody else. Especially now, when her emotions felt so raw after returning to Cornwall. "It's the same as Mum's," she whispered.

"I know. I felt awful when we lost it in the move. As soon as I saw it, I knew I had to buy it. Mind you, I almost baulked at the price. Your mother was always good at picking out pieces that would grow in value." Louis let out a soft chuckle.

Belle hummed her agreement and wished she were at home with her father, where he could wrap his arms around her as they remembered her mother. Then they'd walk into the village to console themselves with freshly baked pastries. But this was her home now and her father was very far away. "What are you up to today?" she asked, eager to move the conversation on to stop her thoughts from spiralling any further.

Once Belle had finished talking to Louis, she switched the kettle on and stared out the window as she waited for it to boil. She'd been thinking about getting a companion to help with the loneliness, and the last couple of days had cemented that thought. A little dog was what she needed to keep her company and once the shop was open, it would come to work with her. Unsure where to start on her quest for a canine companion, Belle decided to text Nick.

If someone wanted to adopt a dog around here, where would they go?

The kettle hadn't even boiled before Belle's phone rang. It was Nick.

"Hello?" she answered, spooning the coffee into her mug with one hand.

"Are you getting a dog?" he asked, skipping any polite formalities.

"I'm thinking about it."

"Have you ever had one?" he asked. Belle could hear him walking around as his heavy boots hit the floor.

"Yes. Well, sort of. We often dog-sat for our neighbours in France."

"Okay. Well, there's a rescue place about an hour away. We could go and look today."

"Nick, you don't have to come with me. You've got work to do." The kettle clicked off, and Belle filled her mug.

"Belle Roux, there is not a chance on this earth that you're looking at dogs without me." His tone was firm.

She chuckled. "Okay. When can you be ready?"

"Give me an hour to finish the coat of primer on your shelves."

"Perfect. I'll meet you by the shop?"

She took the coffee upstairs and picked up the ring her father had gifted her. Belle remembered the blouse her mother had worn the day she bought the ring. It was a pale blue with white daisies on it. The blouse wasn't something Belle would wear. Instead, she'd had a seamstress turn it into a hair ribbon. Belle opened her wardrobe and leafed through the various ribbons, they were hung on the wardrobe's tie rack. Her fingers brushed against the soft fabric. She wrapped the scarf around her bun and then threw on a black vest and a pair of denim shorts. The only piece of jewellery she wore was the ring.

With time to spare, Belle wandered down to her shop. As she waited, she peered inside and saw the plaster was slowly drying and turning a shade of pale pink. Nick had installed the spotlights before re-plastering the ceiling, but Belle hadn't had the chance to see them switched on yet. They would soon be able to decorate and put the new shelving units in. Belle pushed her sunglasses off her face and tipped her head towards the sun, basking in a few minutes of doing nothing.

"Frenchie!" Nick called, interrupting her peace. She cracked an eye open, and a flush rushed through her at the sight of him. His hair was wet, suggesting he'd just climbed out of a shower. He wore a white t-shirt and pastel blue shorts. Belle smiled and pulled her sunglasses on to look at him without squinting. He wore sunglasses, which hid his beautiful eyes, and a pang of something indescribable filled her. She wasn't about to delve any deeper to discover what that something was.

"You ready?" she asked, keen not to linger too

long where Tegen might see them.

"Come on, I've borrowed the keys to my mum's car since my van is full of sawdust." He threw an arm around her shoulders and guided her out of the harbour.

"We could always take my car?" she suggested, enjoying the weight of his arm around her as she nestled into his side.

"I've heard stories about your car, Belle. People can't decide if they're impressed or terrified that you're tackling these winding roads in a left-hand drive. Let's take my Mum's. She said it's fine, and she has aircon."

Belle couldn't argue with that. The car was parked nearby, and Belle laughed as Nick folded himself into the Fiat 500.

"It wouldn't be my car of choice," he said, pushing the seat back as far as it would go.

"I love it," Belle said. She'd wanted one herself but couldn't afford it with opening up the shop.

"What's made you decide now's the right time for a dog?" Nick asked as he manoeuvred the car out of the car park.

"I'm a bit lonely," Belle admitted.

"Oh, Belle." He reached out and took her hand in his. Her hand was soft in his calloused one and his grip was tight. Belle's heart hammered in her chest, and the loneliness that had wrapped around her ebbed away. "You can always call me when you feel like that," he said.

Belle decided not to point out the obvious

reason as to why she couldn't do that. "Thanks, Nick. It'll be nice to have a companion in a dog. To know I'm not the only one in the cottage." She liked the idea of snuggling up with a dog in front of the fire after a long day in the shop. Sometimes her imagination liked to tease her and include Nick sitting on the other side of the sofa. When that happened, she had to busy herself to chase away those thoughts.

Her hand fit perfectly in his, but she knew she needed to stop it. "I've got some sweets in my bag. Do you want one?" She slid her hand from his and ignored the emptiness that filled her.

"Yes, please. Has anyone ever told you that you're the perfect passenger?" he joked.

"My mum would always make sure we had snacks for a car journey."

"She sounds lovely," Nick said.

"I'm assuming you love dogs since you offered to come with me today?" Belle asked, moving the conversation away from her mother. Yesterday had been difficult with the memories the ring had stirred up. She needed an escape from her emotions today.

"Love them. Growing up, we always had a dog. They'd go to work with my dad. Last year, we lost our last one. A Labrador named Buddy. I was eleven when I named him." Nick shot her a smile. "My parents feel they're too old to adopt another, but made it clear they'd help out if I get one in the future."

"Should you sit in the car while I go in today?" Belle joked.

"I don't think I'm ready yet. I need to get my business started and at some point, I'd like to move out from my parents. It wouldn't be fair to allow a dog to get used to living with them and then move it." He sighed before continuing. "Also, Tegen's allergic, which is the real reason why I haven't done anything yet."

"Oh." Belle didn't know what more to say. She turned to watch the scenery pass.

"What kind of dog are you looking for?" Nick asked after a few moments of silence.

"Something small and calm. I want to take it to work with me, so it needs to be well-behaved around customers."

"Of course. Don't be too disheartened if they don't have any dogs that fit your needs on this visit. You can give them your details and we can pop back if one comes in."

Belle nodded and smiled at the way he'd said 'we'.

They pulled up outside the adoption centre and Belle jumped out of the car, unable to contain her excitement for a moment longer. Nick took her hand and led her to the entrance. She didn't know if he did it because he wanted to hold her hand, or if he was trying to calm her down. Belle preferred to assume it was the first option. Inside, a woman greeted them with a smile and asked how she might help them.

"I'd like to register my interest in adopting a dog," Belle said, stepping up to the counter.

"Wonderful. I have a form for you to fill out. You can both take a seat over there." She pointed to a waiting area. "Once you've finished, bring it back to me and I'll pass it on to someone. It should only take them about ten minutes to read through it and then somebody will be out to chat with you." She handed Belle a clipboard with a three-page form on it.

"Okay." Belle nodded, feeling overwhelmed.

"Thank you," Nick called back as he led Belle to sit down. "Do you need some help?" he asked, pointedly glancing at her shaking hands.

"No, it's fine. I'm excited." She took a seat but couldn't stop her legs from bouncing. Belle leaned the clipboard on the chair's armrest and began filling it out. The questions ranged from her living situation, what she did for work, and finally what she'd like in a dog.

Once finished, Belle handed it back to the woman at reception.

"Everyone's a little tied up at the moment," she said, taking the form. "Would you like to go through and look at the dogs while you wait?"

Belle's face lit up. "Yes, please."

"Just through that door." The woman pointed. "I'll buzz you in."

"Thank you," Belle said and went to get Nick.

"We're going to see the dogs. Come on." She pulled on his arm and he followed.

"You can't fall for one based on looks, Belle,"

he warned her.

Belle cleared her throat. "I'll be sensible," she promised.

They followed the corridor to the indoor kennels. Belle instantly knew she was in trouble as she saw the dogs notice their visitors and wander over to the windows.

"Don't," Nick warned as he stared intently at her.

"How on earth am I supposed to pick one?" She pouted.

"Take a deep breath and remember what you wrote on that form." He placed his hands on her shoulders.

Belle looked up at him, and the whirlwind inside her calmed. "Okay. Small, calm, and friendly," she reminded herself.

He took her hand as they walked past the kennels. Belle's heart lurched at every friendly face that peered out at her.

"He's gorgeous, and look how gentle he seems," Belle said, approaching a kennel. The plaque on it said his name was Barney and that he had been at the centre for one week. His gaze met Belle's as she crouched to see him better.

"It says here he's ten weeks old and they think he'll grow to about forty kilos."

"That means nothing to me, Nick," Belle grumbled as she smiled at the fluffy brown dog.

"It's the size of a Labrador, Belle."

"Oh." Belle gave the dog a sad smile and

stepped back. "I think he'd be too big to keep in the shop with me every day."

"Look, what about this little one?" Nick pointed to a kennel on the opposite wall where a dog was curled up in its bed, sleeping.

Belle joined Nick and peered in. It was difficult to see much of the dog as it was curled tightly into a little ball.

"It says here that she's of terrier descent," Nick read from the plaque. "Only three months old. She was dumped by breeders because she was the runt of the litter."

"Does she have a name?" Belle asked. At the sound of her voice, the little dog looked up and blinked its sleepy eyes.

"They're calling her Pearl."

Belle's heart skipped a beat. "This is my dog," she said, her gaze transfixed on Pearl as she stared back at her.

"I think she does tick all of your boxes." Nick was squinting at the plaque.

"Miss Roux?" A man approached them wearing the adoption centre's uniform.

"Yes, that's me." She tore her attention away from the puppy to greet the man.

"I'm Roger, head re-homer here. I see you've met Pearl already. She was actually the one I was going to suggest after reading through your forms."

"She's beautiful," Belle said, turning back to the dog.

"Would you like to go in and meet her?" asked

Roger.

"Yes, please."

Roger pulled out a big hoop with lots of keys attached to it. As he searched for the one to Pearl's kennel, Belle wrung her hands. Nick placed a hand on the small of her back and shot her a smile. She leaned into his touch and her stomach filled with butterflies.

"Hello, little one," Belle said, keeping her voice low, as she stepped into the kennel ahead of the two men. Pearl tentatively stood and climbed out of her bed. She stopped a few steps from Belle and stretched. "I'm very sorry to wake you." Belle knelt on the floor to allow the dog to wander to her. Pearl sniffed along the floor up to Belle's knees, where she stopped and sat, staring up at her. Belle lifted a hand and allowed Pearl to sniff it before she scratched behind the dog's ear. Pearl was white with beige splotches across her body. She had one white ear, and the other was beige. Her brown eyes were kind and bore into Belle's as she leaned into the scratch.

"She's been with us for two months," Roger explained. "A member of the public found her abandoned in a box at a recycling plant when she was only four weeks old. Because she was so small and taken from her mother too soon, we haven't allowed her to be re-homed until now. She's very much a people dog because she was hand-reared. She's a soft little thing."

"I love her," Belle said as the dog put one

paw out onto her knee. Before she knew what was happening, Pearl had jumped onto Belle's lap and curled up.

"It looks as though you've found your match," Roger said, beaming down at them.

"Turn to me, Belle," Nick said and snapped a picture.

Belle had reluctantly said goodbye to Pearl and went to fill out the paperwork. She was eager to bring the pup home but had to follow the protocol. Roger had explained that Belle would need a home visit to check she was suitable.

"Will that have to wait until Monday?" Belle asked as disappointment filled her tone.

"I'm sure I can squeeze in a visit to you tomorrow morning," Roger reassured her.

"Oh, that would be perfect."

"Pearl will need a quick once over from our vet before you take her home. I'll book her in for first thing Monday morning. All being well, you can collect her Monday lunchtime?"

So it was all set. At Monday lunchtime, Belle would be picking Pearl up and taking her home. The entire journey home, all Belle talked about, was the dog, but Nick didn't mind. He dropped her off at the harbour and she went straight to the pet shop to stock up on everything she needed for her new arrival.

CHAPTER FOURTEEN

By the time Belle got home, she only had a couple of hours until she'd arranged to meet Jada and Zoe. She set out Pearl's new belongings for Roger's visit the following morning and then got ready to meet her friends.

At six o'clock, Belle drove towards Padstow Bay, with Jada beside her and Zoe in the back. They'd wound down all the windows and sang along to a 90s CD they'd found stashed in the car's glove box. They reached the bay where a handful of other cars were parked.

"It's a beautiful evening," Zoe commented.

"Isn't it?" Jada smiled at her.

Belle left them to their moment and went to the boot to retrieve the picnic. Jada had arrived with a picnic basket filled with food, much of it leftover from the coffee shop, but she promised them it had all been freshly baked that morning. Zoe had turned up with a patchwork blanket to sit on, and Belle had brought bottles of fresh lemonade and non-alcoholic wine.

"This is ridiculously heavy." Belle groaned as she attempted to lift the picnic basket from her boot.

"Here, let me," Jada said, bumping her aside with her hip. She picked it up as if it weighed nothing.

Zoe wolf-whistled, grabbed the blanket from the boot, and followed Jada onto the beach. Belle hung back. For the first time in her life, she felt like a third wheel. Her fingers itched to text Nick, but she picked up the lemonade and followed the women onto the sand. They'd laid out the blanket near some rocks, which Jada was using as a table to set out the food.

"This looks amazing," Belle said.

"It does. I can't believe Jada made all this herself," Zoe added.

Jada shrugged, and Belle saw the hint of a blush on her cheeks.

"She's an amazing cook, too," Belle said. "Jada gave me a cooking lesson the other night."

"I'm useless at cooking," Zoe said, staring wide-eyed up at Jada.

"Jada, you should give Zoe a lesson." Belle poured the drinks with her back to the women as she crossed her fingers and hoped her plan had worked.

"I'm sure you don't need—" Jada started.

"I'd love that. How does next Thursday sound? I could come to you to save you driving home after, as I'm sure you'll have an early morning in the coffee shop." Zoe spoke quickly, and her words merged into one long jumble.

Belle turned her attention to the food as they arranged the finer details. Spread across the rocks were Tupperware boxes filled with different treats. There was quiche Lorraine, filled paninis, slices of chocolate fudge cake, cheese scones, and a salad with chopped-up strawberries. Jada had even packed a flask of chilled coffee and another filled with ice.

"This is the most over-the-top picnic I've ever had," Belle exclaimed. She was overwhelmed by the choice and didn't know what to put on her plate.

"I'm a feeder."

"Come on. Let's have a little of everything," Zoe suggested.

With their plates piled high and plastic glasses of iced coffee by their sides, they sat in a row on the blanket looking out towards the sea. The few people that had been on the beach when they arrived were packing up to leave.

"There's nowhere like Cornwall in the summer." Belle sighed and dug her toes into the soft sand.

"It's beautiful. So, what have you been up to since I last saw you?" Zoe asked.

"My website has taken off. I cannot thank

you enough. The income should help me during the quieter months. Also, I adopted a dog today."

"What?" The two women snapped their heads to look at Belle.

"Nick and I drove out to an adoption centre to have a look, and I found my perfect companion."

"In Nick or the dog?" Jada teased. Zoe smirked but elbowed Jada in the ribs.

"You two need to shift the focus back to your own love lives." Belle tore a piece of panini off and threw it at Jada. It bounced off her arm and fell onto the sand, where a seagull would no doubt discover it.

"But you do like him?" asked Jada.

"I do, but he has an agreement with Tegen. Besides, I'm not looking for anyone. There are so many enormous changes happening in my life right now. I don't need another." Belle brushed off the sadness that was lurking, waiting to pounce once Nick had finished the work at the shop. How would she feel when she didn't have an excuse to talk to him or see him?

"An agreement with Tegen?" asked Zoe.

Belle picked up a handful of sand and watched as it poured through her fingers.

"It's a friends-with-benefits kind of situation," Jada explained.

"It's irrelevant. I don't want a relationship." Belle squared her shoulders and poured another drink.

"Tell us more about your new dog," Zoe said and shot her a kind smile. "When do they come home? And, more importantly, when can we meet them?"

As they ate, Belle told them about Pearl.

"Bring her into the coffee shop one day for a treat from her aunty Jada."

"Yes. Why don't you bring her over on Thursday, then I can meet her too?" Zoe clasped Belle's hand in hers.

Belle laughed at their reaction. "Okay, we'll pop by for a coffee before you close. We won't stay long, as I'm sure you'll want to start your cooking class."

Neither Jada nor Zoe invited her to join them, and Belle was grateful. She didn't want to gatecrash their first date because they pitied her.

The evening air was warm, and they lounged on the blanket chatting.

"How's the shop refit going?" Zoe asked. She was lying back on her elbows with her foot gently resting against Jada's shin.

"We're moving onto decorating next week. I'm hoping to be open in the next couple of weeks. I'd like to throw an opening party." Belle had been considering it for a while now and really ought to start planning. Two weeks would fly by.

"I'll design posters for you to put up around the harbour," Zoe offered.

"And I'll plan food. I've been wanting to try out some recipes. Perhaps pastel-coloured macarons?"

"That would be wonderful. I don't want any

fussy food, as I need to think about the jewellery."

"Of course. We'll do macarons, strawberries dipped in chocolate, and champagne," Jada announced.

"That sounds wonderful." Zoe sighed, staring into the distance.

"You'll have to get Zoe to help you with a practice run," Belle suggested, sending a wink Zoe's way.

"Yes. You can show me how to cook another night. Let's trial macarons and chocolate-dipped strawberries on Thursday." Zoe clapped her hands.

"Will you invite Nick?" Jada asked.

"Of course. It would be rude not to after all the work he's done." Belle smiled at the thought of standing in her shop wearing a fancy dress, sipping champagne, and with Nick by her side. Then an image of Tegen strutting in ruined the daydream.

"It's going to be wonderful. I have a wedding in August and the dress I'm wearing needs a necklace to finish the look. I can't wait to see what you have in stock," said Zoe.

By the time they trailed off the beach with their empty picnic basket, the sun had set and the roads were dark. They loaded everything into the boot of the car and piled in. Belle took a slow drive back to the harbour and dropped Zoe by her car. She offered to drop Jada closer to home, but she declined, opting to get out with Zoe.

"Text me both when you get home," Belle called before she drove away. She parked in the garage and collected the empty glass bottles from the boot. The dark sky above was clear, and the stars twinkled against the navy backdrop. Belle walked the long way home to pass the pub and put her bottles in their recycling bins. Enough people were milling around that she felt safe. Some were going for a post-meal stroll, while others sat outside the various bars and restaurants sipping glasses of wine. Belle threw the bottles away and winced at the sound of crashing glass as they fell on the heap below.

As Belle rounded the front of the pub, she hung back as Tegen stumbled from the front door. She struggled to regain her balance in six-inch heels on the cobbled floor, and she would have gone over had it not been for a man who wrapped an arm around her waist and steadied her. Belle held her breath as the tall, dark-haired man pulled Tegen against his side and pressed his lips to the top of her head. Belle considered turning and weaving her way through the back streets to avoid them, but the man was already leading Tegen away from the harbour. Once they were out of sight, Belle resumed her walk home. The honeysuckle growing up the front of the pub wafted in the air as she walked past. She inhaled deeply at the scent and her stomach clenched at the sickly smell. Nick had told her he and Tegen were allowed to see other people, but seeing it with her own eyes was jarring. How could Tegen be interested in anyone else when she had Nick?

CHAPTER FIFTEEN

As promised, Roger knocked on the cottage door at nine o'clock Saturday morning. He was impressed to see Belle had everything set up for her new arrival - including a bed upstairs and one downstairs. They discussed the safety issue of the open fire, and Belle promised to retrieve the fire guard from the loft as soon as he left.

"Right, that's everything then," Roger said and stood to leave.

"Did I pass? Can I still bring her home?" Belle asked.

"Of course. I think you and Pearl will be very happy together. I'll see you on Monday."

Once he left, Belle picked up her phone and thought about calling her father. She wanted to share the good news with someone. It rang twice before she remembered he was at an auction and would have his phone on silent. She sent him a quick text telling him not to worry, that she'd only phoned for a chat and she'd call again tomorrow. Without overthinking it, Belle scrolled through her phonebook and pressed Nick's name.

"Hello?" he answered, his voice was gravelly.

"Nick, did I wake you? I'm sorry." Belle held the phone away and cursed. Why had she phoned him?

"It's fine. I should be up now, anyway."

She could hear him moving in bed, and she wondered if a hungover Tegen was lying beside him. Perhaps she'd had second thoughts about going home with the dark-haired man and had gone running back to Nick. "I really shouldn't have phoned you. Don't worry. I'll see you on Monday," she spoke quickly, in a rush to hang up as soon as possible and end her embarrassment.

"Woah, calm down. Give me a second to catch up. You just woke me, remember?" he teased.

Belle groaned. "I'm sorry. I was excited and my brain ran away with itself before common sense could catch up."

"What were you excited about?"

Belle sat on the sofa and curled her legs beneath her. "Roger gave me the seal of approval. Pearl is officially coming home on Monday."

"That's great news. Congratulations." He sounded more awake now, and the excitement was growing in his voice.

"Thank you. I can't wait for Monday." Belle didn't know what to do with herself until then.

"Do you have any plans this weekend?" Nick asked, as though he'd read her mind.

"No. I should start planning the opening party for the shop, but it seems a bit too soon, considering it's an empty shell."

"I've got no plans either. Do you want to help me transport the cupboards and everything today? We can fit them, then it'll be ready to decorate first thing on Monday."

"Nick, you don't have to work on a Saturday."

"I want to, Belle. Besides, it's not work if I get to spend the day with you."

Belle's insides fluttered at his words, and she was grateful nobody could see the soppy smile on her face. "Okay. I'll treat you to some fish and chips for lunch."

"It's a date." Nick's cheery voice came down the phone, and butterflies exploded in Belle's stomach. "I'll pick you up in an hour and we can collect everything from the yard."

"See you soon." Somehow Belle forced the words out despite her dry mouth.

Needing to expel some of her pent-up energy, Belle ran upstairs to get ready. Nick had already warned her his van was filthy. With that in mind, she pulled on an old pair of dungarees that were already splattered with paint and furniture varnish. Ignoring her jewellery, Belle tied her hair back with a pastel green scarf and was ready for when Nick arrived.

He was half an hour late when he pulled up

outside the cottage, and Belle was already halfway through her third coffee. Not wanting to waste the drink, she carried the mug outside with her.

"Morning," Nick called as she climbed in. "You brought me coffee?" He swiped the mug from her hand before she could say anything. "Yuck!" he spluttered after taking a sip. "What is that?" He stared dubiously at the mug.

"It was my coffee." Belle rolled her eyes and blew sawdust off the seatbelt before she put it on.

"That's how you drink your coffee?" He stared at her with an incredulous look on his face.

"I ordered some caramel syrup from Amazon," Belle defended her coffee choices. She'd been enjoying her coffee until he'd taken a big gulp and spat it back out.

"That's disgusting, Belle. Come on, let's get everything into the shop, then I'll treat you to a proper coffee." He handed her back the mug which Belle held out at arm's length, worried the liquid would splash onto her as Nick drove. "Pour it out the window before I drive off," he instructed.

They collected the cupboards and shelves from Nick's yard, and more than once, Belle's heart galloped in her chest as his t-shirt rode up when he lifted something. She gulped and fanned herself.

"Not used to doing anything physical?" Nick grunted as he lifted the new counter into the van.

"Huh?" Belle blinked and pulled her mind back from the gutter.

"Why don't you sit in the van for a minute?

The engine's still on, so it should be cool."

Belle climbed into the van, and cold air rushed over her clammy skin. It was the first day of July and the temperature had shot up.

"All done," Nick announced as he joined her.

"Sorry, I'm not used to working in this heat. At home, we'd close all the shutters and enjoy the cool darkness."

"In France?" asked Nick, reversing out of the yard.

"Yeah. Sorry, I keep forgetting it's not my home anymore." The heat had scrambled her thoughts.

"It will always be your home, Belle. You have more than one."

The harbour was busy, and it took a while to navigate the traffic. They passed the pub and Belle remembered how Tegen had been led away by another man last night.

"Nick?" she asked, her voice barely audible.

"Mmm?"

"I saw Tegen last night,"

Nick's grip on the steering wheel tightened. "What did she say to you?"

"Nothing. She was with someone."

"Okay?" The traffic had come to a standstill and Nick put the car in park and turned to look at her.

"She was with another man."

"We see other people." He shrugged.

"I know, but it was strange seeing. Why

would she want to see someone else when she already has you?" Belle felt the heat in her cheeks as she realised what she'd said aloud.

Nick smirked. "We're ove—" The car behind sounded its horn. They turned their attention back to the road to see the cars in front had moved.

Nick parked the van outside the shop and they unloaded it, neither bringing up Tegen again.

"I'll park around the back," Nick said, gesturing to the van.

While Nick was gone, Belle pulled the bubble wrap off the shelving units and stepped back to admire them. Nick had done an amazing job of creating them. As promised, he'd made some shelves from driftwood. Belle would display some of her costume jewellery on them. He'd made plinths for the glass cabinets to sit on. They would fit them today, then Nick would add some panelling and paint them to match the powder blue walls. Belle wanted everything to flow naturally, to ensure customers were drawn to the jewellery.

"It's going to look beautiful," Nick said, walking in with two coffees from the bakery. "Not quite as good as Jada's, but I got to skip the queue in the bakery." He winked.

"Your mum seems lovely," Belle said, wrapping her hands around the cup. Her clammy skin had cooled, and a chill ran through her.

"She is. Actually, she's invited you round for Sunday dinner tomorrow. Will you come?" He'd turned his back to her and was searching for something in his toolbox.

Belle's mouth opened and closed as she floundered for an excuse. She couldn't have Sunday dinner with Nick's parents. What if Tegen was there? A manic giggle escaped Belle as she imagined sitting around the dinner table with Nick and Tegen opposite her.

"Belle?" Nick asked.

"Sorry, went down the wrong hole."

Nick's brow furrowed. "So, will you come?"

"Oh, um." She stalled for time. "I couldn't. I'm sure your mum already has enough people to cook for."

"Cooking is my mum's passion. Besides, it's only her, my dad, me, and you. It's one extra person." He pulled a hammer from the toolbox.

It was just them. The image in Belle's mind shifted to her sitting beside Nick at the table.

"I'd love to come. What time?" The words had escaped before she could truly think through her answer.

"About one o'clock. Mum usually does dinner for two." Nick muttered around a nail that he had clasped between his lips.

"Okay. Text me the address later." She went back to unwrapping the last few plinths.

The next hour passed in a blur of power tools and expletives. Nick was securing the plinths to the floor to stop them from falling over if someone stumbled into them.

"Will you lay the floor around the plinths?"

asked Belle, searching for a conversation topic that didn't involve dinner with his parents.

"Yeah. We'll make a start on that next week. You might even be ready to open next weekend."

"Next weekend?" Belle screeched, thinking how many things she needed to organise for an opening party.

"Is that too soon? I can slow things down and take a few long lunches," he teased.

Belle's mind wandered to the idea of a long lunch with Nick. It was hot in the shop and Nick's top stuck to him, emphasising his taut muscles underneath. He kept pushing his hair back from his forehead, and Belle watched how his fingers tangled in it and wished they were hers. She grabbed a catalogue that had been pushed through the letterbox and fanned herself with it.

"No, next weekend would be good," she confirmed.

"Brilliant. Are we having a party?"

"If I can get everything arranged in time."

"I better get my fancy shirt ready."

"You mean you need to ask your mum to iron it?" Belle scrolled through her phone and brought up the group chat with Jada and Zoe to let them know they finally had an official date.

"I do all my own washing and ironing, I'll have you know." Nick pointed his tape measure and advanced on her until she was backed up against the new counter.

"Sorry, you seemed like the type." She peered

up at him through her lashes.

"Belle Roux, are you stereotyping me?" His face was merely a breath from hers.

"Maybe." She fought to keep a smile off her face.

His hands wrapped around her waist, and she giggled as he tickled her. She squirmed against his hold, but he was too strong.

"Are you going to apologise?" he asked, his voice barely audible over her laughter.

"I'm sorry for assuming you're a mummy's boy," she choked out between uncontrollable laughter. Tears streamed down her face as she fought her body's reaction to his touch.

"Not quite the apology I was looking for, but I'll let it slide this time," he said. He stopped tickling her and his hands rested on her waist. She could feel the heat from them through her dungarees.

He lifted a hand and used his thumb to wipe away her tears. Belle's eyes darted up to his and her breath caught in her throat as she saw the fire blazing. As if he moved in slow motion, his lips edged towards hers. Belle allowed her eyes to flutter closed. Every nerve in her body tingled with anticipation. His lips brushed against hers and her body relaxed against his.

"What the hell?" someone shouted from behind them.

They sprung apart like two naughty teenagers. Belle had a fierce blush across her face and she noticed the pink tinge to Nick's cheeks.

Belle let out a shaky laugh and leaned against the counter as her wobbly legs struggled to hold her upright. Jada stood in the doorway.

"Jada, how lovely of you to drop in. Aren't you rushed off your feet at the coffee shop?" Belle's tone was forced and overly bright.

"There's a queue out of my coffee shop, but I have staff in. What the hell was this text?" She held up her phone and pointed at the screen.

"We've settled on an opening date," Belle said. The world around her was stilling, and she stepped towards Jada, leaving Nick behind her.

"Next weekend? I'm only doing a trial run on Thursday."

"We don't need to have macarons and dipped strawberries."

"Of course we do." Jada wiped her brow and sat down on the window ledge.

"Am I supposed to know what's going on?" asked Nick.

"I texted Jada and Zoe to let them know we were thinking of opening the shop next Saturday. Jada is… or was, going to cater the party for me."

"I'm still doing it," Jada huffed.

"Brilliant. I'll help in any way I can. What do you need me to do?" asked Belle.

"Wait, Belle." Nick put a hand on her shoulder. "You're going to have enough to do getting the shop ready. You can't commit to helping Jada cater it."

Jada's nostrils flared. "I'm not asking her to

help me."

"Okay, can we all calm down?" Belle massaged her temples as she gathered her thoughts.

"Jada, I'd really appreciate it if you could still cater the opening party. I know it's last minute. You have full discretion to make any changes you feel are necessary. I completely trust your judgement."

"We've got this." Jada nodded.

"Thank you for this," Belle said and crossed the shop to hug her friend.

"I don't know what just happened." Nick stared wide-eyed at them.

Belle and Jada laughed as they broke apart.

"Don't think I was so blinded by stress that I didn't notice what you two were up to when I walked in." Jada wiggled her eyebrows.

Nick cleared his throat, and Belle shuffled her feet.

"I will speak to you soon." Jada pecked Belle on the cheek and left as swiftly as she'd entered.

"Gosh, I need a lie down after that."

"After my kiss or Jada's meltdown?" Nick teased.

Belle wrapped her arms around herself and turned to look out the window. She watched people wandering around and admiring the harbour. Everybody looked carefree, and Belle was filled with envy at the sight.

"We shouldn't have done that," she said with her back still turned to him.

"I enjoyed it," Nick said, but Belle could hear

the change in his tone.

"So did I but that doesn't mean it was right."

"Can we try to ignore it happened?" Nick asked. There was a clutter of tools as he put them back into his box.

"I think that would be for the best." Belle felt a heaviness settle across her chest.

"You'll still come for dinner tomorrow, won't you?"

The sound behind her stopped, and Belle turned to see Nick staring. His shoulders sagged and his eyes, which had burned brightly a few minutes ago, were flat.

"Nick, I'm not sure I should." She wanted to go to him and feel his hands on her waist again, but she kept her feet firmly planted where she was.

"Please, Belle. You're already a really good friend and I don't want to lose that over a silly kiss. It wasn't even a proper kiss."

"It wasn't," Belle agreed, even though her body shouted otherwise. If her legs had shaken like that from brushing lips, then how might she feel after a proper kiss? She pushed those thoughts away.

"I'll see you tomorrow then. One o'clock. I'll text you the address." Nick left before Belle could say anything.

"He couldn't get away fast enough," Belle muttered. As she stood alone in the half-fitted shop, loneliness crept into her bones again. At least she would soon have a furry friend to go home to. Belle gathered their empty coffee cups and went in search of a bin.

CHAPTER SIXTEEN

"What should I wear?" Belle cried down the phone. Outfits were thrown across her bed after she'd discarded them for one reason or another.

"Belle, it's Sunday lunch. Why are you getting in such a panic over it?" Zoe asked. She squinted on the other side of the screen as Belle held the phone up to her wardrobe.

"It's because she kissed him yesterday," Jada said, the hiss of the coffee machine in the background.

"What? Why didn't anybody tell me about this?" Zoe shrieked, putting down her paintbrush.

"Okay, girls, can we not do this now?" Belle groaned. She'd FaceTimed Jada and Zoe out of desperation, needing someone to help pick an outfit, but it was going dreadfully.

"You kissed him and you want us to gloss over that?" Jada asked.

"We can discuss it another time. Actually, no, we can't. Can we pretend it never happened? He has an agreement and I'm not looking for a relationship."

"Who said anything about a relationship?" Zoe smirked.

"If you two carry on like this, I'm hanging up."

"Okay, fine. I need to open in five minutes, anyway. Let's choose this outfit," Jada said.

Belle held the phone up to the wardrobe and slowly panned across the choices.

"What's that black dress?" Zoe asked.

Belle pulled out the dress and heard them gasp.

"It's perfect," Jada said.

"More than perfect," Zoe agreed.

"You don't think it's too much?" Belle bit her lip as she hung the dress up on the wardrobe's door and stepped back to admire it.

Zoe and Jada agreed that it was perfect for her lunch date, to which Belle had rolled her eyes but decided not to argue. They said their goodbyes, and Belle put the phone down on her bed and went downstairs to make a coffee. She had hours until she had to be at Nick's, but she wanted to be ready.

The dress they'd chosen was one Belle had bought from *The Cornish Vintage Dress Shop*.

Belle pushed the door open, and a thrill went through her as the brass bell let out a sharp ding.

"Hi. Welcome to The Cornish Vintage Dress Shop. I'm Rosie. Give me a shout if you need anything," greeted the woman from behind the counter. Her curly red hair cascaded around her shoulders and she wore a beautiful beaded vest with a pair of flared trousers.

"Thank you. I'm just browsing, to be honest. I should probably tell you I'm also checking out my competition." Belle approached the counter and held out her hand for Rosie to shake. "Belle Roux and I'll soon be opening a vintage jewellery shop in Padstow-on-Sea."

"Oh, how wonderful." Rosie clasped her hand and beamed at her. "I have a few pieces of jewellery for sale, but not enough to be considered competition."

"That's a relief," Belle admitted.

"Why don't I make us a coffee and I can fill you in on the good and the bad of running a vintage shop in Cornwall?"

"Yes, please."

Belle wandered around the shop while Rosie went into the back to make the drinks. The racks were filled with vintage clothes spanning a range of eras. Belle's attention was drawn to a black dress.

"That's beautiful. It would look gorgeous on you," Rosie said, emerging with a tray holding two china cups and saucers, and a plate of biscuits.

"I love it, but is it really vintage?"

"Technically, yes, but I can't fathom how 90s fashion can be considered vintage," Rosie confessed. "Why don't you try it on?"

"I couldn't." Belle glanced back at the dress.

"It would be rude to visit my shop without even trying a dress on," Rosie teased as she opened the door to the changing room and beckoned Belle inside.

Belle's eyes widened as she took in the changing room. Her sandals sank into the plush pink carpet which matched the flamingo wallpaper that shimmered under the chandeliers. She placed her handbag on the pink velvet chair and slipped off her leggings and top. She took the dress off the hanger and slipped it over her head. It clung to her every curve and ended below her knee in a soft scalloped flare with a white trim. The skirt hugged her hips and pulled in at her waist. The top was a tight fit with a sweetheart neckline and thin straps, which also had the same white trim. Belle turned to admire herself in the mirror and sucked in a breath at the sight that greeted her.

She stepped out of the dressing room, and Rosie smiled at her. "That dress was made for you," she said.

"I don't know when I'll ever wear it, but I have to have it," Belle admitted.

Belle changed back into her clothes, feeling much less glamorous, and joined Rosie on the shop floor.

"Let me pop the dress behind the till while we have a chat," Rosie said.

They drank their coffee and Rosie talked Belle

through the way her shop ran and the extra services she provided to help her through the long winter months when there would be fewer tourists. The trip had proved invaluable to Belle. She'd purchased a few more items, including a vintage dressing gown, and Rosie was kind enough to give her a discount, telling her that they needed to stick together.

Belle said goodbye and Rosie promised to visit the shop once it was open.

Belle had been too nervous to eat breakfast, and by lunchtime, she was starving. Her stomach growled as she pulled on the dress. It fit as it had when she tried it on. She pushed back the worries that it was too much for Sunday lunch with Nick and his parents and went about finding the perfect jewellery to go with it. Belle chose a small pair of diamond earrings and a matching necklace with a small, pear-shaped diamond pendant. The set had been a present for her twenty-first birthday from her father. Belle slipped on her mother's Art Deco ring. It didn't exactly go with the outfit, but she wanted to feel close to her. She could have worn her mother's sapphire engagement ring, but that felt like too much. Belle pulled her hair back into a low bun and slipped on a pair of heeled sandals. There was no doubt about it. She was overdressed.

With time to spare, Belle picked up her bag

and put her phone and purse in. She walked down to the harbour, enjoying the sound of her heels clicking on the cobbles.

"Hello, Belle. You off anywhere nice?" the pub's landlord asked her as she passed.

"Just off for lunch. See you soon." She waved and continued walking.

Belle popped into the florist to buy some flowers for Nick's mother. The shop was busy, but Belle took her time picking a bunch. Eventually, she settled for six creamy yellow roses with baby's breath surrounding it. They were beautiful, and Belle hoped Mrs Penhale would love them. With the flowers bought, Belle made her way to the house. Her empty stomach did somersaults as she approached. Nick had texted her the address last night, but he hadn't said anything more.

The house was on the second road back from the seafront and looked as though it was once a fisherman's cottage before it had been modernised and extended. Belle walked up to the pale yellow door and knocked.

Nick answered in a pair of jeans and a crisp navy shirt.

"Belle," he stuttered as he took in her appearance.

"Hi, Nick." She was hyper-aware of the way his eyes roamed across her body.

"Sorry, where are my manners? Come in." He stepped aside. The hallway was small and her arm brushed against his and a shiver ran down her spine.

"I bought these for your mum." Belle gestured to the roses.

"There was me thinking you'd bought them for me," he teased and closed the door behind her.

"I didn't think they were your colour."

"No, I'd have preferred beer. Next time."

Belle cursed. "Should I have bought something for your dad?"

"Belle, it's okay. The flowers are more than enough. My parents will be happy you're here. You didn't need to bring anything," he promised her.

"Sorry. I'm not used to this," she admitted. They were still standing in the hallway and Nick was close enough that she could feel the rush of his breath on the top of her head.

"Used to what?" he asked, bending his head to meet her gaze.

"Being invited to Sunday lunch."

Nick placed a finger under her chin and tilted her face up towards his. "Just relax. They're going to love you." His eyes flickered to her lips and Belle's breath caught.

"Nicholas Penhale, are you going to bring your friend in to meet us or are you going to continue to monopolise her?" a female voice shouted from the end of the hallway.

Nick sighed and dropped his hand. "We'll be right there, Mum," he called back. "Come on, let me introduce you to my parents." He placed a hand on the small of her back as they walked into the kitchen. Belle fought to ignore his touch.

"Mum, Dad, this is Belle," Nick announced.

The kitchen was at the back of the cottage and down a few steps. It had a slate floor, but the walls and cabinets were white, reflecting the small amount of light that flowed in from a window on the far wall. Nick's mother stood at the oven stirring a saucepan. Her hair was the same colour as Nick's and it was pulled back into a messy plait. She had a kind face and rosy cheeks. Her apron was covered in pictures of labradors and it shielded a pretty white dress covered in daisies. Nick's father stood on the other side of the kitchen, peeling brussels sprouts. His hair was dark but greying in places and he wore a similar outfit to Nick. Belle could see the familial resemblance around the eyes.

"Mr and Mrs Penhale, it's lovely to see you," Belle said, feeling her cheeks flush as they turned their attention to her.

"None of that Mr and Mrs, my love. Call me Jenny and you can call Jowan Jo." Nick's mother embraced Belle in a bone-crushing hug.

"Thank you for having me, Jenny," Belle said, once the woman had let her go and she could fill her lungs again. "I bought you these." She held the flowers out.

"You shouldn't have. They're gorgeous. Thank you." Jenny took the flowers and went to put them in a vase.

"Lovely to meet you, Belle." Jo walked over and gave her a quick hug.

"You too, Jo. You've got a beautiful home,"

Belle said.

"Thank you. Nick, why don't you give Belle a tour? Dinner should be ready soon," Jo suggested.

"Yes, what a wonderful idea. Show Belle around, and then you can sit at the table for dinner," Jenny called after them.

"Sorry, I don't often bring people back for dinner. My mum's excited," Nick said as he led her back down the hall.

"Do you not have Tegen over?" Belle instantly regretted the question, but it was too late.

Nick scratched the back of his neck as he showed her into the living room. "No. She and Mum don't get on." He shrugged. "Here's the living room. If you stand on your tiptoes and squint, you can see the sea through that gap." He pointed out the window.

"Very impressive." Belle pretended she could see. She turned back to look at the living room. It had a warm and homely feeling with pictures on the wall, a worn cream carpet, and big sofas with lots of cushions scattered across them. The living room led to a dining room with doors that opened out onto the small garden. A round pine table was in the middle with four seats around it and the places were already set for dinner.

"Mum made me lay the table first thing this morning," Nick said.

"I like the daisies." Belle chuckled at the jam jar filled with half-wilted flowers.

"They were the only flowers I could find in the

garden. Come on, I'll show you upstairs and by the time we return Mum will have swapped my efforts with the flowers you bought her."

A twisty staircase led to the cottage's second floor.

"The bathroom's through there." He opened a door, and she peeked in.

"Thanks. I don't need to see the bedrooms." Belle let out a nervous chuckle.

"You don't want to see my bedroom?" He leaned against the wall, his arms crossed, and stared at her. "I quite like the thought of you in my room in that dress," he whispered.

"Nick," Belle gasped.

"Let's go sit down for lunch." He gestured for her to walk ahead of him.

Belle's legs shook as she descended the steep staircase. Nick was close enough behind her that she could feel the warmth emanating from his body and smell his aftershave.

"I'm dishing up," Jenny said from the kitchen.

They sat at the dining table, and as Nick had predicted, the daisies had been replaced by Belle's bunch.

"You're going to be my mum's favourite person now."

"She's lovely."

"She is."

Jo came in, holding a bottle of white wine and a bottle of red. "Which would you prefer?" he asked.

"There's rosé in the fridge, too," Jenny called.

"I'd love a glass of red, please," Belle said.

"Excellent choice. I think we'll all have red. Is that okay, Nick?"

Nick nodded, and Jo filled the four glasses.

"Jenny is going to dish up in the kitchen and bring the dinners in. Is there anything you don't eat?" Jo asked.

"No, I'll eat anything."

Belle took a sip of the wine, and her body relaxed. Nick was beside her and the size of the table meant his thigh was brushing hers.

"This looks amazing," Belle said, as Jenny put a plate down in front of her.

"Thank you, my love." Jenny put Nick's down and Jo followed with their plates. "Dig in. Don't wait for us to get settled."

The roast potatoes were crispy on the outside with fluffy centres, the meat was cooked to perfection, the vegetables roasted until they'd caramelised, and big golden Yorkshire puddings were filled with gravy.

"This is delicious. Thank you," Belle said in between bites.

"I wasn't sure whether it was too hot for a roast, but you can't go wrong." Jenny smiled at her from across the table.

"I can't remember the last time I had a roast. My dad's a rubbish cook and they're not very common in France."

"All snails and frog legs?" Jo asked, only to be chastised by his wife.

"I'm sorry, Belle," Jenny apologised and shot a glare at a snickering Nick.

"It's fine. We mostly ate pastries, to be honest." Belle pressed her lips into a line to stop herself from laughing.

"How's the shop coming along?" Jo asked, his shoulders shaking as he fought back laughter.

"Nick's done an amazing job," Belle said.

"It was an easy job. The electrics were all sound. Just needed plastering and fitting out." He shrugged before loading his fork up.

"The new cabinets look fantastic. I can't wait for everyone to see it once it's been decorated. We're having an opening party next Saturday. You should both come along and see how well Nick's done."

They chatted for a bit as they finished their dinners. Jenny and Jo promised to join them at the opening party, and Belle breathed a sigh of relief. At least she'd have a few people turn up if nobody else ventured inside.

"That was delicious. Thanks, Mum," Nick said as he leaned back in his chair.

"Yes, thank you, Jenny. I can't remember the last time I had a home-cooked meal like that."

"You should come more often." Jenny smiled at her. "You all put your feet up and I'll clear all this and get dessert ready."

"I'll help you, and please don't say no. I'd feel awful if I couldn't at least help you clean up," Belle said, standing to gather the empty plates.

"Thank you." Jenny followed her.

Jenny washed the dishes, and Belle dried them. They spoke about Belle's plans for the shop, and Jenny suggested a couple of local business networking groups to join.

"I'm picking up a dog tomorrow. Did Nick tell you he drove me down to the centre last week?"

"No. Oh, how wonderful. I do miss having a dog around, but Jo and I are too busy to commit. Nick would love one, but he's not been able to with Tegen. I suspect it won't be long until he comes home with one now they're over."

"Nick and Tegen are over?" A lump formed in her throat.

"Yes. Didn't he tell you?" Jenny stopped scrubbing the plate she was holding.

"No. I had a feeling things weren't great between them, but I didn't know they were over." Belle turned to look out the window, not wanting Jenny to read her expression. She didn't know how much to say or how much Jenny knew.

"Well, they are, and I can only think it's a good thing." Jenny resumed the washing up.

"I agree. I knew Tegen at school."

"Yes, she had quite a reputation amongst the parents. I knew your mother, Belle. I didn't know whether I should say anything, as I didn't want to upset you."

Belle was speechless. After they'd moved to France, she'd grown up around people who'd never met her mother. Other than her father, who rarely spoke of her, there'd been nobody to keep Kerenza's memory alive.

"She was a lovely woman, despite her struggles. We would sometimes meet for a coffee after the morning school drop-off."

"Thank you, Jenny," Belle stuttered, not knowing what else to say.

"Belle, I know you hardly know me, but if you need anything, you give me a shout. Kerenza was loved by many here and we'd all like to support you in any way we can. Even if that's just the odd Sunday lunch."

As they finished washing up, they strayed back onto safer topics and Belle told Jenny about the jewellery in her latest delivery.

"You'll have to let me know what you like for when Jo and Nick pop in for your birthday or Christmas present."

"I'll nip by and point out my favourites ahead of time. Right, you go sit down with Nick and I'll dish up dessert."

Belle tried to protest, but Jenny wouldn't hear of it.

"There you are," Nick said, smiling widely at her as she walked into the living room. He was sitting with his father, sipping wine and watching the football.

"I'll go help Jenny with dessert," Jo made his excuses and left.

"What's Mum doing?" Nick asked.

Belle furrowed her brow as she tried to remember what Jenny had pulled from the fridge.

She wanted to ask him about Tegen but knew it wasn't a good time when Jenny or Jo could walk back in at any moment.

"I'm not sure, sorry. I was chatting to your mum too much to pay attention."

"Come sit here." Nick patted the empty seat beside him on the sofa.

"Thank you for inviting me," Belle said.

He threw an arm around her shoulders and pulled her to his side. "Thank you for coming, Belle."

Neither of them spoke as he held her. She rested her head on his chest and felt the hitch in his breath.

Jenny had bought a cake from Jada's coffee shop. She made cups of tea and served it with a selection of clotted cream, warm custard, or Cornish ice cream.

Belle lost all track of time as they ate, drank coffee, and chatted. As she fought a yawn, she realised it had grown dark outside.

"I should make a move. I've got an early morning tomorrow to pick Pearl up." She stretched and stood from the sofa where she'd been making an effort to leave some space between her and Nick, despite the knowing glances from Jenny.

"Of course. I didn't realise that was the time. Nick, fetch Belle a jacket and walk her home," Jenny instructed.

"I'll be fine," Belle argued, but Jenny and Nick wouldn't hear of it.

Belle said her goodbyes as Nick ran upstairs

to get a jumper for her. He returned with his rugby hoodie, complete with his surname printed on the back. Belle didn't allow her thoughts to wander as she pulled it over her dress. Jenny handed her a Tupperware filled with leftovers and hugged her goodbye.

The roads were quiet since the shops had closed hours ago. Belle linked her arm through Nick's as he helped her over the cobblestones in her heels.

"Thank you for coming," he said. His voice was raspy.

"It was lovely."

The darkness was closing in on them, and Belle knew she needed to ask him about Tegen.

"Nick, why didn't you tell me you'd ended your agreement with Tegen?" She finally built up the courage to voice the question that had been rattling around her head all afternoon.

"My mum told you." He let out a heavy sigh.

"Yes, but why didn't you tell me?" They were at the end of her road now, and Belle pulled him to a stop underneath a streetlight. The warm glow lit up his face.

He opened and closed his mouth before scrubbing a hand across his face. "I wanted to tell you, Belle, I even tried yesterday in the van. I didn't want to freak you out. Things with Tegen were awful before you turned up. Actually, in hindsight, they were pretty awful from day one. I thought we were having fun. She could be fun, but then you arrived. I didn't want to tell you because I was worried you'd think I ended it for you. Which I kind of did, but also, I should have done it long before you moved in. I'm not explaining myself very well, am I?"

Belle fought to catch her breath. "I don't know what to say," she admitted.

"This is why I didn't want to tell you. I didn't want to put you in this position."

"So, you're completely single?" she asked, her scrambled thoughts slowly pulling together.

"Completely."

"No more agreements?"

"No more," he confirmed.

"And you like me?" Belle let the question hang in the air as Nick's eyes softened and a small smile played at the edge of his lips.

"I really like you," he admitted.

Belle picked at a piece of thread hanging off the sleeve. She was feeling brave and hoped she wouldn't regret what she was about to say. With a deep breath, she spoke. "Maybe you should ask me out on a date."

Nick blinked as he processed her words. "Would you?" he asked, his eyes glowed with hope.

"You'll have to ask to find out." Belle shot him a coy smile. She might not feel ready for a relationship, but she wouldn't know until she tried.

"Belle Roux, will you go on a date with me?" He clasped her hands in his.

"I'd love to." She beamed up at him and

squeezed his hands.

"I'll plan something. We've got a busy week, but maybe I could come over with dinner one evening? I'm sure you won't want to go out and leave Pearl while she settles in." He was rambling, but Belle adored how considerate he was being.

"Sound perfect. See you soon, Nick." She let go of his hands and walked towards her cottage, leaving him staring after her.

"What about my jumper?" he called after her.

"Goodnight, Nick." She waved but didn't turn.

CHAPTER SEVENTEEN

The roads were busy with Monday morning traffic as Belle drove to the adoption centre. She had the new pale pink plush bed on her passenger seat, ready for Pearl. Nick had texted her that morning asking if she wanted any company, but Belle had refused. This was something she wanted to do on her own.

Everything happened quickly once Belle arrived. The paperwork was ready for her to sign and she handed her card over to pay the adoption fee. Roger walked out holding a rope lead with Pearl attached to the end of it. The little dog trotted along by his side until she spotted Belle and barked.

"Hello, Pearl." Belle crouched to allow the dog to climb onto her lap. Pearl stretched up on her back legs, with her front ones climbing up Belle's top to lick her chin. Belle laughed and scooped the dog up in her arms.

"If you have any problems, then call me, but I suspect you two are going to be fine," Roger said and handed Belle his card.

Pearl settled in the car once Belle had attached her harness to the seat belt. She pawed at the bed before curling up and sleeping as the gentle hum of the engine soothed her. Belle was careful to drive slowly, worried that any sudden movements could jerk Pearl awake.

It was a warm day, and Belle carried Pearl from the car to the cottage. She could hear the coos of people as she passed them and they spotted the fluffy bundle in her arms. Pearl wasn't interested in them as she chewed the collar on Belle's t-shirt.

Once home, Belle snapped a quick picture of Pearl to send to everyone and then left the dog to explore and settle into her new home. As she made a drink, a little wet nose bumped up against the back of her calf.

"Hello," she said and crouched down to scratch the top of Pearl's head. Pearl leaned into her touch. "I hope you're happy with me. I've never had to look after anyone before, so I might make a few mistakes." Pearl looked up at her with her big brown eyes, and for a silly moment, Belle thought she'd understood every word. She let out a yap and launched for Belle's collar, clenching it between her sharp little teeth.

Once Belle extracted her clothes from the

dog's jaws, they curled up on the sofa. Pearl slept on Belle's lap as she drank her coffee and checked the website orders to make a list of the ones she needed to pack and post. She'd lost track of time and when a knock sounded on the front door she jumped and Pearl sprung off her lap and barked.

"I'll be right there," Belle called and ushered Pearl into her bed. "Stay," she commanded and went to open the door.

"Oh, it's you." A rush of air escaped Belle as she greeted Nick.

Before Nick could say anything, a ball of fur hurtled into his ankles and threw him off balance. Belle lurched forward and grabbed his arm before he toppled over.

"Pearl. No."

"Let's get in and close this door in case she gets out," Nick said. He picked Pearl up to stop her from running outside.

Belle stepped aside. It didn't pass her attention that he'd invited himself in.

"What did you bring?" asked Belle, noticing the bakery logo on the paper bags.

"I wasn't sure you'd have time for lunch, so I brought you something."

"Is this an excuse to see me or Pearl?"

"Both," he said without a second's hesitation. Belle felt a simmer of attraction at the sight of Nick standing there in his scruffy work clothes, cradling Pearl in his muscular arms.

"Why don't you introduce yourself to Pearl

properly while I pop these on a plate and make us a drink?"

By the time Belle had made it to the kitchen, the barking had stopped and she could hear Nick's soft voice as he spoke to Pearl. Inside the paper bag, with the bakery logo on, were two sugared doughnuts. The other held sandwiches from Jada's coffee shop.

Belle set the food on the kitchen table and brought Pearl's bed for her to sit on while they ate. The little dog had calmed down now she'd warmed to Nick.

"I love that noise," Nick commented as Pearl padded over to her bed and plonked down onto the soft cushion.

"It's comforting," Belle agreed and took a bite of her sandwich. "Does this count as our first date?" she asked.

Nick coughed and swallowed his mouthful before he spoke. "It can. I hadn't thought of it like that. I planned to treat you to something a little fancier than sandwiches and deep-fried doughnuts."

"I'm teasing you, Nick." Belle chuckled as his face turned from horror to relief.

He cleared his throat. "My mum and dad liked you."

"They were lovely, Nick."

"If you're ever lonely here, Belle, then call me. I'm looking at a flat to rent this evening. It's above one of the shops in the harbour."

"That sounds lovely. Your mum will miss

you."

"She will, but it's time I had my own space and responsibilities. You won't be able to tease me for being a mummy's boy for much longer." He winked.

"Let's wait and see how often your mum pops in to do your housework and take your washing back with her," Belle teased.

Nick grumbled around his mouthful of food.

"I like the colour," Belle said, pointing to the pale blue paint splattered up his arms. Her gaze lingered for longer than necessary on his tanned biceps.

"It's looking really good. Will you pop by tomorrow?"

"I'm hoping to leave Pearl for a couple of hours to lend a hand, but I'm not sure how she'll react."

"Everything's going to plan. No worries if you can't make it in," he reassured her.

"I'll pop by, with or without her. I want to hear all about the flat."

They chatted for a while about the shop and conversation inevitably wandered back round to Pearl, who was sitting up in her bed watching every bite of food they took. With an awkward goodbye, Nick went back to finish the day's painting.

"That was a bit unexpected, wasn't it?" Belle said to Pearl as she washed up the bits from lunch. Pearl yawned and laid down in her bed. Nick had gone to kiss Belle's cheek, but she'd pulled away before his lips met her skin. She hadn't done it on purpose. She'd put the space between them because she couldn't trust the way her body reacted to him.

It was still too warm outside to take Pearl for a walk. Instead, Belle let her out into a shaded area of the courtyard to use the toilet. Belle breathed in the fresh sea air and closed her eyes. It had been a long day already.

Once back inside, she settled down on the sofa to phone her father.

"Hello, Belle?" Louis answered.

"Hi, Dad. Do you have time to talk?"

"Yes. I'm leaving an auction. I've bought you a few more pieces."

Belle stifled a chuckle. "Thank you, Dad. You don't have to."

"I'll stop when you have time to go to auctions. For now, let me help you."

"Thank you. I phoned because I have news. This morning I picked up a little dog named Pearl." Belle told her father all about Pearl but left out the emptiness inside that had led her to the adoption centre.

"I can't wait to meet her," Louis said, and Belle could hear the smile in his voice.

"About that. It's all been a bit of a last-minute rush, but the shop's opening party is this Saturday. Sorry, I should have phoned you sooner, but I've had so much to do. I don't expect you to visit at such short notice. We'll arrange another date for you to come over and see the place." Belle's fingers played with Pearl's fur as she slept on her lap.

"Belle, take a breath." Louis paused while she took a moment. "I'll be there. I thought perhaps Estelle could come, too. I'll rent us a cottage nearby."

"Okay," Belle replied, not sure what more to say. She fought for a breath, but no matter how hard she tried, she couldn't fill her lungs.

"Listen, Belle, I've got to go. I'll text you the details once I've booked a ferry and a cottage. Love you."

"Love you," Belle said, but the line was already dead.

The silence was deafening as Belle cuddled Pearl. She lifted her against her chest and buried her face in the dog's fur. "Oh, Pearl. I don't think I'm ready for this," she cried. The dog wriggled free until she could reach Belle's face and she licked her nose. Belle loved Estelle, but she didn't know how she'd feel about the woman as she watched her step into the empty spot beside her father.

Belle wanted to phone Nick. She wanted to feel his arms wrap around her as he welcomed her into his family home. Belle knew the Penhale family would chase away her loneliness. But she didn't allow herself to message him. She couldn't give in to the feeling. This was her life now, and she had to work her way through it.

"Shall we get some dinner?" Belle said a little while later. As she'd laid on the sofa with Pearl, the day outside had passed and it had grown dark.

Belle's mind was a mess of thoughts and

emotions, but she focused on getting Pearl's dinner ready and then reheated the leftovers Jenny had sent her home with. They ate together in the kitchen and the soft chomps of the dog made Belle feel a little less alone.

CHAPTER EIGHTEEN

Early the next morning, Belle put Pearl in her harness and walked down to the church to introduce her to Kerenza.

"Hello, Mum," Belle said, coming to a stop by her mother's grave. Despite the early hour, there were a handful of eager tourists milling around the churchyard. Belle kept her voice low, not wanting to draw attention to her tear-stained face. Pearl nibbled on her sandals as she sank to the ground. "I wish I could talk to you. You'd roll out the picnic blanket on the living room floor, make us jam sandwiches, and promise me that everything's going to be okay." Belle held her breath, but nothing happened. The air remained still and the gentle hum of the sea could be heard in the distance.

Belle cringed at a voice behind her. She instantly knew who it belonged to.

"Gosh, you always were odd, but sitting in a graveyard crying is a new low, even for you."

"What do you want, Tegen?" Belle wiped her eyes and pulled a growling Pearl into her arms.

"What are you doing?" asked Tegen, looking down her nose at Belle.

"Not that it's any of your business, but I'm visiting my mother's grave."

For a rare and brief moment, Tegen's scowl was replaced with a softness, but she quickly covered it. "Nick ended our agreement," she said and tapped her foot on the ground.

"I'm sorry to hear that," lied Belle.

"You're not. I just wanted to say that if you want my sloppy seconds, then I'm fine with it." Tegen inspected her nails, and Belle didn't know where to look.

"What?" she stuttered.

Tegen let out an exasperated sigh. "We're hardly going to be best friends forever, are we? If you want him, you can have him."

"Okay. Thanks, I guess?" Belle bit back her retort.

"It's my way of saying sorry about how I treated you at school."

"Are you sorry?"

"Yes. When I was eighteen, I fell in love with this second hand Tiffany necklace. It was silver with a heart on it. I cried for three days before my dad would buy it. That was when I realised you weren't all that strange for liking antiques. It's not all smelly, ancient artefacts. Anyway, see you around." Tegen waved and jogged out of the graveyard.

"Well, that was odd," Belle said to Pearl, who had since fallen asleep in her arms. "You know, Pearl, I think I've been a bit stupid for letting Tegen's opinion affect the way I see myself. All this time I thought her opinion mattered, but she's shown me how little weight I should attach to any of her thoughts."

At home, Belle gave Pearl her breakfast and nipped upstairs to get changed for the day. She couldn't shake the feelings that her encounter with Tegen had stirred up. Tegen had always been shallow, but Belle hadn't realised how bad it was. Their conversation just now had made her see how pointless it was to let Tegen's childhood taunts hang over her like a dark shadow. Her opinion meant nothing, and Belle's shoulders sagged with relief as the weight lifted from them. For years she'd carried the pain with her, but she could let it go. Belle reached for an old pair of leggings and a t-shirt. There was a soft patter of paws as Pearl climbed the stairs. The dog plodded into Belle's bedroom and jumped onto the bed, where she promptly made herself comfortable.

It took Belle three attempts to leave the house, but

every time she got to the end of the road, she could hear Pearl frantically barking from inside the cottage. After the third try, she gave up and brought Pearl to the shop with her. Belle made a note on her phone to look into local dog trainers, and Pearl trotted happily at her feet as they walked to the harbour.

"Leaving her went well?" Nick asked as she approached the shop. He was sitting on the doorstep drinking coffee. Pearl let out a little yap and ran to him, smothering his face in licks as he tried not to spill his drink. Belle laughed at the scene as Nick was lovingly assaulted by the bundle of fur.

"She barked every time I walked down the road. I'll have to get someone in to help."

"My mum's probably still got the details for the person we used. I'll ask her tonight."

"Thanks." Belle picked Pearl up and followed Nick into the shop. "It looks amazing."

Nick had painted all the walls, the counter, and the plinths. The spotlights were on and the shop was illuminated.

"It's a beautiful colour," Nick said. "The painting is almost finished. I've got a couple of areas to go over this afternoon. Then I can lay the floor tomorrow."

"I'm not much help with Pearl." Belle sighed and scratched behind the dog's ear.

"Belle, I've been telling you the entire time that I've got this." Nick stood beside her and his chest brushed her arm as he turned to stroke Pearl.

Belle breathed in the smell of his aftershave and resisted the urge to lean into him.

"Belle?" Nick's voice broke through her thoughts.

"Sorry, what was that?" She blinked to clear her mind.

"I asked if you have a desk to go in the office?"

"Oh, no. I need to get one." Another thing to add to her to-do list.

"I can run out and pick one up from Ikea or somewhere?" he offered.

That brought Belle's attention into focus. "Ikea?" she fumed, causing Pearl to bark.

"Yeah. It's a bit of a drive to Exeter, but I don't mind."

"Nicholas Penhale, I will most certainly not be buying any furniture from Ikea." Belle huffed.

"What's wrong with Ikea?"

"Nick, this is a vintage jewellery shop. I've spent my entire life surrounded by antique furniture. I'm not about to buy flat-pack MDF."

"Oh."

"Is that how you're planning to furnish your flat?" Belle narrowed her eyes. He'd texted her last night after the viewing to say it was perfect and he'd said yes to it on the spot.

"Umm, no?" He scratched the back of his neck.

"I'll need to find a local auction to buy some stock soon. We can get your furniture at the same time." Belle nodded as the plan came together.

"Do I get a choice in this?"

"Nope." Belle smiled and wandered through to the office to get a feel for what size desk she needed.

"So, I guess Swedish meatballs and flat-pack furniture are off the menu for our first date?" he asked as he followed her.

"Don't even joke about it." Belle kept her face towards the office to hide her smile.

"What about dinner at a nice pub twenty minutes away?" He stood behind her, and Belle could feel the heat radiating from him.

"That sounds perfect," she said.

"Good, because I've booked us a table for tomorrow evening. My parents have said they'll look after Pearl."

Belle turned. He was so close that her nose brushed his chest. She tilted her head up to him and a jolt rushed through her body.

"You've thought this through."

"I have."

"What time is the table booked for?" she asked.

"Seven."

"I'll drop Pearl off and pick you up at six."

"I've never been picked up by a woman before." His lips were almost brushing hers and Belle's heart hammered in her chest.

"I'll see you tomorrow." Belle stepped around him and back into the shop. "You've got a lot to get on with. I won't distract you any longer." She needed to put some distance between them.

"Bye Belle. Bye Pearl," he called after her, a smirk on his face.

It was almost lunchtime. Belle wandered across the harbour to see Jada. Pearl was sleepily nestled in her arms as Belle carried her, since the ground was too hot for her paws. The coffee shop was busy, but Belle found a table in the corner. She waited while the queue went down. Jada spotted her and gave her a wave. While she waited, Belle watched families come and go. She saw a family of three enter the coffee shop and join the queue. The parents looked exhausted, but the little girl bounced up and down as she peered through the glass cabinet to decide what cake she wanted. A lump formed in Belle's throat as she saw them interact.

"Belle, come on. The auction starts in an hour and it's a fifty-five-minute drive away!" Louis shouted.

"I'm coming," Belle shouted through the closed door. She pulled at her messy ponytail to finish the look and stepped out of the bathroom and into the hotel room.

"You look lovely, darling," Kerenza said. She was sitting on the bed, waiting.

"Shall we go?" Belle asked, watching as her father paced around the room.

"Finally!" he huffed, his French accent shrouded

the words as frustration oozed from him.

Belle hung back with her mother as Louis checked out.

"I like your hair," Kerenza said, linking her arm through Belle's.

Eleven-year-old Belle fought the urge to shake her mother off. If the girls at school saw her now, then she'd never hear the end of it. Thankfully, they were nowhere near home and nobody knew her. "I fancied trying something new."

"It suits you. You've done the winged eyeliner very well."

Louis ushered them into the car and barely gave them enough time to put their seatbelts on before he pulled away. Realising her father wasn't in the mood, Belle put her earphones in for the journey to the auction house. She felt guilty for making them late. Last week, Belle had seen the girls from school sporting the latest fashion trends and wanted to try it on herself, but knew she'd have to wait until there was no chance of bumping into them.

"Why don't you run in and I'll park the car?" Kerenza suggested as they reached the busy car park.

"Good idea. I'll see you in there." Louis raced inside.

Belle reluctantly pulled her earphones out and got out of the car with her mum.

"Do you want to head inside with your dad? I'm going to grab a coffee, then I'll join you." Kerenza locked the car and glanced longingly over to the sign that said café.

"I'll come with you," Belle said, ignoring the way her heart yearned to enter the auction house and explore the treasures.

"Okay." Kerenza quickly hid her shock and led Belle into the café.

The café was like many Belle had sat in while her father filled out auction house forms. Pine tables and chairs were covered in plastic plaid tablecloths with pots of dusty fake flowers in the middle. An elderly woman stood behind the counter, wearing an apron that matched the tablecloths. She gave them a kind smile and handed them a menu.

"Can I have a slice of cake?" Belle asked, looking at the Victoria sponge displayed on a stand by the till.

"Okay," Kerenza agreed and pointed Belle to a table while she ordered.

While Belle waited for her mother to pay, she got out her phone and scrolled through the numerous anonymous texts. Each one stung, but she kept her face passive.

"I'm sorry you have to spend your weekend traipsing around auctions," Kerenza said as she placed a tray on the table. There were two slices of cake and a pot of tea for two.

Belle pressed her lips together as she took a mug and poured her tea.

"What's wrong, Belle?" Her mother reached across the table and squeezed her free hand.

"It's nothing, Mum," Belle bit back.

"Belle Alice Roux, you are a terrible liar."

"I don't want to talk about it." Belle picked up

the fork and broke off a piece of cake. It was claggy in her mouth as she forced herself to chew.

"Is it those girls at school again?"

Belle hesitated, and Kerenza sighed.

"What are they saying to you now?" she asked.

"I didn't say it was them," Belle protested.

"It was written all over your face."

Belle scrunched shut her eyes.

"Belle?" Kerenza moved to the chair beside her and wrapped an arm around her shoulders.

Silently, Belle pulled her phone out and handed it to her mother so she could read the messages the girls from school had sent.

Kerenza's face fell and Belle could see her becoming angrier with every message she read. "Why didn't you tell me?" she asked gripping Belle's hand in hers.

Belle shrugged. The cake she'd eaten had settled like lead in the pit of her stomach. "It's fine, Mum. They're right. I am weird. Who actually enjoys spending their weekends looking at antiques?"

"Belle, you enjoy it, and it's fine for you to enjoy it. Everyone's allowed their own interests, even if it's different from other people their age. These girls are shallow and stupid."

"I think I'd like to stop spending my weekends looking at antiques." Belle had crossed her hands on the table and sat up straight.

"Is this why you put on all this makeup and did your hair differently today?" Kerenza put the phone on the tabletop and slid it over to Belle.

"Yes. I need to find some other interests."

"You have interests. It's not that you can't find more, just don't drop what you love because of some silly, spiteful girls at school. There's more to life than school, Belle, and one day you won't even remember these girls. Never be afraid to be you."

Belle considered her mother's words. "I cannot wait for the day I can't remember them." She pulled her hair from the ponytail that was pulling on her head and giving her a headache.

"Come on, eat your cake and drink your tea. We need to check on your father before he blows the budget." Kerenza pushed the plate towards her and Belle tucked into the cake.

Belle shoved the memories back as Jada crossed the coffee shop to her table. The lunchtime rush had dwindled while Belle was lost in her thoughts, and Jada had left her staff to serve the last few customers.

"Is this Pearl?" cooed Jada.

"Yes. Pearl, meet your Aunty Jada." Belle held her up for Jada to greet and give her one of the coffee shop's homemade doggy treats.

"Zoe is going to be incredibly jealous when she hears I met Pearl before her." Jada chuckled and took the spare seat.

"Are you okay to sit with me? If you're busy,

I'll get some lunch to go and leave you be."

"I'm due a break. I put our order in, so it should be over in a minute." Jada already knew Belle well enough to know her usual order.

"How are things with Zoe?"

Jada's stare became distant as a soppy smile spread across her face. "She's been over every night since the beach picnic."

"Oh, my gosh. Look at you two."

"I'm afraid you'll be third wheeling for a while," Jada said, with not an ounce of guilt on her face.

"Actually, I might not be since I have a date tomorrow evening."

Jada let out a silent scream. "Who with? Wait, that's a silly question. It's obviously Nick. Isn't it?"

"Yes, it's Nick. He's taking me to dinner while his parents look after Pearl."

"You have to let us know how it goes," demanded Jada.

"Of course I will. Jada, am I doing the right thing? I don't think I'm ready for a relationship. I'm scared to let another person get close to me. Losing my mum was so painful and I can't face that again."

"You can't go through life without feeling loss, Belle. I can't begin to imagine how awful losing your mum was, but she wouldn't want you to shut yourself away from life. If you're going to pick someone to take a chance on, I think Nick is the perfect option."

Belle sucked in a shaky breath. "I'm scared,"

she admitted.

Jada reached across the table and squeezed her hand. "We're all scared, Belle, just for different reasons. Don't jump ahead. Enjoy your date with Nick and take it one step at a time."

CHAPTER NINETEEN

Belle missed going to the shop on Wednesday, but she didn't get time to pop in. She'd spent the day visiting a woman in Port Isaac who upcycled and restored furniture. Eventually, Belle settled on an antique oak desk that had been lovingly restored. If she was honest, she wasn't sure if she missed the shop or Nick, but she wasn't ready to delve deeper into her feelings. By the time Belle had to get ready for her date, Pearl was exhausted from trotting after her all day. She curled up on the bed and slept as Belle fretted over her outfit and makeup.

It was another warm July day, and the evening promised to be balmy. Belle opted for a short black dress with a deep v-neck. She slipped on a pair of black heeled sandals, and put her hair in a bun before wrapping a black silk scarf around it.

"Is this too much?" she asked the sleepy dog, who opened one eye before letting out a soft huff and going back to sleep. Belle didn't know what that meant, but she wasn't going to change. She went to her jewellery box to focus on her favourite part of getting ready.

Belle took out the Art Deco ring her father had sent and slid it onto her finger. She matched it with a pair of earrings from the same era with a pearl in the centre and a pretty gold decoration around it. Belle put on a simple gold chain necklace with a round cut ruby pendant that would glow in the evening sunshine. She picked one of the small gold watches and did the clasp up. Belle snapped a picture and sent it to the group chat.

Ten seconds later, her phone rang.

"Hello?" Belle answered.

"You look amazing. Don't you dare get second thoughts and change," Zoe shouted down the phone.

"I second that," Jada called from the background.

"Are you sure it's not too much for dinner at the pub? I've never been taken out on a date like this, and I'm not sure what to expect." Belle perched on the edge of the bed and Pearl moved to her side.

"Trust me, you look perfect. Nick won't know what to do with himself. When do you have to leave?"

Belle glanced down at the delicate watch. "I need to go pack Pearl's bag and leave. I'll text you when I get home tonight. Love you both."

For a tiny dog, Pearl needed a surprising amount of stuff for her evening out. Belle wasn't sure if Jenny would still have any dog bowls, so she packed them, a blanket, some treats, and a tin of her dinner.

Multiple people watched her as she walked through the harbour to Nick's. Pearl trotted by her side, garnering attention from everyone she passed. They were a few minutes early when Belle knocked on the door.

"Belle, you look gorgeous. Come in," Jenny greeted her.

"Thank you, and thank you for having Pearl." Belle looked around for any sign of Nick, but she was alone in the living room with Jenny.

"It's no bother. We're looking forward to having a few hours with her so we can spoil her rotten." Jenny knelt to greet the dog. Pearl gave her hand a tentative sniff before she leaned into the stroke. "I think Nick is still getting ready. You're welcome to go up and get him."

Belle blushed at the thought of being in Nick's bedroom while he dressed. "I should probably make sure Pearl is settled first," she mumbled, dropping the tote bag with the dog's stuff in it.

"Does she have a routine yet?"

Belle talked Jenny through Pearl's non-existent routine and explained how attached she had been the last couple of days.

"No worries. It will do her good to be away

from you for a while," Jenny reassured her as she set down a bowl of fresh water.

"Hello," Nick said from the doorway. Pearl immediately ran to him and launched herself into his arms. Belle stood staring, unable to look away. Nick wore beige chinos and a white shirt. He'd had a haircut, but it was still long enough for Belle to run her fingers through. She shook her head at the thought.

"You look very nice," she said, mindful that his mother stood beside her.

"Thank you. You look gorgeous." He sent her a smile that made the hairs on her arms stand up as a delicious shiver ran through her body.

"Come on, you two, or else you'll be late. Here are my car keys. Give me a text if you want us to have Pearl overnight." Jenny took Pearl from Nick's arms and handed him a set of keys.

"Thank you. See you later, Pearl." Belle kissed the puppy goodbye and allowed Nick to lead her out of the house.

He took her hand as they made their way across the harbour. Nick beamed as they walked through crowds of people. She heard a few people shout hello to him, but she kept her attention on each step she took.

"You really do look amazing," he said as they cleared the crowds.

"Thank you. You do, too." She squeezed his hand.

Nick drove to the pub, and Belle put the radio

on quietly in the background. She drummed her fingers on her leg as they drove away from the sea and into the Cornish countryside.

The pub was a beautiful old white-washed building on the edge of the road. Nick parked and took Belle's hand.

"Wait until you see the garden. I've booked us a table outside, but if it gets cold, we can move." He glanced down at her bare legs and Belle noticed his sharp intake of breath.

They were shown through to the pub garden, and Belle immediately knew why Nick had chosen to take her there. The pub sat on the top of the hill and the garden overlooked the rolling fields below for as far as the eye could see. They were given a table on the edge and handed menus.

"Nick, this place is amazing," Belle said, looking around. Being midweek, it wasn't too busy, and it truly felt as though they had this corner of Cornwall to themselves.

"Isn't it? I grew up coming here with my mum and dad. They had their first date here." He cleared his throat and shifted his attention from her to the menu in his hands.

"Thank you for sharing it with me," Belle said as she fought the bubble of emotions rising inside her.

They ordered their drinks and food. Nick's foot kept bumping against Belle's under the table.

"I bought a desk today," Belle said, pulling her phone out to show Nick a picture of it.

"That's what you chose instead of a pine Ikea flat pack?" He asked. He squinted as he zoomed in on the picture.

"Are you honestly telling me you'd prefer something mass-produced over that? Tell me now, Nick, so I can walk away before either of us develops feelings."

"I think it's a bit late for that, Belle," he murmured and handed her back the phone.

Belle froze.

"Take your phone, Belle," prompted Nick.

She shook herself and took the phone from him, her fingers brushing his.

"I was joking, by the way." He sipped the beer the waiter had delivered.

"About having feelings for me?" Belle grasped the stem of her wineglass so tightly she was surprised it didn't shatter.

"I would never joke about that." He reached across the table and took her hand in his. "Belle, I was joking about the furniture. You've got amazing taste."

"Thank you." Belle threaded her fingers through his. "You have feelings for me?" she asked.

"I do. Maybe it's too soon to be admitting it, but there's no point pretending. I don't want to play games with you. Since the moment we met, I was attracted to you and the more I've got to know you, the more I've come to realise how amazing you are."

Belle's chest rose and fell rapidly with each breath. "I don't know what to say." His eyes clouded over and he went to pull his hand back, but she gripped it harder. "No, that's not what I meant." The words came out in a tumble as she tried to explain herself. "I'm overwhelmed. I didn't expect this…" She gestured between them.

"I don't want to rush you into anything." Nick sighed and rubbed a hand across his face. "I'm not very good at this."

"Neither am I. Let's take this one day at a time, okay?"

Their food came, and it was delicious. Belle had ordered the whipped goat's cheese and beetroot salad with a side of fries, while Nick had ordered a burger.

"This is amazing, Belle groaned around her mouthful.

"It is," Nick agreed.

"So, tell me more about your parents. You said they had their first date here?"

"My mum and dad grew up around the harbour and went to school together. They hung out with the same friends, but my dad didn't ask Mum out until they were about nineteen. He brought her here for a drink and they've been by each other's side ever since."

"That's lovely. Jenny said she knew my mum when we were at school."

"Mum mentioned it. I can't remember Kerenza, if I'm honest. How did your parents meet?"

Belle finished her mouthful as she remembered her mother telling the story of how she'd met her father. "Dad used to travel the world in his early twenties buying and selling antiques. He met my mum when he was in London. Mum was visiting to look at universities and they bumped into each other, quite literally. Dad walked right into Mum. He was so focused on getting to the auction on time that he wasn't watching where he was going. She was carrying a cup of tea, which went everywhere, covering both of them. Dad felt awful. He ushered her into a nearby café to dry off, and he ordered her a fresh cup. They spent three hours in that café chatting and Dad missed the auction. He said that was how he'd known she was the one. No other woman could make him forget about antiques."

"Your dad sounds like a good man," Nick commented as he wiped his fingers on a napkin.

"He is. You should get to meet him on Saturday. He's coming for the opening party." Belle didn't mention that Louis was bringing Estelle, and she suspected something was going on between the two of them.

"I'm looking forward to the party." Nick bumped his foot against hers and reached to take her hand.

"So am I," Belle said, but her deflated tone didn't match the words.

"Belle?" Nick asked.

"I won't see you once the shop is open," she admitted, her stare fixing on their joint hands.

"You'll still see me. I'll be working at Jada's

straight after the shop. I can pop in on my lunch breaks. I'm sure Jada would encourage some long lunches." He winked and rubbed his thumb across her knuckles.

Belle chuckled. "That sounds lovely."

The waiter cleared away their dirty plates and returned with dessert menus. Neither Belle nor Nick wanted the evening to end, so they shared a slice of cake and ordered coffee. The light slowly dwindled, and the torches scattered around the garden were lit, but they were oblivious to the goings on around them. Belle's gaze was fixated on Nick as he recalled stories of some of the jobs he'd worked on with his dad.

"I wonder how Pearl is," Belle said as they waited for the waiter to bring the bill over.

"She'll be curled up on the sofa having tummy tickles." Nick pulled his wallet out as the waiter approached.

"Do you want to go halves?"

"No. It's my treat."

Nick wrapped his arm around Belle's waist as they walked back through the pub and out to the car park. He walked her to the passenger side of the car and encircled her with his arms as she turned to face him. Even with her heels on, he still towered above her. Nick tilted his head towards her and Belle's arms wrapped around his neck. Her eyes fluttered closed as he brought his lips down to meet hers. Belle's body was on fire as her lips met his and moved against them. She took a step forward to close the space between them until her chest was pressed against his. Nick gripped her waist with one hand as the other cupped her face.

Someone drove past and beeped. They sprung apart.

"Sorry," Nick muttered.

Belle rested her head against his chest while her pulse slowed, and the world stopped spinning. Her voice shook as she assured him there was nothing to apologise for.

"Shall we head back? Do you want me to drop you at the cottage, or do you want to pick Pearl up?"

Belle considered the question as she climbed into the car. She knew what he meant. Did she want him to go home with her?

"Could we pick Pearl up? Sorry, I know it means you have to go back and forth." The lust-filled fog had lifted and she could think clearly. Her body screamed to invite him back, but she couldn't. They'd just agreed to take things slowly and she couldn't lead him on if she wasn't ready for this.

"Of course." Nick's voice was strained, but he shot her a smile and nodded.

"Thank you."

The radio switched on with the car, and Belle sank back into the seat as the latest summer hits played. Her mind was awash with flashbacks of the kiss they'd shared. It would only take a few words and he'd go home with her.

"I've had a really nice time tonight," Nick said, his voice just loud enough to be heard over the music.

"So have I." Belle's face relaxed into the smile that tugged at her lips.

They collected Pearl, who was dozing on the sofa between Jenny and Jo. Nick had nipped in to collect her while Belle waited outside. She was too embarrassed to go inside with her smudged lipstick and flushed face.

"Pearl," Belle called as the little dog bounded up to her.

"I left all her bits. I'll drop them round to you tomorrow," Nick said.

"Thank you. You don't have to walk us back. We'll be fine on our own." It was late, but there were still people around.

"I want to, Belle. Besides, it's a great excuse to spend a bit longer with you." He took her free hand and walked by her side.

Pearl followed slowly, sniffing from one patch of concrete to another, and neither Belle nor Nick were inclined to hurry her along. Each time they stopped for more than a few seconds, Nick stole a kiss.

"We're never going to make it home," Belle joked as her legs wobbled.

"I know, and I have to be up early to put your flooring down." He wrapped his arm around her waist and they turned into Belle's road.

Nick walked her up to the doorstep and kissed her before he stepped back.

"Will I see you tomorrow?" he asked, his voice raspy.

"I'll pop by," promised Belle.

"Good. Thank you for a wonderful first date." Nick smiled. "See you tomorrow."

"Bye." Belle fumbled for her keys as Nick walked back down the street. She let herself into the cottage and leaned against the closed door to catch her breath. Pearl let out a frustrated yap from her feet.

"Sorry, let's get you out of this harness." Belle pulled herself together enough to sort Pearl and get them both some water.

Once she'd changed into her pyjamas and climbed into bed with Pearl curled up beside her, Belle checked her phone. She had multiple messages from Zoe and Jada asking how the date had gone, but she ignored them and opened Nick's messages and texted him.

Thank you for an amazing night. See you tomorrow xx

Once she'd sent the message, Belle opened her group chat with Jada and Zoe. She wondered if it was too late to call them, but decided to try it, anyway. She hit the button to call them both, but only Jada answered.

"Hey, you," Jada answered.

"How was your date?" Zoe asked in the

background.

"Shorter than yours, by the sounds of it," Belle teased.

"She won't leave," Jada joked. Belle heard a kerfuffle on the other end of the phone, followed by laughter. "Okay, I don't want her to leave," admitted Jada.

"Anyway, enough about our date. How was yours?" asked Zoe.

Belle tangled her fingers in Pearl's fur and leaned back on the pillows. "It was amazing."

"Tell us everything," Zoe demanded.

"Is he a good kisser?" Jada asked.

"He's an amazing kisser."

"Then why are you calling us instead of kissing him?"

Belle sighed. Trust Jada to get straight to the point.

"It was perfect. Almost too perfect." Belle sighed as she finally let down the wall, which had been holding all her worries in place. "There wasn't a single awkward silence between us. He makes me laugh and smile. And the way he kisses me makes my legs go weak."

"So, what's wrong?" Zoe asked. Her voice was louder and Belle could imagine that she'd taken the phone from Jada before she could say anything stupid.

"I don't know if I want this."

"You don't want him?"

"I want him. My body is screaming out for

him. But I can't fall for him. I can't go through the pain of losing another person I love." Belle felt as though a rug had been pulled from beneath her.

"Belle, there's no saying you'll lose him." Zoe's voice was soft, and it brought a fresh set of tears to Belle's eyes.

"But there's no saying I'll keep him. No matter how much you love someone, you can always lose them." Belle swallowed a sob.

"Is this about your mum?" Zoe asked.

"I can't lose someone else." Belle's voice shook.

"Oh, darling. I wish we were there to squish you in a Jada and Zoe hug," Zoe said.

"We're only around the corner. We could come now," Jada suggested.

"Thank you both, but I'm fine." She paused for a moment. "Sorry, I didn't mean to cry down the phone. It was an amazing night, but I'm struggling with my emotions. I thought it would be a fun night out. I didn't expect to realise I was falling for him."

"Who can blame you? He's seriously hot. I can't wait for him to start the work on Jada's courtyard."

"Excuse me? Is that the real reason you've basically moved into mine?"

Belle chuckled and used her sleeve to wipe her wet cheeks. "Thank you for not making me feel like an annoying third wheel."

"Never." Jada and Zoe replied at the same time.

"I should get some sleep. I'm sure I'll feel better in the morning once I've had a chance to get my head around everything."

They said their goodbyes, and Belle wrapped an arm around Pearl as she let herself drift off to sleep.

CHAPTER TWENTY

There was a knock on the front door, and Pearl's high-pitched bark echoed around the bedroom.

"What on earth is going on?" Belle threw her dressing gown over her pyjamas. Pearl barked and growled until they reached the door, where she backed up behind Belle's legs and peered around them. Belle's shoulders relaxed when she spotted Jada and Zoe.

"Morning," she called, opening the door. Pearl ran to greet them and Zoe instantly scooped her up, smothering her in kisses.

"We thought you might like a coffee and a girly chat." Jada held up a takeaway cup with the cafe's logo on it.

"Couldn't you have done it at a reasonable

hour?" Belle groaned, closing the door behind them.

"Afraid not. Zoe has to head back home soon, and I've got a coffee shop to run," teased Jada.

"Come on, let's sit out in the courtyard. I've got some supermarket croissants in the bread bin. Let me grab them." Belle opened the door to let everyone out.

Jada handed Belle a coffee and took a croissant.

"How are you feeling today?" Zoe asked as she threw a ball for Pearl to chase.

"I've not had the chance to gather my thoughts." Belle rubbed the sleep from her eyes and hoped her neighbours didn't look out their window to see her eating breakfast in her dressing gown.

"We don't have to talk about him," Zoe said and picked at the pastry.

"How's the plans coming along for my opening party?" Belle asked, eager to move the conversation away from Nick and her feelings.

"Everything's on track," Jada confirmed.

"I'm going to print your flyers when I get home, then I'll hand them out when I come back this evening," Zoe said.

"You don't have to distribute them. I can do it myself."

"I'm happy to do it. It'll give me something to do while I wait for Jada to close up for the evening."

Belle picked at her croissant. It was clear things were moving fast, but she wouldn't question them about it. If it felt right, then she was happy for them.

"When does your dad get here?" asked Zoe.

"They should arrive late Friday night, so I won't see him until Saturday."

"They?" Jada asked, her brow furrowed.

"He's bringing Estelle." Belle forced herself to swallow the mouthful of croissant.

"I think I remember you mentioning Estelle. She's your dad's friend or colleague, right?" asked Zoe.

"Yes to both, but I have a suspicion that things might have changed since I left," Belle admitted. She hadn't told anyone, and as the words left her mouth, Belle wished she could take them back. Saying it out loud made it feel real, and the pain clouded the memories she had of her mother.

"Has there not been anyone since your mum?" Zoe scooted her chair closer to Belle and wrapped an arm around her shoulders. Belle shook her head.

Jada stood and went to Pearl, who was shaking a toy between her teeth.

"Oh, Belle. Your dad deserves to be happy." Zoe's voice was soft.

"I know. I'm just not ready." Belle's lip quivered, and she took a deep breath. Coming back to Cornwall had dredged up Belle's grief, and the emotions felt raw.

"You've had lots of changes in your life recently. We're here, Belle. Whatever happens, you'll always have me and Jada to talk to."

"Thank you. I've never had friends like this before. It's nice."

"It's a first for me, too," Jada admitted from across the courtyard.

"Whatever happens, we've all got each other." Zoe reached her hand out for Jada to join in a group hug. Pearl barked from the ground, and Belle picked her up.

The moment was interrupted by another knock on Belle's front door.

"Why is everyone up this early?" Belle groaned and went to see who it was.

It was Nick. He stood there bleary-eyed and holding a bag of Pearl's belongings.

"Morning," he said as he raked a free hand through his hair. He took in her dressing gown, and Belle could see his throat bob as he gulped.

"Morning." Belle smiled as her mind wandered back to the way his hands had grasped her waist as he kissed her last night.

"I brought Pearl's stuff round." He held out the bag.

"Thanks. She's been using one of my best bowls to drink from. Do you want to come in?"

He glanced behind her at the sound of laughter. "Did I wake you?" he asked, looking back at her attire.

"No. Zoe and Jada woke me when they came around with coffee."

"Oh." Nick let out a breath and his body visibly relaxed.

Realisation dawned on Belle. "Oh my gosh, you didn't think I'd had someone stay over, did you?"

Nick opened and closed his mouth and scrubbed at his eyes. "I didn't know what to think," he admitted.

Belle stepped forward to close the gap between them and rested her hands on his chest. She could feel the thrum of his heartbeat beneath her fingertips. His arms encircled her waist, and he rested his chin on top of her head.

"Sorry. I shouldn't have jumped to conclusions." He sighed. "I haven't stopped thinking about you since I left last night."

"I haven't stopped thinking about you either." Belle wriggled in his hold to tilt her head to look at him. He captured her lips with his, and Belle's body ignited under his touch.

A crash behind Belle sent them pulling apart.

"Oops. Sorry," called Zoe. Pearl came running in and launched herself at Nick.

Belle stepped back in a daze to allow the dog to greet him. She pressed her fingers to her lips and turned to see Zoe in the kitchen doorway surrounded by pastry crumbs.

"I tripped over Pearl on the way to the bin," she explained, as a blush crept up her neck. "That was hot," she mouthed at Belle.

Belle fought the urge to throw herself face down onto the sofa and pretend her friend hadn't walked in on her kissing Nick.

"What's going on in here?" Jada asked,

appearing in the kitchen.

"I ruined their moment," Zoe explained. She was kneeling down, picking up the crumbs.

"There's a dustpan and brush under the sink," Belle said absentmindedly as she turned back to look at Nick, who had his face hidden in Pearl's fur as he fussed her.

"We should probably go," Jada said, pushing Zoe towards the door.

"Sorry about the mess," Zoe said as Jada pulled her along.

"Bye," Nick and Belle called after them. Nick was the first one to crack and burst out laughing. Belle followed shortly and threw herself onto the sofa when she couldn't stand any longer.

"Do you think they left any food?" Nick asked once he'd gained control over his laughter.

"Probably. I put out a big packet of croissants. I doubt they've eaten them all. Go through to the courtyard with Pearl. I'll be out once I've cleared up the crumbs."

Belle retrieved the dustpan and brush from under the sink and swept the mess on the floor. She was grateful for the distraction while the fire inside her dampened.

"Still a few pastries left," Nick commented as she joined him.

Belle picked one up and bit into it with a sigh.

"These are good," Nick said.

"They're not as good as the ones in France."

"You'll have to show me one day."

Belle felt the initial wave of panic roll in, but excitement pushed it back. She could imagine walking into the village with Nick, holding hands and telling him about her life there. They'd sit outside the boulangerie with espressos and pastries. Pearl would curl up at their feet and they'd watch the world pass them by as they enjoyed each other's company.

"Belle?" Nick asked. He'd put his pastry down and was watching her.

"Sorry?" She blinked and hoped he couldn't see the longing on her face.

"You didn't say anything, and I was worried I'd said the wrong thing."

"No. You said the right thing."

"Good." He looked at his watch. "I should get going." He rubbed his hands to get rid of the crumbs on them. "I only popped round at this time so I could get an early start in the shop."

"Sorry, I distracted you." Belle stood with him.

"It was a welcome distraction." He cupped the side of her face in his palm and Belle's breath caught.

"Shall I pop by in a bit?" she asked.

"Probably best not to. I've got a lot to do and I think you'd be too much of a distraction." His hands moved to the back of her head and he kissed her until her knees went weak and she grasped at his shoulder to keep her upright.

"Definitely too much of a distraction," he muttered as he pulled back, licking his lips.

"Sorry," Belle said, not trusting herself to say anything more.

"I'm going for dinner with some friends tonight. I won't see you until tomorrow."

Belle swallowed down her disappointment. "That's okay," she said, not meaning it.

"The shop will be finished by the end of today. I can help you move the stock in tomorrow?"

"I'd like that."

"Why don't I come over early and cook you breakfast?" he offered.

"That sounds perfect." Belle reached up on her tiptoes and pressed a chaste kiss to his lips.

"I'll see you tomorrow then." He gripped her dressing gown belt and pulled her against him, kissing her one last time before he left.

Belle held onto the doorframe as she watched him walk down the road and disappear towards the harbour.

By the evening, Belle was up to date with postal orders and had got the stock ready for the shop tomorrow. It was starting to feel very real now. She picked up the necklace on the coffee table. It had been upstairs in the safe with the rest of the jewellery for the shop, but Belle wasn't sure she could part with it.

"I can't believe Dad's going to miss this auction," Belle shrieked as she gathered her overnight bag and followed her mum out of the cottage.

"He's beside himself," Kerenza said, locking the cottage door and opening the car's boot to stow their bags.

"I told him not to risk the ferry at this time of year," Belle said with a wisdom beyond her fourteen years.

"He was desperate to pick up that Louis XV console table."

"And he didn't even win it," Belle scoffed.

"I know. Come on, get your seat belt on or we'll be too late to check in."

Kerenza drove out of the harbour and onto the motorway towards Exeter. They were heading to London for an auction.

"Dad promised me he'd be here," Belle groaned.

"I know he did, darling, but you know how his work is."

Belle sighed and turned to look out the window. She'd been doing a paper round for the last few months to save up for this auction. Despite all the spiteful comments from the girls at school, Belle kept working, even through the torrential rain and gale-force winds. Her father had promised to take her to spend some of her hard-earned wages. The auction was focused on artwork and jewellery. It seemed like the perfect combination for a father-daughter trip. Instead, Louis had gone to France for an auction followed by a networking event, and his ferry home had been cancelled due to the weather. It wasn't unexpected since it was November.

Kerenza had said they'd simply drive to London and Louis would meet them the following morning, then they could go together. However, with the state of the weather forecast, it looked as though tomorrow's ferries would also be cancelled.

The rain lashed against the car as Kerenza drove slowly through it. They stopped for dinner at a service station and eventually made it to their Premier Inn. It was dark and windy as they crossed the car park to the hotel. Kerenza insisted Belle go straight to bed, but with the wind howling outside, she couldn't sleep. At some point, she heard Kerenza disappear into the bathroom on the phone to Louis. Her voice was low, but Belle could make out her mother's side of the conversation.

"Don't be ridiculous, Louis!" she hissed down the phone.

Making as little noise as possible, Belle rolled over in the bed so she was closer to the bathroom door.

"I can take my daughter for a night away. I'm not going to do anything stupid."

Belle lay completely still as something heavy hit the bathroom floor. She grasped the duvet in her fists as her mother walked back into the bedroom.

"Sorry, did I wake you?" Kerenza asked. Her smile was overly bright in the dimly lit room. "I dropped *my phone. Think I cracked the screen."*

Belle slept terribly that night as the howling wind kept waking her. Every time she woke, she saw her mother lying awake beside her. Eventually, the alarm went off, and Belle and Kerenza dragged their tired bodies from the bed.

"We don't have to go, Mum," Belle said as she pulled on a jumper. Kerenza was frantically typing on her mobile. A large crack spanned the length of the screen, but it was still useable.

"No, this is your treat, Belle. You've been looking forward to this for months. Your father has texted me to say his next ferry has been cancelled. I'm afraid he's not going to make it."

Belle had already guessed he wouldn't, but still, her heart dropped at the confirmation.

"Come on. Let's go downstairs for breakfast and then we can ask at the desk about which trains we need to get."

Belle had a bacon sandwich followed by a croissant with marmalade from the buffet. Meanwhile, Kerenza had a cooked full English.

"Dad would be rolling his eyes at you right now," Belle said as she tore off a piece of croissant and smothered it in marmalade.

"I know. I'll sneak a couple of pastries into my handbag before we leave." She winked at Belle, who smiled, knowing her father would still eat the stale pastry.

Once at the venue, they wandered around the lots before the auction began. Everything was crazy expensive and Belle's excitement drooped.

"What about this one?" Kerenza asked, pointing to a glass case on the opposite side of the room to where Belle stood admiring a sapphire brooch.

Nestled against a blue silk backdrop was a gold necklace. The chain was thin and delicate, with an intricate gold pendant. It was understated, but beautiful.

"It's got a guide price of two to three hundred," Kerenza read from the brochure.

Belle considered the piece. "It's Edwardian," she said.

Kerenza glanced back at the brochure to read the description. "You're right. You really know your stuff, Belle," she said and squeezed her shoulder.

"Okay. This is the one. What did Dad want us to look out for?"

The auction began. Belle and Kerenza had taken seats fairly near the front. Neither had been to an auction without Louis, and they were nervous. After a phone call with her father, Belle had deduced that there was nothing here of any interest to him. If she didn't get the necklace, it would be a wasted trip. The lot came up and Belle sat on her hands to stop herself from bidding too early. The auctioneer started at one hundred pounds, but there was no interest.

"Belle," Kerenza hissed.

"Be patient," Belle uttered the words her father had said to her countless times.

The price dropped to eighty pounds and still, there was no interest. When it dropped to sixty, Belle *nudged her mum in the ribs to hold up their sign. She was too young to bid by herself. In a matter of seconds, the auction ended and Belle got the necklace for a bargain. She grasped her mother's hand and squeezed.*

With no interest in any of the other lots, they sat through the auction and Belle enjoyed watching as each item was snapped up by an eager buyer. It was a completely different experience without the mixture of nerves and excitement in the pit of her stomach as she waited for a certain lot to come up.

"Your dad's finally on a ferry. He's going to go straight home, but he's booked us into the hotel for another night because the weather's awful," Kerenza explained. She'd phoned Louis while Belle popped to the toilet. They'd finished all the paperwork for her necklace and handed over the money, and Belle had wanted to put the necklace on and admire it in the mirror.

"Okay." Belle nodded. She wondered if that was the truth, but didn't ask any questions. She glanced through the glass doors to the street outside, where rain splattered against the pavement and rubbish was blown past, caught up in the wind.

"We're a short tube journey away from central London. Shall we treat ourselves to some lunch and then a wander around Harrods to look at the expensive jewellery?"

Belle held the pendant between her thumb and

finger. She couldn't sell it. There were too many memories attached to it. The auction in London had been the last one she'd been to with her mother. They'd gone into Central London and had pizza at a chain restaurant. After they'd washed their greasy hands, they wandered into Harrods and admired the jewellery. Belle's eyes had widened at the prices. A kind shop assistant had noticed her interest and had shown her a few expensive pieces.

Pearl nudged her arm and climbed onto her lap. Belle unclasped the necklace and put it on. "I wish you could be there on Saturday, Mum."

CHAPTER TWENTY-ONE

Belle was up early on Friday morning, not wanting Nick to catch her in her dressing gown again. She wore a navy and white striped vest with a pair of high-waisted denim shorts and her hair tied back into a bun. Pearl wore a matching striped collar with one of Belle's silk headscarves tied around it. They'd already popped out for an early morning walk after Nick had texted saying he was running late. Belle walked to the churchyard to say good morning to her mother. She still wore the necklace. It was the only piece of jewellery Belle had put on.

At eight o'clock, Nick arrived with a bag filled with the contents to cook a full English. He had dark shadows under his eyes and his hair was askew as if he'd just rolled out of bed.

"Good morning." Belle beamed and reached up on her tiptoes to kiss him. He kissed her back, but it lacked the passion that had been building between them for the last couple of days. Disappointment filled her as he pulled back.

"Sorry. I'm feeling a little delicate," he explained and followed her through to the kitchen.

"I'll make you a coffee. Do you want any help? I'm not a very good cook, but I can stir beans or something." She got out two matching mugs. After another online sale, she'd treated herself to some new homeware.

"No, thanks. A coffee will be more than enough help." He unpacked the items from the shopping bag as Pearl clambered over his feet for attention.

"Did you have a good night?" Belle asked as she picked up the dog while the kettle boiled.

"It was really good. Another one of my friends has started his own business, so we went out to celebrate us both finishing our first jobs." Nick was rummaging around the kitchen cupboards, getting out pans.

"That's nice."

"It was great until they realised how often I mentioned your name." He raised his eyebrows at her and smirked. "They turned it into a drinking game. And that is why my head is pounding this morning and my mouth feels like I've had sand for breakfast."

Belle chuckled. A warmth spread across her

chest at the idea of him talking about her. Nick was standing at the hob, heating oil in the frying pan. She brushed her chest against his back and wrapped her arms around his waist.

"Hmm," he hummed and leaned into her touch.

As the kettle boiled, he turned to give her a quick kiss before she went to make their drinks.

"I could get used to this," Belle said as she finished her last bite of breakfast. It had been delicious, and she'd watched Nick perk up as he ate.

"It's a very nice view across the breakfast table for me." He drained his mug of coffee and leaned back in the chair with his eyes closed. "Sorry for turning up still hungover."

"We've all been there. Besides, maybe I should be apologising to you. If it wasn't for me, you wouldn't have got yourself involved in a drinking game."

"That's true. Right, are you ready to head to the shop?"

They'd agreed to double-check all the safes before they transported the jewellery. Nick had suggested they make multiple trips to avoid transporting it all in one go.

"I'm sure it's fine, but we don't want to risk anything happening. Let's take the most expensive items first before anyone realises what we're doing," he'd suggested.

They left Nick's van outside the cottage and walked down to the shop, allowing Pearl to trot along in the shade. Belle ached to reach out for Nick's hand, but she stopped herself. The harbour was a small place, and the residents gossiped. If she was seen holding his hand, then everyone would know by the end of the day.

"We can sneak kisses in the office."

Belle blushed at the thought. "I'm going to hold you to that."

"You better do. Belle, I don't mind if people know we're dating."

They'd reached the shop and Belle's fingers fumbled with the key as she tried to get it in the lock. "It's not that, Nick. I'm scared. It feels like a lot of pressure if people know we're together. This is all new, and I don't want everyone getting involved." Belle's mind wandered back to the churchyard and her chat with Tegen.

"I understand." He took the key from her and unlocked the door with his steady hand.

"I'm sorry, Nick. You deserve someone who's proud to walk down the road holding your hand."

"As long as you hold my hand in private, I don't mind. If you count this morning, we've only been on two dates. We don't need to rush into anything. Besides, there's something quite sexy about sneaking around." He wiggled his eyebrows at her and ran into the shop before she could shout after him.

Belle followed, preparing a witty retort, but all her thoughts were scrambled as she took in the shop's interior. After flicking through numerous catalogues, Belle had settled on white wood flooring. It was real wood that had been whitewashed. All the original dinks in the wood were still present, and Belle loved how it showed its past life. The powder blue walls and plinths all blended in to create a seamless backdrop for the jewellery. Nick had cut, sanded, and whitewashed driftwood to make the perfect shelves to display some of the vintage items. He flicked a switch, and the spotlights turned on. Light bounced off every surface.

"What do you think?" he asked, standing in front of the blue counter, which he'd added gold trim to.

"Nick, it's amazing. I can't believe this is the same shop." Belle turned around on the spot, taking it all in. The bay window at the front allowed natural light to flood in and Nick had angled some cabinets towards it, so the light would catch on the gems. He'd done more than refit the shop. He'd helped her to realise her dream. It didn't feel like her father's shop anymore. *The Cornish Vintage Jewellery Shop* was hers.

"It was your vision. I brought it to life." He shrugged as if it was nothing.

"Thank you." She smiled and put Pearl on the floor.

"We should move the stock in. I kept the packaging for the flooring. I thought we could put the jewellery inside, then it'll be less obvious what we're doing."

Belle's heart was full. "You've thought of

everything." She reached up on her tiptoes to press a kiss to his lips but pulled back before they could lose themselves in it.

Over the next couple of hours, they made multiple trips back to the cottage to collect the jewellery. Once it was all safely put away in the shop's safes, Belle locked the door and pulled the shutter down across the window.

"Are we having a lock-in?" Nick asked, his brows raised. "We should have at least got some snacks in."

"I need to do a trial run of where I'm setting out the jewellery." Belle had left the cheaper pieces on top of the glass cabinet in the middle of the shop. She spread the items out and stepped back to look around, trying to decide the best way to display them.

"Shall I take Pearl out for a walk and get us some lunch?" suggested Nick. "I'll be quick, so I'm back for when you unload the safes."

"Okay." Belle nodded absentmindedly. "If I put those there, the light should reflect off them," she muttered to herself, oblivious to Nick and Pearl leaving.

"Are you sure you like it how it is?" Nick asked. He was sitting on the shop floor leaning against the counter and Pearl was curled up in his arms, fast asleep.

"Hmm. Now you say it, I'm not sure about this sapphire necklace."

Nick let out a grown. "I was being sarcastic."

"I'm only winding you up. It's perfect. Let me snap a couple of pictures, so I remember the setup tomorrow. You don't have to stick around, you know."

"I want to help. Besides, I thought you could treat me to some dinner after today." He winked at her, and Belle suppressed a laugh.

She took a few pictures, and with Nick's help, returned everything to the safes. He left the office while she locked them.

"What do you want for dinner?" she asked as she locked the door to the office. If someone wanted to break in, then it wouldn't deter them, but she hoped it would buy some time for the alarm system to alert the police.

"Shall we get some fish and chips and take them back to yours?" Nick held the front door open for her.

Belle locked up and took Nick's arm as they wandered down to the chip shop along the front of the harbour. Nick waited outside with Pearl while Belle ordered two portions of fish and chips. They strolled back to her cottage with the steaming parcels. Pearl's nose twitched as the smell of their dinner drifted down to her.

"I'll pop the kettle on," Nick said as they got back.

"Okay. I'm going to run upstairs and get

changed into something more comfortable." Belle put the food down on the kitchen counter.

"Lucky me." Nick winked at her before he turned to fill the kettle up.

Belle's cheeks flamed, and she stuttered. "No, I didn't mean…" she trailed off.

"I know what you meant, Belle. Don't worry. Go get changed before our dinner gets cold."

Once upstairs, Belle splashed her face with cold water and changed into a pair of leggings and an oversized t-shirt.

"I gave Pearl her dinner," Nick said as Belle walked back into the kitchen.

"Thank you. Shall we have this on our laps in there?" Belle nodded her head towards the living room. "My legs could do with a rest." She'd been wandering back and forth from the office to the shop floor all day and her calves burned.

"Sounds good. Here you go." Nick handed her a plate with a portion of fish and chips on it. "Go ahead. I'll bring your tea in."

"Thank you." Belle gave him a sleepy smile and went to sit in the living room. Pearl joined her after she'd cleared her bowl.

"Once the shop's open, I need to learn how to cook. I'm constantly eating takeaway food," Belle admitted as Nick joined her on the sofa. She unravelled the paper and a rush of steam escaped.

"Why don't you come over for Sunday lunch again?"

"I'll be working in the shop."

"I forgot about that. Do you not have any staff yet?" Nick handed Belle the bottle of tomato sauce he'd found in her fridge. She took it and squeezed some on the side, unlike him, who'd covered his dinner in it.

"I can't afford to employ anyone yet. I'll see how finances are at the end of summer."

"I'll help if I'm free," Nick said around a mouthful of food.

Belle chuckled. "I appreciate your offer, but you probably don't know the difference between a pearl and a diamond."

His brow furrowed. "No, you're right. I don't have a clue. I'll have a chat with Mum about having Sunday dinner later, then you can come after work."

"You can't do that."

"Why not? She won't mind. She loved you." He shrugged and loaded his fork.

"Promise me you won't ask. It would make me feel awkward."

"Okay. I won't. I'll bring you round some leftovers instead. How's that?"

Belle nodded. "That would be lovely. Thank you."

They finished their dinner and Nick took the plates out to the kitchen and washed them up. Belle flicked through the television channels and found a film to put on in the background.

"I found some chocolate in your fridge," Nick said as he walked back in with a bar of milk chocolate.

They settled down to watch the film and Pearl curled up in Belle's lap. Nick wrapped his arm around Belle and she leaned her head against his shoulder. She was just nodding off when her phone beeped from across the room. Belle groaned and every muscle in her body fought her as she rose to get it. She passed Pearl to Nick and grabbed her phone. Her hands shook as she read the message.

"Belle?" Nick asked.

"Sorry." Belle shook herself. "It's my dad."

"Do you usually look horrified when your dad texts you?"

"He's texted to say he's off the ferry." Belle sat beside Nick and Pearl clambered back onto her lap.

"I'm confused. Isn't that a good thing?" Nick had turned the volume down on the television.

"Yeah, it is. Well, it would be if he were on his own. He's bringing Estelle." Belle's voice shook as she said Estelle's name.

"Who's Estelle?" Nick reached out to hold her hand.

"She's my dad's friend. They worked together, and they became friends. As time went on, she became part of the family." Belle's mind wandered to the first day out they'd had with Estelle. She'd wanted to show them the French countryside and had packed a picnic.

———

"You will love it," Estelle told Belle, her words thick with a French accent.

"You will, Belle. Your mother loved it here," Louis said, climbing into the front of the car beside Estelle.

Belle nodded from the backseat. They'd been living in France for a year now, and with every day, her memories of home faded. Belle's attempts at learning the language had all fallen flat and sometimes, when she was with Louis and Estelle, she felt like an outsider. Not that either of them ever purposely did anything to make her feel that way. She didn't fit in with their ways because she wasn't from here.

The lush green fields passed them by, but Belle wasn't interested in any of it. Before her father had announced Estelle was taking them out for the day, Belle had planned to reorganise the antiques in the barn and make an inventory. Instead, Louis had insisted she join them on a trip. From the front seat, Louis and Estelle spoke in French, and Belle put her earbuds in and turned her iPod to the maximum volume. Tears prickled in her eyes, but she refused to succumb to them.

Estelle had stopped the car on the edge of a field that overlooked a valley. Beyond a field of lavender, there were vineyards for as far as the eye could see.

"Let us stop here and lunch," Estelle said, switching back to English.

Belle traipsed behind them as they found a spot under a tree. Estelle pointed out the local landmarks in the distance, but Belle's expression didn't waver from *the sulky pout she'd had ever since her father woke her that morning.*

"I packed wine, and how do you say it? Fizzy orange for Belle." Estelle smiled as she spread out a chequered blanket beneath the tree they'd chosen to sit under.

"Wine. Aren't you driving?" teenage Belle bit back.

"Just a small glass with lunch." Estelle smiled, but Belle glared. She hated the way the woman's dark, sleek hair shone in the sunlight. It was the opposite to her mother's unruly curls that had stuck out in all directions, no matter the weather.

"I'll have fizzy orange with Belle," Louis said and placed a hand on her shoulder. Belle shook it off and wandered into the field while Estelle set out the picnic on the blanket. Across the field was another, but this one was full of lavender. Belle wandered to it and climbed over the fence to walk through the blooms. The air was delicious from the lavender's scent and bees buzzed from one plant to another. For the first time that day, Belle's scowl was replaced with a smile. It was beautiful, and she couldn't help but imagine her mother's reaction. Kerenza would have grabbed her hand and pulled her into a run down the rows. The air would fill with their joyous shrieks until they tumbled to the ground in a pile. Belle could imagine her father watching them from the top of the field and laughing, ready to hand them each a drink when they returned.

"Belle?" a voice called from behind.

Belle tensed at the sound of the French accent.

She tried to ignore it and pretend she hadn't heard anything, but Estelle called out again. The smile dropped from Belle's face, and she turned to look at the woman in her tight white jeans and striped vest. Estelle shaded her eyes with one hand as she waved to Belle with the other.

"What does she want?" Belle muttered to herself and slowly dragged her feet back to the field's entrance.

"Belle, that is private!" Estelle shouted as she grew closer.

"I did realise that when I saw the fence and climbed over it," Belle said, not bothering to raise her voice.

"Come." Estelle gestured. She squinted against the sun and beckoned Belle closer.

Reluctantly, Belle climbed over the fence and stood beside Estelle.

"You do not like me," Estelle said.

"There was me thinking I was doing a brilliant job of hiding my feelings," Belle snapped.

"Belle, I am not your mother. I want to be friends."

"I don't want any friends." Belle turned her back to Estelle and leaned her elbows on the fence. She watched as the lavender swayed in the breeze, dislodging bees who frantically flew to their next perch.

"Louis told me you love antiques. I'd like to talk to someone about them." Estelle joined Belle at the fence.

Belle breathed out a huff of air and glanced sideways at Estelle. "Do you like my dad?" she asked with all the confidence of an interfering fifteen-year-old.

"We are friends." Estelle nodded.

"Just friends?" Belle narrowed her eyes.

"Friends," Estelle confirmed.

"Then why do you need me as a friend if you already have my dad? He can talk to you about antiques."

"You are a woman. It is different."

"Do you like antique jewellery?" Belle asked, tentatively turning to Estelle.

"This bracelet is antique jade." Estelle held out her arm and showed Belle the bangle on her wrist. It had a gold clasp that glistened under the midday sun.

Belle's jaw dropped at the sight. "They're worth a fortune," she exclaimed. Her fingers ached to touch it, but she kept them firmly at her sides.

"This was less because it's damaged." Estelle pulled the bangle off and turned it over to show Belle where it had been repaired. Someone had filled the crack with gold.

"It's beautiful."

"I have more. My whole house has antiques."

"Can I come round one day?"

"Of course." Estelle frowned and gesticulated with her hands as she sought the right words. "You and Louis come for dinner next weekend?"

"I'd like that." Belle gave her a weak smile.

"Your father is safe, Belle," Estelle whispered and winked.

The heaviness that had wrapped around Belle's

heart lifted at the confirmation. She'd judged Estelle too
soon and assumed she had feelings for her father.

"Shall we have some lunch?" Belle cocked her
head towards the tree at the top of the field where her
father sat watching them.

"Yes. Come." Estelle held out her hand and Belle
grasped it.

"Belle?" Nick asked, pulling her back into the
moment.

"Sorry, I lost myself in my memories."

"What were you thinking of?"

"A year after we met Estelle, we all went for
a picnic. I was fifteen, had just lost my mother, and
was scared that I would lose my father. I wasn't very
nice. She had a chat with me and promised me they
were friends. I trusted her after that. We bonded
over antiques and over time, she became like an
aunty or older sister. She'd take me shopping when
I needed new clothes, or sit with me as I pored over
magazines deciding what new hairstyle I wanted to
try." Belle sucked in a shaky breath. "I trusted her,
Nick."

Nick pulled her against him, much to the
annoyance of Pearl, who was snoozing on her lap.
"And you don't trust her anymore?" he asked as he
brushed his lips against the top of her head.

"I don't think she and my dad are 'just

friends'." Belle sniffed and squeezed her eyes shut.

"Has your dad not dated anyone since your mum?"

"Not that I know of."

"That's a long time, Belle. Maybe he's lonely. Especially now you've moved back to Cornwall."

Belle pulled back and blinked a few times as she stared at Nick. "I don't want him to be lonely. It's not that he's seeing someone. It's who he's seeing. Estelle promised me they were friends, nothing more. We built a friendship based on that." A tiny part of Belle knew she was being unfair, but she felt as though she'd fallen back into being a teenager. However hard she tried, she couldn't pull herself out of the mood.

"Perhaps you're jumping to conclusions," reasoned Nick.

"Perhaps." Belle nodded, but the sickening feeling in her stomach suggested otherwise.

"I think you need to talk to your dad about it, Belle."

"I know." She sighed and pinched the bridge of her nose.

"Maybe you should get an early night. You've got a big day tomorrow."

"Will you stay?" As soon as the words left her mouth, Belle knew she shouldn't have said them. "Sorry, I shouldn't ask that of you."

"I'll stay." He took her hand and squeezed.

"Thank you. I don't want to be on my own." Belle stood and stretched. "I'll take Pearl into the courtyard for a wee. Be back in a minute."

Belle carried Pearl outside. As she sniffed around in the darkness, Belle took in a few deep breaths. The evening air filled her lungs and calmed her thumping heart. She raked a hand through her hair as she replayed the last half an hour. They'd been having such a lovely evening until she'd ruined it with her reaction to her father's message. Belle was twenty-four, she had no right to say who her father could or couldn't date. She just wished it was anyone but Estelle. The only woman, other than her mother, that Belle had trusted, loved, and confided in. Pearl let out a yap, forcing Belle to take a step back from her thoughts. The little dog wagged her tail by the back door, asking to be let in.

"Good girl," Belle said, and let the dog back into the kitchen. She pulled her treats from under the sink and gave her a bedtime biscuit.

"Do you have a spare toothbrush?" asked Nick, wandering over to the doorway.

"Probably not."

"No worries. I'll use my finger and some toothpaste."

"Nick, please don't feel you have to stay. I'm feeling much better now. I'll be fine on my own tonight."

"I'm more than happy to stay, Belle. Is the spare bedroom set up, or do I need to make the bed?" He had his back to her, getting a glass of water so he couldn't see the shock that crossed her face.

"I thought you could share with me?" Belle's

voice trembled. Maybe she'd got the wrong end of the stick.

"Oh. Okay," Nick said.

"The water's overflowing." Belle watched as the water flowed from the tap and down the sides of the full glass. "I can make up the spare bed for you." She went to move, but he called after her.

"No. Sorry, I didn't want to jump to conclusions." He put the drink down on the counter and dried his hands on a tea towel.

"I want to sleep, Nick. Nothing else." Belle glanced down at her feet as a blush rose on her cheeks.

"I'd like that, Belle. Don't be embarrassed." He put a finger under her chin and tilted her head up. "There'll be plenty of time for anything more in the future," he promised before he kissed her.

CHAPTER
TWENTY-TWO

An alarm echoed around the room and Pearl howled along to it. Belle groaned and pulled the duvet over her head.

"Sorry," a voice mumbled from beside her.

Belle's eyes sprung open, and she threw the duvet off her face to see a rumpled Nick rolling over to turn the alarm off.

"I forgot you stayed," Belle muttered as she scooped Pearl up to stop the howling. They'd have the neighbours knocking soon, complaining about the racket.

"Am I that forgettable?" Nick turned the alarm off and stretched, pulling the duvet from Belle.

"I'm stressed." Belle sighed, not in the mood

to revel in Nick's teasing. His face grew serious, and he reached out to tuck a stray strand of hair behind her ear.

"Belle, today is going to be a huge success. Don't let your dad or Estelle sour this moment for you. This shop is your dream, and you deserve to enjoy today." His thumb rubbed her cheek and Belle leaned into his touch.

"I know."

"None of this feeling sorry for yourself. Now, why don't you get up and get ready? I need to run home for a shower and a fresh set of clothes. I'll take Pearl with me to give her a walk. We'll be back in about an hour, okay?"

Belle nodded. She watched as he climbed out of bed in only his boxers. He had his back to her, but Belle couldn't look away as he dressed. Nick leaned down and kissed her before he left. She wrapped her arms around his neck and kissed him back until Pearl wriggled between them. Reluctantly, Belle said goodbye and got out of bed. She made a coffee and left it to cool while she jumped in the shower.

With her hair air drying, Belle got out her outfit for the day. She'd chosen it a few days ago and had opted for something plain to show off her jewellery. It was a white playsuit that Belle had bought from a charity shop. It was missing a belt, so she threaded a navy silk scarf through the belt loops and tied it in a knot at the front. Belle slid her mother's sapphire engagement ring on. She wished she'd thought to get her nails done, but there hadn't been time. In her safe, Belle owned a pair of sapphire earrings and a necklace. The necklace was a simple, pear cut pendant on a chain, which would stand out against the bright white of her outfit. The earrings were also pear cut, but they were simple studs. Belle tied her hair back, not wanting it to hide the jewellery. She threw some makeup on and glanced at her appearance in a mirror. Her eyes glowed and the corners of her mouth turned upwards in anticipation of the day.

As promised, Nick returned an hour later.

"Close your eyes," he called from the doorway.

Belle paused in the kitchen and closed them. "Okay," she called back. She could hear Pearl's paws tapping on the floor, followed by Nick's heavy footsteps.

"Pearl, sit," Nick said. "You can open them now."

Belle peeled open her eyes to see Nick standing in front of her, holding a paper bag from Jada's coffee shop in one hand and Pearl's lead in the other.

"Look at her collar," Nick prompted.

Belle's gaze fell upon Pearl's new collar. It had her name in the middle, printed gold on a beige tag. On either side of the tag were pastel-coloured beads. It was very pretty and fitting for the dog of a jewellery shop owner.

"It's perfect. Did you buy it?"

"I got it online." He beamed at her.

"Thank you." Belle bent down to pat Pearl on

the head before she pecked Nick on the lips.

"Is that all I get?" he teased.

"Later," she promised. Her words held more confidence than she felt.

"I like the sound of that. Come on, Jada sent me off with some breakfast. She said she'd meet us at the shop in an hour to help set up. Actually, she said both she and Zoe would be there. I think Zoe was upstairs in the flat." Nick raised his brows.

After breakfast, they went to the shop to get ready for the midday opening. Belle had received texts from her father and Estelle wishing her luck and saying they'd see her soon. She'd closed her phone and shut it in the drawer of her new desk. It looked lovely in the middle of the office. There was still lots to do in the room to make it feel like her space, but it was already worlds away from the room Belle associated with that fated phone call.

"How are you feeling?" Nick asked, joining her. He'd been busy setting out Pearl's bed and water bowl behind the counter and settling her into the space.

"It feels like a lot of pressure on one day." She sighed.

"Just get through today, Belle. Then the fun begins and you get to spend every day surrounded by your jewellery."

A knock on the door was Jada and Zoe.

Belle let them in and they carried boxes of food, champagne glasses, and balloons. With wide eyes, Belle watched them bring everything into her tiny shop.

"I don't think we're going to need that many glasses," Belle said, watching as Nick carried in a third box.

"It's easier not to argue with Jada. If she thinks you're going to need that many, then let her go with it," Zoe advised.

Belle nodded and showed them into the office, where they could stack the glasses in a corner.

"That's everything," Nick announced. "I'll lock the door while we set up, then Belle can unlock the safes and put the jewellery out."

Belle took a deep breath while Nick connected his phone to the speakers and put on a 90s cheesy hits playlist.

Jada set out the food, Zoe hung balloons around the entranceway, Nick helped in any way he could, and Belle set out the jewellery working from the pictures she'd taken last night. Pearl watched from her bed as everyone scurried around.

"This looks amazing," Zoe said, as she stepped back to admire everyone's work.

"Look at the balloons! Zoe, they're fantastic." Belle stared at the blue and gold balloons that Zoe had fashioned into an arch above the doorway.

"I've got a poster for the back of the door. Hold on." Zoe ran into the office before returning with a cardboard tube. "Give me a moment to stick it to the back of the blinds. I thought it would be perfect for people to get a picture under the balloons with your poster in the background."

"Zoe, you're a genius," Belle exclaimed. A warmth rushed through her at how her new friends had pulled out all the stops for the shop's opening day.

"Give me a second."

Belle glanced over to the table Jada had set up with food. She'd brought a small fold-up table with her that she'd covered in a gold tablecloth. Vintage plates were laid out with a selection of chocolate-dipped strawberries and macarons. The strawberries were dipped in dark chocolate and Jada had decorated them with edible gold flakes. Meanwhile, the pale blue macarons were stacked in towers on either side of the strawberries.

"Jada, my mouth is watering looking at these. Thank you." Belle threw her arms around the woman, who instantly hugged her back.

"I'm so glad we pulled it together in time. You should have seen the first batch of macarons. They were an absolute disaster."

"I'm sure they weren't—"

Belle was interrupted by Zoe, who had finished putting the poster up and had wandered over to them. "No, Belle, they were awful." She laughed and put an arm around Jada.

"I couldn't have done this without either of you. Thank you." Belle pulled them both into a hug.

"Shall I open a bottle of Champagne?" Nick

offered, glancing at the bottle Belle had left on the counter.

"Yes. I'll grab us some glasses." It took Belle two trips to gather four champagne flutes, as she didn't want to risk dropping them. Someone had taken the time to tie blue silk bows on the stem of each glass. Every little touch had been thought of.

"To Belle," Nick said, holding his glass up. Zoe and Jada echoed his words.

"To everyone," Belle said, as she blushed.

They clinked glasses and a rush of excitement flooded Belle as she took her first sip and the bubbles danced across her tongue.

"Shall we unlock the door and put the board out to let everyone know you're open?" Nick asked.

Belle buried her face in Pearl's fur and took a deep breath. "Okay, let's do this." They'd been open for two minutes when Belle's first customers walked in. It was a young couple on holiday. Nick poured them each a glass of champagne, and Belle pointed them towards the table of sweet treats. They both picked a macaron and nibbled at them as they wandered around looking at the jewellery. Zoe and Jada had taken their champagne and were also wandering around, looking at the jewels on display. Nick had swapped the 90s playlist for something more subdued.

"Could I try this on?" the woman asked, pointing to a gold bracelet in one of the glass cabinets.

"Of course." Belle handed Pearl to Nick and

pulled the keys from her pocket to unlock the cabinet. It was a gold tennis bracelet adorned with cabochon opals.

"It's gorgeous," the woman said as she handed her champagne glass to her partner to allow Belle to slip the bracelet on. The opals stood out against her delicate tanned wrist.

"The opal matches my engagement ring," the woman turned her wrist, admiring the piece. "It's what I've been looking for to make up my wedding jewellery. I'll have it." The woman held her wrist out for Belle to take it off.

"Wonderful. I'll pop it behind the till for when you're ready." Belle locked the cabinet and wandered back to where Nick waited for her.

"They didn't even look at the price," he whispered.

Belle smothered a chuckle. "You'd be surprised how many people don't," she told him as she found a velvet box for the bracelet and wrapped it in tissue paper before putting it in one of her branded bags.

In the end, the couple also purchased a pair of opal earrings to match the bracelet. The man paid without uttering a word, and Belle wished them a lovely day.

"They spent over a thousand pounds without a second thought." Nick's jaw had dropped.

"I should have sent them towards the café," Jada commented. "Speaking of, I should probably get back. If we stay any longer, Zoe is going to talk me into buying her that peridot ring." Jada cocked her head towards the shelf by the window.

"It's very pretty. If it's not sold by next week, I might treat myself. I'm waiting for an invoice to be paid." Zoe looked wistfully back at the ring.

"Come on, you. Best of luck. Let us know how the day goes." Jada blew her a kiss and Zoe sent her a wave as they wandered out of the shop.

Once they'd left, Belle went to the shelf and picked the peridot ring.

"Are you saving it for her?" asked Nick. His gaze hadn't left her.

"It's her birthday next week. I'm going to give it to her. After all the help she and Jada have been, it's the least I could do."

"Do I get to choose a peridot ring?" Nick asked, fluttering his lashes at her.

"I have some signet rings if you'd like one."

"I don't need any jewellery, Belle, but I will take you up on the offer of a night with you." He wrapped his arms around her waist as Belle searched behind the counter for a ring box to put Zoe's gift in.

She giggled as his fingers tickled her sides. He pulled her against him and dropped a kiss on the top of her head. Belle let out a sigh as she relaxed against his hold.

"That's a lot easier on my accounts," Belle teased.

"I won't be eas—" Nick broke off and let go of her as the door opened and two people walked into the shop.

Belle's breath caught in her throat as she took in the man and woman standing in her doorway.

"Dad." Her voice shook. Louis stood ahead of Estelle with his hands by his sides and a huge grin across his face.

"Belle, this is fantastique. I'm so proud of you." He looked around the shop before his attention returned to her.

"Dad." She walked round from the counter and threw herself into his embrace. "I've missed you," she said as she hid her face in his chest.

"It's been too quiet at home without you." He hugged her. "And there's been nobody to stop me overspending at the auctions. I made a big loss last week." Belle pulled back and her father winced.

"Dad! How many times do I have to tell you?" Belle sighed, but she couldn't stop the smile that took over her face. She'd worried he would have changed in their time apart, but he was the same as he'd always been.

During their reunion, another customer had walked in and Nick had poured them a glass of champagne.

"Why don't you go and introduce yourselves to Nick," suggested Belle. Her father glanced over at the man behind the counter and then back at her with his eyebrows raised. "He's a really good friend," she said, avoiding her father's gaze.

Louis stepped aside and gestured for Estelle to walk ahead of him.

"Lovely to see you, ma chérie. We'll catch up with you in a moment." Estelle squeezed her hand before she crossed the shop to where Nick stood. Belle sucked in a deep breath and went to greet her newest customer. It was a man looking for a gift for his wedding anniversary.

"We have some beautiful necklaces," Belle suggested.

"Thank you, but he's not much of a necklace wearer. Do you have any gold bracelets that would fit a wrist similar to mine?" He held up his wrist for Belle to inspect.

"I'm sorry." Belle wanted the ground to swallow her.

"It was an easy mistake, especially considering I was browsing your beautiful ruby earrings when you approached me. I'm sure my husband would love them, but I'm not sure he's ready for the gossiping at work." He sent her a wink and Belle relaxed.

"I've got a very small men's selection over here. There's not much at the moment. I wasn't sure what the demand would be." She showed him over to the cabinet in the far corner. Belle caught a glance of Nick handing her father and Estelle a glass of champagne. Louis had crouched down to fuss Pearl and Estelle was talking to Nick.

Ten minutes later, the man left with a gold bracelet wrapped in one of Belle's bags. He'd promised to pop by in the next couple of weeks to drop some hints to his husband for his birthday present, and Belle had promised to have more men's stock.

"Second sale." Nick held up his hand for Belle to high-five.

"Two sales already. Congratulations, Belle." Louis held his glass up for her to cheers. Belle glanced around for hers but couldn't find it. Nick handed her his.

"Nick was telling us how he renovated the shop. He's done an amazing job. It looks nothing like it did in my day," Louis commented as he walked over to one of the cabinets and peered inside.

"It's beautiful, Belle," Estelle said. She placed a hand on Belle's arm and smiled at her. Belle returned the smile, but it didn't reach her eyes. Estelle wore black silk trousers, a white t-shirt, and kitten heels. Her dark hair was slicked back and her perfect pout was covered in bright red lipstick. She looked wildly out of place in Padstow-on-Sea. It was jarring seeing Estelle in the one place that was filled with memories of her mother.

"Thank you," Belle choked out.

Pearl let out a small bark and Belle picked her up, grateful for the distraction.

"I think she's missed you while you've been busy," Nick said. Belle glanced up at him, and her body relaxed as he took her hand. His eyes held a question, and she nodded to him to let him know she was okay.

"She's lovely, Belle," Louis said, wandering back to the counter.

"Thank you. You're welcome to go and look at the office."

Louis gestured for Estelle to follow him and they went through to the back.

"How're you doing?" asked Nick once they were out of earshot.

"Okay, I think. It's nice to see my dad, but there's an awkward atmosphere." Belle's shoulders sagged. "I want it to be like it always was between us." Pearl wriggled in Belle's arms and lunged to lick her nose.

"You need to have a proper chat and clear the air."

"I know. I'm dreading it." Belle nibbled at her lip.

"It's your dad. It'll be fine." Nick squeezed her hand.

"I can't believe what you've done to the place. It's unrecognisable," Louis exclaimed as they joined them back out in the shop.

"Is that a good thing?" Nick asked. He'd let go of Belle's hand.

"Yes. Really good. I think you're going to be very happy here." Louis glanced between Belle and Nick.

"I think so, too." She smiled.

Another customer walked in and Nick brought them a glass of champagne.

"You're busy. We won't get in your way. Why don't we go out for dinner tonight to celebrate? Nick is welcome and we can find somewhere dog-friendly," Louis said. Belle noticed the way he reached back for Estelle's hand.

"Okay." Belle nodded, but her insides turned to ice. "Why don't we go to The Cornish Arms?" Belle suggested. She felt numb and wanted her father and Estelle to leave as soon as possible.

"Perfect. See you later." Louis leaned in and kissed Belle on the cheek. She stiffened and tightened her grip on Pearl.

"Au revoir," Estelle called as she followed Louis out of the shop.

"Oh, she looks very glamorous," the customer commented as Estelle left.

"She's French," Nick replied quickly and shot Belle a sad smile.

"Do you have anything French?" the woman asked, looking at Nick with quizzical eyes.

Despite the mix of emotions rippling through her, Belle laughed at the look of panic that crossed his face.

"We do. Follow me," Belle said, handing Pearl to a relieved Nick.

The woman left with a beautiful citrine brooch that Belle had picked up at a flea market in Provence.

"Strange how nobody wears brooches these days," mused Nick as he watched the customer leave.

"What?" Belle asked absentmindedly. The whole time she'd been talking to the customer, her dad's invitation to dinner had rattled around her head.

"What's wrong?" asked Nick. He refilled his glass for her.

Belle pushed it away. "I shouldn't, not if I'm going out tonight."

"Where are you going tonight? I thought you promised me your company."

"My dad invited me for dinner. Actually, he invited both of us."

"Are we going?" Nick handed her the glass again, and this time, Belle accepted.

"You don't have to come with me, Nick. It's going to be awkward."

"I wouldn't want to be anywhere but with you."

"Thank you. It means a lot." She took a shaky sip of the champagne.

"My mum texted me earlier and said she'll pop by after the lunchtime rush with some sandwiches for us."

"That would be amazing." Belle's head was swimming with the second glass of champagne, and there were only so many sweet treats she could stomach.

"You're going to need more stock soon," Nick commented.

"I know. It's going far better than I'd imagined. My dad's brought some pieces with him from various auctions."

"Probably best not to fall out with him until you've got them then," Nick joked, and Belle choked on a mouthful of champagne. He wrapped an arm around her shoulder. "Belle, whatever happens, Estelle can never replace your mother, nor can she replace the memories you have of her."

"I know. My dad deserves to be happy. I just wish it was with anyone but Estelle." She let out a sigh before plastering a false smile on her face as another customer walked through the door.

The day was busy with a steady stream of people coming into the shop. Some people browsed, others took cards and promised to look on the website, and a surprising amount of people left with a special piece of jewellery. Belle's heart had soared as she'd overheard a little girl asking her mother about a ring.

"Who do you think wore it, Mummy?" the girl asked.

"I'm not sure. It's a beautiful piece. Look at the size of that diamond. It was probably someone very important," the mother had replied.

"A princess?" The little girl's face lit up at the question.

"It could be." The mother had smiled.

As promised, Jenny popped in with some lunch for them. She insisted on Nick accompanying her around the shop as she pointed out anything she liked and reminded him that her birthday was next month. When she left, Nick glanced longingly at the pearl necklace his mother had looked at.

"She liked that, didn't she?" he asked.

Belle had noticed the way Jenny's eyes kept wandering to the piece. She'd asked Belle the price and moved swiftly on.

"You can have it for half the price," Belle said as she unlocked the cabinet.

Nick reached to stop her. "Belle, you can't do that."

"I can. Say it's from both of us. The fifty per cent discount is my half."

By the time Belle turned the sign on the door to 'closed', her feet throbbed and the very last thing she wanted was to go out for dinner with her father and Estelle.

CHAPTER TWENTY-THREE

"Why is it so difficult to find something nice to wear?" Belle groaned.

"What's wrong?" Nick asked, leaning against the doorframe. He'd come running upstairs after she huffed and threw herself on the bed, making more noise than she'd intended.

"What do you wear to dinner when your father's about to tell you he's dating the closest thing you've had to a mother since your own died ten years ago?" Belle's words all merged into one, and Nick's brow furrowed.

"This isn't you, Belle." He sat beside her on the bed and took her hand in his. "It's going to be okay. Don't jump to conclusions. It's just dinner with your dad."

"I'm sorry. You must be counting down the hours until you can go home."

He squeezed her hand. "I'm not going anywhere," he promised.

Belle put her mother's jewellery back in the safe before she pulled on a short white dress with scalloped edges. She glanced towards the Art Deco ring but decided against it. Instead, she put on a simple pair of small gold hoops and a gold necklace with a citrine pendant that Estelle bought her the first time they went to an auction together. Belle swallowed the emotions rising inside her and focused on brushing her hair.

They walked down to The Cornish Arms, and Belle could feel people looking at her as she walked beside Nick.

"You look lovely," he said.

"Thank you." She shot him a sad smile.

"In a few hours, you'll be back home," Nick reminded her and took her hand in his.

"Maybe I should have offered to have them around for dinner. Then we wouldn't have to do this in public." Belle glanced around the pub, looking for Louis and Estelle.

"At least this is neutral territory. They're over there." Nick motioned towards the back of the restaurant area.

"You sure you want to do this?" Belle asked.

"Very sure. Come on." He led the way to the table, with Belle trailing behind.

As they approached, Louis stood. He pulled

Belle into an awkward embrace before he shook Nick's hand. Belle noticed they'd changed their clothes. Her father was dressed smartly and Estelle had changed into a red shift dress. As she stood to greet them, Belle noticed the heels she wore. Over the last ten years, Belle had admired Estelle's fashion choices, but now they reminded her how different she was from Kerenza.

"Do you need anything for Pearl?" Louis asked, scratching the dog on the head.

"No. I've got everything she needs in my bag." Belle busied herself with setting out a blanket and some water for Pearl. The little dog curled up on the blanket and drifted off to sleep after her busy day in the shop.

"She's got the right idea," Nick joked, breaking the awkward silence that had settled around the table.

"I know. We've had a busy day. I can't wait to sleep." Belle stifled a yawn.

"Did you have many more customers?" Estelle asked.

Belle looked at Estelle, and she saw the plea in her expression. "Yes, quite a few," Belle recalled the handful of customers and described each piece of jewellery they'd bought.

"I've got a suitcase of jewellery for you. I'll drop it round to the shop tomorrow before you open."

"Okay. Thanks, Dad."

They ordered their food and Belle ripped her

napkin to shreds as Nick talked with Louis.

"Belle, are you okay?" Estelle asked. She reached across the table, but Belle snatched her hand away.

"No. I'm not okay. Can we stop this pointless small talk and get straight to the point?" She huffed. Pearl looked up from her blanket at the change in Belle's tone.

Louis groaned, and Estelle sat back in her chair.

"Just get it over with," Belle prompted. She drummed her fingers on the tabletop as she waited for them to confirm what she already knew.

"Belle, darling, please don't be like this," Louis begged.

"Don't tell me how to feel, Dad." Belle spat. Nick placed a hand on Belle's thigh and she took a deep breath. "I'm not a child. You don't have to protect me anymore. Tell me the truth and then we can all move on."

"Fine. Estelle and I are dating." The table fell silent as Louis's words sunk in.

Belle sucked in a shaky breath as the words echoed around her head. She'd known they were together, but having her father confirm it felt like somebody was squeezing her heart.

"How long has it been going on for?" Belle asked, using all her energy to keep her voice level.

"I've known Estelle for over twenty years."

Belle blinked as she processed the information. Her mother had died ten years ago.

They'd only known Estelle for ten years. Hadn't they? Nick squeezed her thigh, but Belle was numb to it. Her hands shook, and she fought to catch her breath.

"What do you mean, twenty years?" she ground out. Pearl walked over to Belle, pawing at her leg. Belle picked her up and cradled her in her arms as she waited for her father to explain.

"I met Estelle at an auction in France twenty years ago." Louis stared down at his empty glass of beer, refusing to meet Belle's gaze.

"You told me you met her when we moved to France."

"I'm sorry, Belle."

"Were you cheating on Mum?" Belle pulled Pearl tighter to her chest as she waited for an answer.

Louis sighed and looked from the glass to Belle. "Yes."

The pub around her melted away as the single word shattered Belle's heart. Everything she'd believed growing up had been a lie. Her father had been her everything. She'd looked up to him and wanted to be like him. Belle had watched the way her parents were together and knew one day she wanted it for her adult self. Everyone had referred to them as soulmates as they laughed and danced together. Belle remembered the long evenings spent on the beach when she was young. Louis would pull Kerenza into his arms and dance with her on the sand to the sound of the crashing waves as the sun set behind them. But it had all been lies. Bile rose in Belle's throat as she realised every memory she had with her mother was built upon a lie.

"Did Mum know?" she croaked out.

"Belle, don't."

Estelle reached out and took Louis's hand in hers. Belle ground her teeth together. "Were you happy when Mum died? It was the perfect excuse for you, wasn't it?" Belle spat across the table. The words spewed from her and she couldn't stop herself. "Without Mum, you were free to move in with your French bit on the side. You moved me to France and tried to replace my mother with that woman." Belle jabbed her finger in the direction of Estelle. Nobody around the table spoke, but Nick's hand remained on Belle's thigh.

"I'm sorry, Belle."

"It's a bit too late to be sorry." Belle stood and gathered Pearl's things, throwing the water in the nearest plant pot. She stood at the end of the table and turned her gaze to Louis and Estelle. "I don't want to talk to you again for a very long time."

Belle knew the tables around them had heard her outburst and she could feel their eyes on her as she left, but she couldn't find the energy to care what anybody thought.

"Belle," Nick called after her as she left the pub and stopped to put Pearl on the ground.

Despite the warm evening, Belle couldn't stop the shivers that vibrated through her body. She waited for Nick to catch up with her, but she didn't want to talk to him.

"Are you okay?" he asked, wrapping an arm around her.

Belle's body stiffened, and she stepped back from his touch. "No. I need to be alone. I'll talk to you tomorrow?" She sniffed.

"Are you sure? Belle, I don't think you should be alone."

"I'm not alone. I have Pearl. See you tomorrow." Belle walked away before Nick could say anything more. She couldn't bear to be around anybody with the emotions tearing through her.

The walk back to the cottage was a blur. Pearl trotted along by her side, and Belle walked without seeing where she was going. Her eyes were misted, and her mind kept replaying her father's words. The sickening realisation that he'd been seeing Estelle for the last twenty years churned in her stomach. Belle stumbled through the cottage's front door. With the door locked behind her, she sank down with her back against it and clasped a hand over her mouth to stifle a sob. Ten years of pent-up pain and grief spilt from her as the tears tumbled down her cheeks.

Belle felt herself suffocating under the heavy weight of grief on her chest and it brought her back to the day she'd lost her mum.

———————

"What is it?" asked Belle, as Louis put the phone down

with shaking hands. She was standing by the heater trying to dry off after getting caught in the rain. Louis wiped a hand across his face before he turned to look at her. His face was blank.

"It's your mum," he said as his voice cracked.

"What's wrong with Mum?" Belle pulled a hairband from her wrist and tied her damp hair up to stop it from dripping down her back.

His mouth opened and closed, but no words came out.

"Dad?" Belle's voice trembled. She reached a hand towards him, but her feet wouldn't move.

"We need to go to the hospital." His eyes searched wildly around the room.

"Okay. Let's put everything in the safes."

"No. Leave it."

"What's going on?" Belle asked again. Fear flooded her stomach at her father's order to leave the antiques.

"I'm sorry, Belle." Louis' eyes filled with tears as he raked a hand through his hair.

"Dad?"

"She's dead, Belle."

Belle's entire world changed with those words. Louis started throwing things into his satchel as Belle stared unblinkingly at him.

"Do you have your school bag?" he asked, but Belle wasn't listening. She moved her gaze to the heater, watching the orange light flicker.

"Belle?" He shook her shoulder, and she jumped.

"What?" Her mouth was dry and her throat hurt

as she forced the word out.

"Do you have your school bag?" he asked again.

Belle held it up to show him.

"Good. Come on." Louis ushered them out of the shop. The winds were howling across the harbour and rain pelted down. Within seconds, Belle was soaked through and the tears that rolled down her face mixed with the rainwater. "Do you want me to drop you off at home?" he asked, his fingers fumbling the key in the lock.

"No. I want to come with you."

"Belle, I don't think you should. I'll leave you with someone. Who can I leave you with?" His brow furrowed.

"I'm coming with you, Dad." Belle slipped her hand into his and squeezed.

They sped down the roads to the hospital, and Belle pressed her lips together as her nails dug into her palms.

The hospital lights were too bright. Belle squinted as she followed Louis down the endless corridors. Her school shoes squeaked against the tiled floor as she rushed to keep up. They reached the reception desk and Louis told her to wait to the side while he asked where to go. There was an overwhelming smell of disinfectant that filled her nostrils. The woman behind the counter looked at Louis with a sympathetic gaze as she gesticulated the route to him.

"This way," Louis said, taking a door to the right.

Belle followed her father a few paces behind.

Every step was becoming more and more difficult. A sob stuck in her throat and her legs buckled beneath her. Louis continued for a few strides before he noticed her collapsed in a heap. He knelt and held her as Belle cried for the emptiness inside of her, which seemed all-consuming.

"I shouldn't have brought you here." Louis pressed a kiss to Belle's head. He helped her stand, and with shaky legs, Belle staggered over to a chair.

"What happened?" she asked. It took Louis so long to respond that Belle wondered if the endless white corridors had swallowed her words before they'd reached his ears.

"Belle, I can't," Louis trailed off.

"Dad?" Belle wiped her eyes and looked at her father. His cheeks were tear-stained and the pain in his eyes was palpable.

"She walked out to sea."

Belle glanced out of the window. It was almost dark outside by now, but she could make out the way the trees swayed in the shadows and the sound of the heavy droplets of rain pounding on the glass.

"Why would she swim in this weather?" a naïve Belle asked.

"She didn't go into the sea to swim, Belle." Louis left the truth unsaid as Belle's young mind slowly pieced things together.

"No," she shrieked. "Mum wouldn't do that. She wouldn't leave us." Louis gathered her in his arms, but she pushed against his chest. "They're wrong, Dad. It's not Mum. You have to go in there and tell them. She

wouldn't leave us."

Louis didn't say anything. He hugged her tighter until her shrieks turned to sobs. Belle didn't know how long they sat like that, but eventually, she became numb. The tears dried up, and she sat up straight in the plastic chair. Louis left her in the chair as he slipped into a side room.

Belle sat alone with her fingers crossed. Even when her muscles cramped, she didn't uncross them. A silly part of her thought that she could change the outcome if she kept them crossed. But the moment Louis emerged from the room, she knew from the look on his face that there had been no mistake. Her mother had killed herself.

Belle scrambled to her feet with Pearl in her arms. The little dog still licked at the tears rolling down her cheeks. After her father's confession tonight, Belle wondered if her mother had known. Maybe that was why she had killed herself. That realisation was like a knife twisting in an opening wound. Belle dragged herself to the bedroom and climbed into bed, still wearing her dress. She pulled Pearl against her and rested her tired head on the pillow.

CHAPTER
TWENTY-FOUR

Belle's eyes were swollen, and she struggled to prise them open. She felt her way to the bathroom, almost tripping over Pearl, and went to the cupboard above the sink. Inside were a handful of toiletries. Last week, Belle had treated herself to some under-eye patches, which claimed to help with puffiness. She splashed her face with water and then stuck the eye masks on. Belle looked at herself in the mirror and recoiled at her reflection.

"It's okay. I don't have to be at the shop for another two hours," she muttered to herself and for the first time truly appreciated Sunday opening hours.

The kettle boiled as Belle let Pearl out into the courtyard. She went in search of her phone and found it in her tote bag, discarded against the front door. There were multiple texts and missed calls, but Belle didn't feel ready to talk to anyone. She opened the messages from Nick, not bothering to read them, but texted him to say she was okay but needed some space. He tried to call, but Belle declined.

"Shall we get you some breakfast?" she asked Pearl, who had wandered back inside. The dog let out a small bark before stretching. "I'm sorry for being such a mess last night. Did it exhaust you?" Belle chatted away as she prepared Pearl's breakfast. She was simply going through the motions. Last night, Belle had fallen into the chasm of pain and she didn't think she'd ever be able to claw her way back. Numbness was her only hope.

Belle dressed in shorts and a top but didn't put any jewellery on. She did her best with makeup to cover her swollen face, but as hard as she tried, you could still see the telltale signs of a night of crying.

Once at the shop, Belle washed up the used champagne glasses from yesterday and stacked them in the boxes in the office. She left the balloons up but folded down the table that had displayed the sweet treats. Every one of them had been devoured yesterday. Belle set out the jewellery for the day before she opened. She turned the sign on the door and breathed a sigh of relief. Now that she was open, her dad wouldn't risk dropping the expensive jewellery off with customers around.

An hour later, Belle's phone pinged with a

text from Nick.

Do you still want me to drop off some leftovers for dinner tonight? x

Belle stared at the message until the words all blurred into one long jumble. She needed to decide what to do about Nick.

"Morning," Jada called from the doorway, and Belle put her phone down. She'd reply to Nick later. "I thought I'd collect the—" Jada came close enough to see Belle's face. "What happened? Was it Tegen? I'll push that girl off the harbour wall if she's hurt you."

"Jada, calm down. It wasn't Tegen."

"Not Nick?" she asked.

"No, not Nick either. It was my dad." Belle sucked in a deep breath to steady herself before she said the words out loud. "My dad announced he's been seeing Estelle for the last twenty years."

Jada's face dropped as she did the sums in her head.

"He cheated on your mum?" she asked.

Belle nodded, not trusting her voice.

"Oh, sweetie." Jada let herself around to Belle's side of the counter and enveloped her in a hug. "I'm sorry," she said.

"I'm fine," Belle protested as she pulled back. She blinked to clear the tears before Jada could notice them.

"Nobody would be fine after finding that out, Belle."

"I'm still trying to process it."

"Has Nick helped?"

Belle chewed her lip. "I told him to go home last night."

"You don't have to deal with this alone."

"I can't let him in. I've lost too many people already. I can't lose him."

"Belle, if you push him away, you will lose him."

"It's better to do it now than in a few years." Belle squared her shoulders and rolled her neck. Saying it out loud confirmed to her that it was the right thing to do.

"Don't make any rash decisions," Jada instructed. "I'll pop around tonight after closing time. You need to talk to someone."

Belle tried to protest, but Jada wouldn't hear it.

"I'll see you later," she said and walked out without collecting the glasses she'd popped in for.

The shop was the perfect distraction, and the steady stream of customers kept her mind from wandering. She focused on the jewels as she picked them up and showed them to customers. Belle's favourite sale of the day had been a Colombian Emerald stone. It wasn't often that Belle bought uncut stones, but this one had caught her eye. It was a deep, saturated green that radiated light. The piece was stunning and had ended up in the middle of a furniture auction, so Belle got it for a fraction of its value. The woman had walked into the shop in a dress the exact shade of the stone. Her eyes lit up as she spotted the jewel nestled against a black velvet cushion.

"I heard about your shop from a friend who popped in yesterday. She knew I'd been looking for a stone like this," the woman explained as Belle undid the cabinet to show her.

"Thank you for popping in." Belle forced her face into a smile. Her insides should have been fizzing with excitement, but nothing stirred.

"This is perfect. I'm hoping to get it set into a necklace for my fortieth birthday," the woman explained.

"It will look gorgeous." Belle went through the motions of wrapping the jewel and charging the customer.

As the day came to a close, Belle glanced around the shop and realised she needed to think about ordering more stock. She had a handful of pieces in the safes but not enough to keep the shop fully stocked if sales continued like this.

Belle locked the door after the last customer and realised she'd never replied to Nick's message this morning.

Sorry, it's been busy in the shop. Jada's coming around tonight, so don't worry about the leftovers.

She'd need to speak to him soon and tell him they couldn't see each other again, but she was happy to put that off for a little longer.

Belle put the jewellery back in the safe while Pearl followed her, enjoying racing around the shop floor with no customers around. There was a knock on the front door, and Belle froze. Surely Nick had got the hint from her text message.

"Hello?" she called out as she locked the office door.

"It's me," Jada's voice floated through the door.

Belle raked a hand through her hair and went to let Jada in.

"Sorry," Jada said as she shook her umbrella before walking into the shop. It was warm outside but had been raining for the last couple of hours. "I'd hoped to get away from the coffee shop early enough to help you close up, but it didn't go to plan. We had a last-minute order for paninis. Honestly, who goes into a coffee shop at quarter to five and orders ten paninis to take away?"

"Sounds busy." Belle glanced at her phone as the screen lit up. Nick had replied, but she ignored it.

"Sorry, I'm waffling."

"No, it's me. I'm terrible company." Belle couldn't relax into a conversation because the slip of attention could cause the wave of emotions to crush her and she didn't think she possessed the energy to come back from it this time.

"I bought some bits to cook dinner for you." Jada held up a bag.

"Thanks." Belle's stomach rumbled at the mention of food. She'd left home before having breakfast and had skipped lunch.

"Can I help with anything?" Jada asked.

"Nope. Let me double-check that the safes are locked and then we can leave."

They strolled back to the cottage and Belle kept checking over her shoulder, in case Nick was around. Thankfully, they had nothing to worry about and didn't bump into anyone on the short walk.

"Where's Zoe?" Belle asked. She'd followed Jada into the kitchen and opened the backdoor to let Pearl have a sniff around. It was shaded from the worst of the rain, and Pearl's feet were already wet.

"It's her mum's birthday," Jada said, unpacking the bag.

Belle nodded, not trusting herself to reply.

"I forgot the wine. Do you have any?" Jada groaned and turned the bag inside out as if a bottle would magically appear.

"I haven't. Do you want me to run out and get you a bottle?" Belle offered, although it was the last thing she wanted to do.

"No, I thought you might appreciate a drink."

"Best not to. I need to be completely in control."

"Do you want to talk while I prepare dinner?" Jada pulled out one of the seats at the kitchen table and gestured for Belle to sit.

"I don't know where to start." Belle pulled her feet up onto the chair and wrapped her arms around her knees.

"This has been triggered by your dad's visit, right?" asked Jada. She was chopping an onion and blinking furiously as her eyes watered.

"Yeah. He came over for the shop's opening, but he brought someone with him. Estelle is…was, my dad's friend. Although it turns out she's more than a friend. They've been dating for twenty years." Belle told Jada about how Estelle befriended her when they moved to France, and over the years, she'd become the closest thing Belle had to a mother.

"That's awful. I'm sorry they betrayed you like that."

"There's more. When I got home last night. I had a flashback to the day my mother died. Have I ever told you what happened?"

Jada shook her head.

"She killed herself. I think she knew about my dad's affair and that drove her to it."

"What makes you think that?"

It was a reasonable question, but Belle didn't have a response. Truthfully, she didn't have any evidence to back up her theory. She was purely basing it on a feeling.

"Belle," Jada began but was interrupted by the hiss of oil in the pan.

"I know, it's silly, but I can't shake the feeling I have. My mum was always happy and smiling." Ever since her mother's death, Belle couldn't fathom why her mother had killed herself.

"Have you spoken to your dad since?"

"No. I don't know how I'll ever speak to him again. He could be the reason my mum's dead. How can I ever forgive him?" Belle bit her lip until she tasted blood.

Jada left the food to simmer and sat down opposite Belle. "You probably don't want to hear this, but I think you're making a lot of assumptions here."

Belle nodded and waited for Jada to continue.

"You need to talk to your dad and ask about your mum's mental health. She might have been the smiliest person you knew, but you were a child when you lost her, Belle. It might be that your mother was really good at hiding her struggles from you."

"I don't want to talk to him." Belle let out a huff.

"It doesn't have to be now. You deserve some time to let all this sink in. Aside from cheating on your mum, your dad also betrayed you by allowing you to develop a close relationship with Estelle without telling you the truth."

"It hurts, Jada." Belle looked up from her hands and focused her bleary gaze on her friend.

"Oh, sweetie." Jada pulled her into her arms and held her as Belle cried.

Belle didn't fancy food, but she knew she had to eat, so she gratefully finished the plate of shepherd's pie that Jada dished up for her.

"Thank you for looking after me," Belle

mumbled as she pushed a pea around the tabletop.

"What have you said to Nick?" Jada sat perfectly still as she waited for a response.

"I told him I needed some space," Belle said, staring at the pea.

"Don't shut him out."

"I need to end things with him. Although, it's hardly ending it when we've only been on one proper date." Belle swallowed back a tide of emotions.

"Belle, don't do this. I know how much he means to you and it's obvious he adores you. Don't hurt yourself more by doing this."

"I have to." Belle's lip quivered, but she pressed them into a line to stop it from happening again.

"You can't shut yourself off from the world. I know you've had a difficult time and you've been hurt, but it'll be an empty life if you don't let anyone in."

"It hurts too much. I can't love anyone else." Belle squashed the pea between her fingers and dropped it onto her plate.

"Sleep on it. Don't do anything until you've had enough time to think it through." Jada took their plates and went to wash them up.

"I'll do that. Thank you for dinner. I'm sure you've got lots to get on with at home," Belle said, standing to show Jada to the door.

"I can stay if you want?" Jada dried her hands on a tea towel and appraised Belle.   "I'm going to run a bath and have an early night. The shop's closed tomorrow, and I'm going to have a nice relax."

Jada left, and Belle ran herself a bath. She settled Pearl on the bed with a new chew and then grabbed her phone and sank into the bubble-filled bath. Belle was finally ready to go through the numerous texts she'd received over the last twenty-four hours. She started with the messages from her dad.

I'm sorry, Belle. Please talk to me x
Belle, please x
I need to talk to you x
Belle, I'm heading back to France on Wednesday. Please talk to me before then x
I didn't mean to lie to you x

Belle couldn't bring herself to read any of the others. She took a deep breath and texted her dad to let him know she had the day off tomorrow and they could talk. As much as she didn't want to see him, she had questions that she needed answering, and Belle wanted to do it when she could look him in the eye and know if he was lying. With the text sent, Belle moved on to Nick's message.

I'm here when you want to talk x

It was a short message and got straight to the point, but it brought a lump to Belle's throat. She knew it wasn't fair to keep stringing him along. He deserved to know she had no interest in a future for them. She had to message him and let him know.

CHAPTER TWENTY-FIVE

Belle was in bed with a cup of tea and a bar of chocolate when someone knocked on her front door. She instantly knew who it was. Pearl barked, and Belle almost spilt her tea as she clambered to the door. It was Nick. His hand was raised to knock again as she yanked the door open.

"Pearl, stay," Belle called to stop the little dog from charging out of the cottage to throw herself at Nick. "You better come in," she said.

He nodded and closed the door behind him, giving Pearl a polite tickle behind her ear. Belle sat on the sofa and grasped her mug in both hands as she readied herself for the conversation they were about to have. Her swollen eyes stung, her head pounded, and her heart felt as though it had been trampled enough for one day.

"Well?" Nick asked. He stayed standing and crossed his arms as he looked at her. His lips pressed into a line.

"I thought I said everything in my message." Belle shrugged and sipped her tea. She'd been busy building a wall between her and her emotions, and she wouldn't allow him to see the pain behind it.

Nick scoffed and got out his phone before he read her message aloud. "Thank you, Nick. I appreciate everything you've done for me since arriving in Padstow-on-Sea. I'm not looking for a relationship. I think it's for the best if we don't see each other again." His eyes were ablaze as he looked up from his phone and their gazes met.

"I think I made myself clear." Belle recoiled at the coldness in her tone but kept her face expressionless.

"Talk to me, Belle."

"I texted you so I didn't have to talk to you." She drummed her fingers on her mug and let her gaze wander around the room.

"Belle," he pleaded. Nick sat beside her and turned his body to face her.

"There's nothing more to say." Belle sank her nails into her palms as her voice wobbled.

"Is this because of your dad?"

"I don't want to talk about it." Her cool facade cracked as her voice shook again. She traced the rim of her mug and kept her stare fixed on it.

"Belle, please."

"I can't do this. I can't lose another person."

"You won't lose me."

Belle sniffed and put her mug down before she turned to face him. Pearl was curled up on the sofa in between them. "Nick, you can't promise me that. You've still got your parents. You don't know what it's like to lose your mum at fourteen. It tore me apart and ripped my heart to shreds. She killed herself, Nick. Fourteen-year-old Belle woke up every morning wondering if it was her fault. I blamed myself for getting bullied at school and worried that the stress of it was too much for my mother to deal with." Belle swallowed and took a shaky breath before she continued. "Now, I find out that the two people who supported me through my darkest days lied to me. Their affair might have been the reason my mother killed herself. I spent most of my teenage years blaming myself. Do you know how many nights I cried myself to sleep? I kept it to myself because I was terrified that if I voiced my worries to my father, he'd realise the truth and he'd hate me because I was the reason my mother was dead."

Nick sat completely still and listened to her. The wall Belle had carefully built had come crashing down and with it came an unbearable pain. She'd never confided in anyone about her guilt over her mother's death. Ten years she'd carried it with her, and it had festered, rotting her heart until she was sure nobody would want her. Then Nick came along and made her feel like someone worthy of love.

"I can't do this, Nick. I've lost everyone I've

ever loved and I can't put myself through it again. You don't want to be a part of this." Belle's hands shook as she clasped Nick's. His fingers wrapped around hers and she fought with every ounce of energy left not to let the tears fall. "We'll only hurt each other. Hardly anyone knew we were together. You could go back to Tegen. I'm sure she'd take you back if you grovelled."

Nick's face dropped. "Get back with Tegen? Why would I want to do that? Belle, I don't just like you. I'm falling in love with you. I know you've been through a lot and you've still got a lot to work through, but you're everything I've ever wanted. I've never felt happiness like I do when I'm with you. You're a beacon of light in my life and I already can't imagine you not being in it."

Belle pulled her hands from his grasp. "Don't." She turned her head. "It's for the best."

"I'll be here when you're ready, Belle," he promised.

"What if I'm never ready?" She pulled her knees up to her chest and hugged them, hoping the action would fill the void inside.

"You will be. I might not have known you for very long, but I know you well enough. You keep fighting, Belle. One day you're going to wake up and realise that you've won the fight." He leaned forward and pressed a kiss to her forehead. Belle's heart skipped a beat as his soft lips pressed against her hot head. "This isn't a goodbye forever." He stroked Pearl one last time before he let himself out of the cottage.

Belle stared after him. Pearl rolled onto her back, and Belle absentmindedly tickled her tummy as she replayed the conversation with Nick. She'd opened up to him and shown him the ugliest depths of her soul and he hadn't run away. Belle picked up her mug and went to make another cup of tea. She locked the front door again and carried Pearl back to bed. As Belle lay there watching the shadows, her mind wandered to her mother.

"Mum?" Belle shouted, racing through the cottage in search of her mother. She'd not been at the harbour to collect her from the school bus as promised. "Mum?" she shouted again, climbing the stairs. As Belle stilled on the landing, she heard sobs coming from her parents' bedroom. She dropped her schoolbag and peered around the door. Her mother was curled up on top of the sheets with her head buried in a pillow. From the way her body shook and the muffled sniffles, Belle knew she was crying.

"Mum?" she called from the doorway, scared to take another step into the room.

Kerenza slowly lifted her head from the pillow. It was dark in the room with the curtains still drawn, but Belle could still make out her mother's tear-stained face and shied away from it.

"Belle, darling. Is it that time already?" Kerenza pushed herself up from the bed and wiped her face with

the backs of her hands.

"The bus dropped me off half an hour ago. I waited for a bit, but when you didn't come, I thought I'd walk home." Belle cleared her throat. She took a step into the room and saw the medicine box next to her mother's bed. Maybe she was unwell.

"I'm sorry. I must have dozed off and lost track of time. How was your first day at secondary school?" Kerenza smiled and Belle relaxed as her mother looked like herself again.

"It was okay." She'd wanted to tell her mum about how nobody would sit next to her on the bus, or how she'd spent her lunch break alone sitting behind the science building because the girls from her old school had made her cry in her first class of the day. Instead, she didn't mention it because she didn't want to upset her mum any more.

"I bought a chocolate cake to celebrate. Shall we have it for dinner?" Kerenza stood and held out her hand. She still wore her pyjamas.

"Okay." Belle nodded and took it. Her stomach was knotted from the day and the last thing she wanted was a sickly, sweet chocolate cake, but she didn't want to disappoint her mother.

Kerenza brought her duvet downstairs and spread it out on the floor before she grabbed every cushion from the sofa and piled it on top. She cut them each a huge slab of cake and put Beauty and the Beast on television. Belle took a bite of cake. It was from the local bakery and should have been light, fluffy, and delicious. Instead, the sweetness overwhelmed her *tastebuds, and she fought to swallow it.*

"When's Dad home?" Belle pushed a piece of cake around the plate with her fork.

"He phoned earlier to say the auction has been pushed back a day, so he's going to be away for longer," Kerenza said, her tone overly bright. "That's okay, though, isn't it? We'll be fine without him here." Her eyes were wide and held a wild edge to them.

"Of course." Belle nodded and already knew that she'd open her lunchbox tomorrow to find another slice of cake inside.

Belle pulled Pearl closer as the ghost of the memory fled. Perhaps she'd remembered life with her mother through rose-tinted glasses. As an adult, she now recognised the signs that her mum had been struggling. Belle didn't know whether it was her mental health or if Kerenza had known about Louis's affair. She'd hidden that memory in the depths of her mind, and Belle didn't know how many more there were.

"I don't know what's real anymore," she sobbed into the darkness.

CHAPTER TWENTY-SIX

Belle reached for some paracetamol and swallowed them down with last night's cold tea. She winced at the sun shining through the window where she'd forgotten to close the curtains. Pearl wagged her tail and scrabbled around on the bed, waiting for Belle to give her some attention.

"Good morning," Belle said and tickled the dog behind the ears. Pearl leaned into the touch and yawned. "I'm sorry. Did I keep you awake with all my tossing and turning last night?"

Belle's phone buzzed. It was a text from her father asking if he could pop round in an hour. Belle sighed and replied, saying that would be fine. Her emotions felt as though they'd been set on fire, but she couldn't avoid this conversation. As she went about her morning routine, Belle tried to silence the questions that she wanted to ask her dad. There was no point getting in a state before he even arrived. She threw on a summery maxi dress, tied her hair up, and glanced at her jewellery but didn't put any on.

At nine o'clock, there was a knock on the door, and Belle answered it to see her dad standing on the doorstep.

"Good morning, Belle," he said, giving her a timid smile.

"Hi, Dad," she mumbled, looking down at her feet. "Do you want to come in?" Pearl was peering around her legs at their visitor.

Belle looked up in time to see Louis glance behind her into the cottage. His smile drooped, and he rubbed a hand across his stubble. "Why don't I take you out for breakfast?" he suggested.

"Okay." Belle wasn't hungry, but she didn't fancy sitting in the cottage surrounded by ghosts of the past as they talked.

"The car's at the bottom of the road."

Belle grabbed some bits for Pearl and slung a tote bag over her shoulder. The sun hadn't burnt through the morning cloud yet, so the ground was cool enough for Pearl to walk between them.

"The shop looked lovely," her father said as they approached the car.

"It's everything I dreamed it would be," Belle muttered.

"Shall we see if the beach café is still there?" Louis asked as he drove out of Padstow-on-Sea. Belle knew which beach café he meant. During school holidays, they would go there when the antique shop was closed on Monday and Tuesday mornings. It would always be the two of them since Kerenza was at work.

"Okay." Belle kept her gaze on the road ahead as she swallowed the lump in her throat.

"I wonder if they'll still do those bacon petits pains."

"Bacon butties, Dad."

"All this time and I still get my French and English mixed up."

"I guess you mostly speak French these days," came Belle's barbed response.

"Belle." Louis sighed.

"You can't buy me a bacon sandwich and pretend the last twenty years didn't happen. It doesn't work like that, Dad."

"I know, but it's not as black and white as you think it is."

"All I know is what I've been told. If I don't know the whole story, it's your fault."

"It is."

The radio filled the silence as Louis drove to the beach. There were a few early morning swimmers, but the car park was almost empty.

"You sit down and I'll order." Louis pointed her towards the tables.

Belle chose one that had a view of the beach. Pearl dug a hole in the sand underneath the table and curled up in the shade. While she waited, Belle watched a couple of surfers on their boards. One jumped up effortlessly, while the other fell straight into the water. They came back to shore and sat on the sand, laughing and gesticulating with their hands. Belle wished she could swap places with them for the next hour.

"Here you go," Louis announced, setting down the food and drinks on the table. "Two coffees and two bacon butties, one with ketchup and the other with brown sauce." He pushed the one with brown sauce towards Belle. "I got a sausage for Pearl. Is she allowed it? They said it's one hundred per cent meat, nothing added."

Belle nodded and watched as Pearl held the sausage between her paws and sniffed at it before she deemed it safe to eat.

"Nick seemed nice," Louis said, stirring sugar into his coffee.

"This conversation isn't about Nick." Belle took a bite of the sandwich before she lost what little appetite she had.

"You must have questions, Belle. What do you want to know?" Louis pushed his glasses up the bridge of his nose.

Belle chewed as she thought about where to start. "Why did Mum kill herself?" She needed to know the answer before she could wade through the rest of her thoughts.

Louis sighed and wiped his hands on a napkin. "We did our best to shield you from your mother's mental health struggles. I knew your mother struggled with depression very early on in our relationship, but I loved her and I could see the way she sparkled, despite the dark clouds that sometimes stole her away. There were good days and bad days. Mostly good days. After we had you, she struggled, but I did everything I could to help her. She got better at hiding her low moods and pretending everything was fine." He paused and stared out to sea. "You started coming to auctions with me to give your mum a break. Then you'd finish school and come to the shop. It was easier as you got older and could do things for yourself. You knew she took antidepressants. I even remember you coming home from school one day and saying you'd been teased about it."

Belle opened and closed her mouth. As a child, she had known her mother took pills to make her happy. As an adult, Belle hadn't thought any more about it, but now it was blindingly obvious what those pills were.

When she didn't say anything, Louis continued. "I loved your mum, Belle, but I came to feel like her carer."

"Is that why you cheated?"

"Yes. I met Estelle at an auction and we realised how much we had in common. For the first time in a long while, I had fun without any responsibility. I know how selfish that was. I was a husband and a father, but I'd forgotten who I was."

Belle put down her half-eaten sandwich, unable to take another bite as her stomach churned.

"Why didn't you leave? You could have given Mum the chance to be happy with someone else."

"I couldn't leave, Belle. What would have happened to you? And I didn't know what your mum would do if I left."

"She killed herself anyway. Maybe you leaving would have been the kinder option." Belle saw the pain that shot through her father's face from her words.

"I was wrong, Belle, and I live with that every day. I wish I could go back and do things differently." Louis picked at the crust on his sandwich. "I don't think she knew about Estelle," he said, focused on the bread he was tearing apart in his fingers.

"Are you sure?" Belle caught his eyes. She needed to watch him to know he was telling the truth.

"I've wracked my brains and I'm sure she didn't know." He held her gaze.

"Why didn't she let us help her?"

"I wish I knew. Belle, your mother was an amazing woman, and she did everything she could for us, despite her demons. I don't believe that anything we did led to her suicide." Louis tentatively pushed his hand across the table and Belle reached out to take it.

They sat for a moment and Belle let her father's words sink in. All those years she wondered if she was responsible for her mother's death when really her mental health problems had been far worse than Belle had known. The revelation was bittersweet because nothing could ever bring her mother back.

"I'm sorry I lied to you about Estelle," Louis ventured. Belle pulled her hand back and sat up straight as she readied herself for the conversation.

"Estelle was special to me, Dad. I never would have opened up to her like I did if I'd have known she was your girlfriend."

"I know, and that's why I didn't tell you. You came to life in Estelle's company. I watched you bond with someone over your love of antique jewellery. You couldn't speak the language, and she was the only person you had. I couldn't bring myself to ruin that for you. We stopped seeing each other for a few years after your mother's death."

"You did?"

"Yes. However terribly I behaved, I did still love and care for your mother. I was heartbroken. Estelle and I agreed to be friends, and she helped me establish my business in France."

"I know I was a child, but I wish you'd been upfront with me from the beginning. All these lies have caused me so much pain."

"I'm sorry." Louis stood and pulled her into his arms. Belle felt like a child again as her father held her.

Their coffees had grown cold, and the food was forgotten. "Shall I get us some fresh drinks?" Louis suggested.

"Yes, please." Belle nodded and blew her nose on a napkin.

"I'll get some more tissues, too."

While he was gone, Belle stared out to sea, not really seeing it. Slowly, she was coming to terms with the fact that nobody was to blame for her mother's death. They'd all been living with their own guilt and doing their best. She wanted to hate Estelle, but as hard as she tried, she couldn't stir the emotions. Belle couldn't lose anyone else. She had no choice but to forgive them.

They drank their coffees, and the beach filled up as Belle told her father more about the shop and the pieces she'd sold in its two days of being open.

"I still have the pieces I bought for you. I can drop them off at the shop tonight?"

"Maybe Pearl and I could come back with you for a bit?"

Louis blinked. "Of course you can, but Estelle will be there."

"I know. I want to talk to her. Too much has happened for you to go back to France without us talking."

"Shall I text Estelle and tell her we'll be back in the next hour?"

The drive back to Padstow-on-Sea was relaxed. They drove with the windows open and Pearl stood on Belle's lap with her nose poking out of the gap. There was still so much to process, but she would do that once Louis and Estelle had left. For now, she wanted to enjoy their familiarity and spend the afternoon as if her emotions hadn't just waged a war inside her.

They drove through the harbour and Belle felt a pang of regret as they drove past Nick's home. She pushed it back and locked it away with everything else she needed to process.

"It's this one here." Louis pulled onto the driveway of a small cottage at the end of the road. It had an unspoilt view of the sea.

The front door opened before they'd got out of the car. Estelle stood there, her usual flawless self. She wore white linen trousers without a hint of a crease, a pale green silk blouse and her hair was tied back with a scarf. Her face broke into a smile as Belle climbed out of the car.

"Bonjour, Belle," she said, her accent thick.

"Hello, Estelle." Belle handed Pearl to her father and went to the cottage's front door.

"I'm sorry," Estelle said as she searched Belle's face.

"Thank you." Belle stepped into Estelle's outstretched arms. She wrapped her arms around Estelle and held on.

Pearl barked from her father's arms, and Belle stepped back and took her. Estelle stepped aside to let them into the cottage. It was beautiful and light inside, with big windows overlooking the stunning views of the Cornish coast.

"This place is lovely," Belle commented and set Pearl on the floor. She instantly put her nose to the ground to inspect their new surroundings.

"It is," agreed Estelle. She'd taken the tote bag from Belle and was filling up Pearl's water bowl.

"I put the jewellery in the loft. I'll go get it. Estelle, why don't you put the kettle on?" Louis disappeared upstairs, leaving the two women alone.

Belle waited for it to feel awkward, but the atmosphere didn't change. She felt how she always had in Estelle's company.

"I am sorry, Belle." Estelle paused the way she always did when she was translating words in her head. "We wanted the best for you, but it was all so complicated."

"I know. I'm hurt that you both lied to me, but I know it was a difficult situation."

"Belle, I didn't know of your mother when I met Louis."

"He lied to you, too?"

"Not lied. Just wasn't completely open. I wasn't open with him about my husband at the time."

Belle's jaw dropped. She hadn't known Estelle had been married.

"He was an awful man, Belle. He hit me."

"You don't have to tell me this, Estelle."

"No. We need the truth." She handed Belle a mug.

Belle sniffed the contents. It was mint tea.

"Let us sit," instructed Estelle. She pointed Belle to the kitchen table, which was positioned next to a window.

Belle blew on her drink as she waited for

Estelle to continue.

"I met Louis at an auction and for the first time, someone spoke to me. We talked for hours and discussed our love for various periods. Then he took me for dinner and we ate and drank wine. Not once did I anticipate a punch. It was addictive, Belle. The next time he came, we met again. I didn't tell him about my husband, and I never asked him about his life back in England." Estelle sighed wistfully.

"From what Dad told me, you both needed an escape. I wish things had been different. Mum didn't deserve to be treated like that, but I can see why Dad was scared to leave her. There's so much going around my head." Belle's voice caught.

"I know, and I'm sorry for the part I played." Estelle reached across the table and squeezed her hand. "Who was that handsome boy you brought to dinner? He was hot, non?"

Belle laughed. "Non is French, Estelle."

"He is so hot I forgot myself." She fanned herself and winked.

"Estelle!" Belle shrieked, and Pearl jumped at the noise. "He is lovely, but I'm not ready for a relationship. I don't even know if I ever want one."

"You can't protect your heart forever, Belle. It has a mind of its own."

"I could build a wall around it."

"No. That is not you, and you would be unhappy. Don't be unhappy, Belle."

"What if I let him into my heart and he broke it?"

"What if he didn't break it?" Estelle countered. "Think about it," she said before Louis returned with a suitcase.

"It's all in here." He put it down on the kitchen floor and unzipped it.

Belle watched in wonder as her father opened the suitcase to reveal boxes of jewellery with bubble wrap and air-filled pouches scattered around to keep everything safe. Pearl's nose was already exploring, and Belle sank to her knees to rummage.

"Look at that box there," Estelle said, pointing to a large square box that looked as though it held a necklace. Belle opened the box and found a garnet rivière necklace in yellow gold. "It's nineteen century," Estelle explained, kneeling opposite Belle.

"It's beautiful." Belle carefully lifted the necklace from its box and gasped as the light flooding in caught on the deep red jewels and they flared with yellows and greens. It was a stunning sight and a calmness spread within Belle as the light danced through the oval cut jewels.

"I found it in a... what do you call them? A second arm shop."

Belle chuckled, and Louis hid his smirk by turning to fuss Pearl. "I think you mean second hand shop," Belle offered.

"Whatever it is called." Estelle waved a dismissive hand. "I found it in this shop and the woman had no clue that the jewels were garnets. She thought they were coloured glass for costume jewellery. I paid her double the asking price of ten euros and she was happy enough."

"Twenty euros for this?" Belle could hardly believe her ears.

"That was not all. She knew nothing about jewellery. Open that black ring box. There's an aquamarine ring in it."

It was a tearful goodbye when Louis drove Belle home that evening. She'd stayed and had dinner with them. Estelle had made French onion soup and had cooked some leftover fish for Pearl. They'd dropped the jewellery off at the shop on the way home and ensured it was safely locked up.

"I'll visit once summer is over," Belle promised.

"You'll always have a home with me, Belle. If you change your mind about the shop and Cornwall, you can come home." He hugged her, and Belle didn't want to let go.

Belle put the television on and cuddled Pearl on the sofa. It was late, but she knew she'd only toss and turn for the next few hours if she went to bed now. She checked her phone and saw a text from Nick. It simply said *I hope you had a good day x* She smiled but didn't reply.

"What shall we do with our day off tomorrow, Pearl?"

The little dog snuffled in her sleep.

CHAPTER TWENTY-SEVEN

"I brought you breakfast," Jada said to a bleary-eyed Belle.

"Jada, it's seven in the morning on my day off. What are you doing here?" asked Belle. Pearl hadn't even stirred when the knock on the door echoed throughout the cottage. She was still curled up on the warm duvet upstairs.

"Oh, I'm sorry. I didn't think. I saw you in the car with your dad last night and I thought you might need someone to chat to this morning. I can go." Jada went to turn around, but Belle reached out a hand to stop her.

"No, don't go. I do appreciate you thinking of me and popping around. Is Zoe not with you?"

"She stayed at her parents' again." Jada busied

herself by unpacking the pastries she'd brought.

"Is everything okay?" Belle went to make the drinks.

"It's fine. You've got enough going on."

"Jada, you're my friend. Please tell me what's wrong."

"She said we're moving too fast." Jada huffed and sat down.

"Wasn't she the one that practically moved in with you after the first date?"

"Exactly! I agree it was too fast, but now it feels as though she's backed off completely."

"Maybe some space will do you both good? It's obvious Zoe likes you. I don't think she's going anywhere, anytime soon. Maybe she got scared and realised she didn't want to lose you."

"Isn't that what you've done with Nick?" Jada's knowing eyes bore into her.

"Don't change the topic. This is about you and Zoe."

"We're both down in the relationship dumps, aren't we?" Jada broke a croissant in two and handed a piece to Belle.

"You need to stop overthinking everything." Belle set two mugs down on the table.

"Only if you promise me, you'll also stop overthinking." Jada raised her brows and held out her hand.

"Okay. No more overthinking," Belle agreed and shook her outstretched hand. "These croissants are amazing."

"Thanks. I've been practising for a while now. I thought you might enjoy a little taste of home."

Belle's eyes misted over and she squeezed Jada's hand. "Thank you."

"How are things with you and Nick?"

Belle sighed. "We're not together, but we're not completely broken up. He texted me last night, but I didn't reply."

"Why not?"

"Because a huge part of me wants to find him and throw myself into his arms. My heart wants to hand itself over to him and tell him to keep it safe. Then there's my brain that says I can't lose someone else I love. I've spent my entire life in my own company. Why stop now?"

"Belle, keeping to your own company hasn't saved you from pain." Jada's voice was soft, but the words stung.

"You're right." Belle leaned back in the chair and squeezed her eyes shut. "I've been an idiot, haven't I?"

"Belle, I love you, but you've been the biggest idiot I know. Nick adores you, and I don't think he would purposely hurt you."

"I really like him." Belle chewed her lip.

"Life's all about taking chances. You took a huge one coming back to Cornwall and opening your shop, but look where it's got you."

"I need to call him." Belle patted her pocket, but her phone wasn't there.

"Why don't you invite him around for

dinner?" Jada rested a hand on her shoulder.

"Okay. I'll call him and invite him over."

Belle went upstairs to get her mobile. Pearl lifted her head and regarded her as she stumbled into the room and tore the charger out of her phone, knocking over an empty glass on the bedside table. Pearl let out a growl and stretched.

"Sorry, Pearl. Jada's downstairs. Why don't you go ask her for a morning tummy tickle?" Belle said as she frantically scrolled through her phonebook. She stopped at Nick's name and her finger hovered above it. With a deep breath, she hit call.

"Hello?" Nick answered, his voice thick with sleep.

"Nick, it's Belle." She sounded timid and her hands shook, but she pushed herself to keep speaking before she changed her mind. "Will you come round for dinner tonight?"

"Good morning, Belle. I'm fine thanks, how're you?" teased Nick. Belle could hear the creek of a mattress in the background and a wave of fear crashed over her. What if he wasn't alone?

"I shouldn't have phoned," her voice quivered.

"No, Belle. I shouldn't have teased you, I'm sorry. I'd love to come for dinner tonight. Shall I bring a takeaway?"

"No, I'm going to cook."

Nick was silent for a few seconds too long. "Belle, don't take this the wrong way, but can you cook?"

"You'll find out tonight. Be here for about seven?"

"Okay."

"Brilliant. Perfect. Thanks," she rambled.

"Take a breath, Belle."

"Sorry. I'll see you tonight."

"I'm looking forward to it. Bye, Belle."

He hung up before Belle could force any words from her mouth. She sat on the edge of the bed and put the phone back on charge. Her hands shook and her body quivered with excitement.

Belle went back downstairs on shaky legs. "Jada, can you write down the recipe for that curry?"

"Of course. Hand me a notepad." Pearl was curled up on Jada's lap, enjoying the attention.

"Nick's coming around tonight and I've promised to cook for him."

"Do you want me to throw it together for you, then all you have to do is reheat it?"

Belle sat down with a huff. "Why does nobody think I can cook?"

They reached a compromise, and Jada accompanied Belle into the harbour to buy the ingredients for dinner. Their first stop was The Green Grocers by the Sea.

"I should have looked in your fridge before we left," Jada huffed.

"There's nothing in there." Belle held Pearl

since she wasn't technically allowed in the shop.

"Onions, potatoes, tomatoes, green beans," Jada muttered to herself as she threw the ingredients into a basket.

The next stop was the supermarket outside of the harbour. Belle stayed in the car while Jada ran inside to get everything. She came back laden down with bags and a fresh sheen of sweat across her forehead.

"You don't have to do this," Belle said as she helped lift the bags into the boot.

"I want tonight to be perfect for you," Jada said once they were back in the car. "Besides, I need a distraction. Zoe texted me, asking me out on a date tomorrow evening," Jada confessed.

"That's brilliant news."

"She said she still wants to see me, but she wants us to slow it down. I think she's scared that if we move too fast, we'll run before we can walk and it will kill the relationship before it's even started."

"It sounds like she wants to be with you."

"I know." Jada let out a breath and smiled.

They got back to the cottage and unpacked the shopping bags. Jada had thought of everything from naan bread to two bottles of red wine.

"That's everything ready for dinner. Now, what about you?" Jada chewed a nail as she gave Belle a once over.

"What about me?"

"You're a blank canvas, Belle, and that's fine, but I don't think it's really you. I've seen the effort you put into picking your clothes and jewellery. What about a haircut?"

Belle's head was spinning with the morning's events. "A haircut?" She pulled at a strand of hair. She did have lots of split ends and she couldn't remember the last time she'd had a trim.

"Treat yourself. I'll stay here with Pearl and you run down to The Hairdressers by the Sea."

The old Belle would have said no, but she was determined to become comfortable in her own skin and a haircut seemed like a good place to start. Belle said goodbye to Pearl and Jada, and wandered back into the harbour. She felt lighter today, as though all the worries that had been stacked on her shoulders had tumbled off and she didn't have the energy to gather them up. It was both freeing and exhausting.

The hairdresser was around Belle's age and smiled as she walked in.

"Do you have time for a walk-in?" Belle asked. She did her best to square her shoulders and appear confident.

"I do. I'm Tamsyn. Take a seat." She pointed Belle to the chair in front of a mirror.

"Thank you. I'm Belle."

"What did you want doing today?" Tamsyn asked as she wrapped a black cloak around Belle's shoulders.

Belle's mouth opened and closed, but nothing came out. She hadn't thought that far ahead. "I'm not sure. I fancy a change."

"Hmm, you'd look lovely with a bob. Is your

hair always this wavy?"

Belle nodded.

"What about a long bob with a full fringe? I think it would suit your face shape, and I can show you which products to use for a more tousled look. It'll highlight its natural wave."

"I'd love that."

Belle relaxed into the chair while Tamsyn chopped away at her hair. When she was done, Belle hardly recognised the woman staring back at her in the mirror.

"There we go." Tamsyn pulled the cloak off and shook the hair from it.

"It's perfect. Thank you." Belle couldn't look away from her reflection in the mirror.

Belle left with another appointment booked in six weeks and a promise to meet Tamsyn for a drink during the week.

"You look amazing," Jada said as Belle walked into the cottage.

"Thank you." Belle giggled as Pearl launched herself into her arms and sniffed at her hair before licking her cheek. "I think Pearl approves."

While she'd been at the hairdressers, Jada had prepped some bits for dinner. "I thought I'd do enough to make it easier for you tonight." She'd diced the onion and popped it in a bowl in the fridge, and she'd measured out the spices into a ramekin, so all Belle needed to do was pour them into the pan.

"Shall we have a coffee and you can help me decide what to wear?" Belle suggested.

"I've already put the kettle on."

They settled on a white shirt with the sleeves rolled up and a midi skirt with cream and orange stripes. Belle got out a simple pair of diamond earrings and a matching necklace. She left the outfit and jewellery laid out on the bed for when she got ready.

"I should go." Jada glanced at her watch. It was one she'd bought from Belle's shop a couple of weeks ago. "It's Nick's first day doing the work on my courtyard. I should see him before he leaves to get ready for his hot date tonight."

"You won't mention me, will you?"

"Of course not." Jada pulled Belle into a hug.

"Thank you for today," Belle said.

"Whatever happens, Belle, you've got me."

Belle sniffed. "And you've got me, Jada."

Once Jada had left, Belle got Pearl ready for a walk. She'd popped into the florist on her way back from the hairdressers and bought some flowers to put on her mother's grave.

"Hi, Mum." She placed the flowers on the ground. "I wish I'd known how much you'd struggled, although I'm not sure what I could have done." Belle sucked in a shaky breath and sank to her knees. "I've forgiven Dad and Estelle. I'm sorry if that hurts you, but they're all I have left and I can't lose anyone else." Belle watched as Pearl picked up a small twig and settled down on the path to chew it. "Nick's coming around for dinner tonight. I really like him, Mum. I think I'm finally ready to risk my heart."

Belle sat in the graveyard for a while, enjoying the peace as Pearl shredded a twig.

CHAPTER TWENTY-EIGHT

Belle smoothed down the skirt. It flowed over her curves. She rolled up the shirt's sleeves and left the top buttons open to show off the diamond pendant. Her hair still looked as it had when she'd left the hairdresser's. Belle had spent some time on her makeup. She felt good about herself, and a glance in the mirror sent a thrill through her. This was the confident woman she wanted to be. Her smile slid from her face as the smoke alarm echoed throughout the cottage. She ran downstairs to find the curry bubbling furiously on the hob. It splattered up and across her white shirt.

"No," Belle cried, knowing she'd never get the red splodges out. She blew her new fringe out of her eyes and turned the heat down on the hob, then grabbed a tea towel to wave in front of the smoke detector.

"Do you need any help with that?" Nick called above the piercing noise. "I heard the alarm and let myself in."

Belle suppressed a groan and handed him the tea towel while she opened the backdoor. Pearl had burrowed under the duvet when the smoke alarm went off and hadn't been seen since.

"Wow, you look amazing," Nick's voice was raspy. He reached to take the batteries out of the smoke alarm, but his eyes were firmly on her.

"Thanks." She blushed.

The piercing noise silenced.

"That's better." Belle sighed and glanced back to their dinner. Curry was splattered all over the worktops and the splashback. She groaned and grabbed a cloth.

"How's dinner?" Nick glanced behind her at the mess.

"It's cooking."

"What's causing the smoke?" Nick asked as he stepped closer. The kitchen was still filled with thick smoky air and Belle's eyes watered, despite the fresh air pouring in through the door.

Belle tried to shoo him away, but he stood his ground. "I'll figure it out," she promised him.

"Are you cooking naan bread on an open flame on your gas hob? It's the colour of charcoal." Nick sounded horrified. He used a couple of forks to pick up the unrecognisable food from the hob and put it in the sink, where he doused it with water.

"The packet said they took ten minutes in the oven, so I thought I'd speed it up." Belle stifled a giggle at Nick's serious expression.

"You nearly had a nasty fire on your hands. I'll put those batteries back in before I leave."

"I'm not a very good cook," she admitted.

"Lucky for you, I didn't fall for your cooking skills. I like your new hair." He stepped closer. Nick reached around her to turn the hob off, and Belle's breath caught as he brushed against her. "I also love your outfit."

"It's covered in curry. I should soak it."

"Why don't you go get changed and I'll finish dinner?"

Belle glanced down at her splattered shirt and nodded. She disappeared upstairs and pulled on a pair of wide-leg jogging bottoms and a vest. So much for making an effort. The evening was a disaster, and she hadn't even spoken to Nick yet.

"We should have got a takeaway," Belle said as she threw her clothes into the washing machine with a large scoop of stain remover.

"It tastes amazing," Nick mumbled around a mouthful. "I got the roast potatoes out of the oven and added them to the curry. Then I popped the rest of the naan bread in to cook."

"Thanks. Between us, we can cook a meal."

"Shall we eat outside?" he suggested. It was a beautiful evening, and it seemed a shame to waste it sitting in the shady, smoky kitchen. Belle busied herself with laying the table and pouring wine.

Pearl was still hiding upstairs, and Nick went up to see her while Belle dished up. The curry slopped everywhere as she tried to ignore the thoughts of Nick upstairs in her bedroom.

"How are you, Belle?" Nick asked when they were sat opposite each other.

"I'm getting there." She focused on loading her fork with food. "I've forgiven my dad and Estelle. I'm not sure things will ever go back to how they were between us, but I realised they're all I have. I can't stay mad at them forever."

"That must have been difficult." Nick reached across the table, but he quickly pulled his hand back. "Sorry," he muttered.

Belle cleared her throat and put her cutlery down. "The last few days have been a roller coaster of emotions and revelations. I'm sorry that you got caught up in it." She reached across the table and took his hand in hers. Her skin tingled underneath his touch and she fought to keep her concentration on what she had to say. "I've been living in my mother's shadow for a very long time. Even before she died, I knew there was something wrong. She'd always have a new harebrained scheme she'd cooked up, and I'd go along with it to keep her happy. I never spoke up for myself and then I went along with life in France." Belle paused. Nick was looking at her with raw emotion across his face. His thumb rubbed comforting circles on her hand and she took a deep breath to continue." I'm rambling. What I'm trying to say is that I've spent a lot of my life living for other people, but coming to Padstow-on-Sea allowed me to be myself. I don't know Belle Alice Roux very well. I know she likes antique jewellery, dogs, and fish and chips on the harbour. I need to get to know myself."

"I'll support you any way I can."

"Thank you." Belle stood and pulled Nick up with her. "There's one more thing I know about Belle Roux," she said as she walked around the table to stand in front of him. Belle took both of his hands in hers and looked at him. Their gazes met, and a thrill flowed through her. "I know that she loves Nicholas Penhale."

Nick stared at her. His eyes filled with an emotion Belle couldn't decipher.

"Say something," she said.

He stood, letting go of her hands and wrapped his arms around her waist, pulling her body flush against his. Belle rested her hands on his chest. She could feel his heartbeat thrumming underneath her palm.

"Belle Alice Roux, I love you." He laughed and pressed a kiss to the top of her head. "I want to be by your side as you learn who you are. I'll be here every step of the way. Belle, you're kind, caring, funny, and a terrible cook. I love you for who you are, even if you can't see yourself properly." He bent down and kissed her.

EPILOGUE

Rain hammered against the shop's windows and Pearl let out a small whine before she buried deeper into her bed. The radio played in the background, reminding them it was the wettest Christmas Eve they'd had in several years. Belle tightened the belt on her cardigan and turned the little heater up another notch. Pearl had a pink jumper on that Jenny had knitted, but she was still worried the dog would be cold. Nick had promised that in the summer he'd look into replacing the windows to stop the draughts.

The bell rang, and a customer walked in. Their coat dripped water onto the mat, and Belle sighed at the idea of mopping the floor again.

"Merry Christmas," she called out.

"Merry Christmas," the man replied. "I've left my Christmas shopping to the last minute."

"We're still open, which means you've still

got time," Belle kept her voice light even though she'd lost count of how many times she'd said the same thing today. "Are you looking for anything in particular?"

"I think my wife popped in during the week and fell in love with a ring."

"Okay. Do you know which one?" Belle hopped down from her stool and walked around the counter.

"It was red. I think she mentioned something about it being Edwardian." His brow furrowed.

"Is your wife's name Cindy?"

The man nodded, and Belle led him over to a cabinet on the righthand side of the shop. "It was this garnet cluster ring." She unlocked the case and pulled out the ring. The gold band had an intricate line design around it. Cindy had fallen in love with the piece and asked to try it on, but had eventually decided it was too much money to spend on herself.

"She loves history and jewellery, so this is the perfect gift." He nodded and inspected the ring.

"Her face lit up when she tried it on."

"I'll take it." He handed the ring back, and Belle wrapped it for him.

"Have a lovely Christmas," she said to him as he left. The door closed and Belle grabbed the mop from the back office to wipe down the muddy footprints on her white floor. "Right, I think it's time for a coffee. Would you like a chew?" Belle asked Pearl, who looked up from her fleece-lined bed and licked her lips.

Before Belle could slip out from behind the counter, the bell above the door rang out and she let out a sigh. It wasn't that she didn't appreciate the last-minute Christmas rush, she just didn't want to mop the floor again. Belle's face lit up when she realised who it was.

"We bring lunch," Jada announced as she entered the shop, with Zoe following behind her. They were soaked, despite Zoe leaving an umbrella at the door.

"And coffee." Zoe held up a paper bag that looked as though it might disintegrate at any moment.

Pearl barked at the sound of their voices. "And treats for you, Pearl," Jada called.

Belle watched as they took off their coats and left them dripping on the umbrella stand. Then they both slipped off their shoes and pushed them to the side so nobody would trip over.

"I could kiss you both for doing that." Belle exhaled once she knew her clean floor was safe for a little longer.

"It's been a nightmare at the coffee shop. We've been mopping all day. We closed half an hour ago and thought we'd bring the leftovers to you for a Christmas Eve picnic." Jada plonked a paper bag down on the counter. "Help yourself," she instructed and headed into the back to wash her hands.

"Coffee's in this one," Zoe said before she followed Jada.

Belle took out the coffee and saw someone

had written their names on them. There was even one for Nick. She took a sip of her gingerbread latte and smiled. At the bottom of the bag was a sausage for Pearl cut into bite-sized pieces.

"The paninis are all the same. Take whatever one looks the best," Jada instructed. She and Zoe walked back in with extra stools. They often popped in and Belle had ordered more seating, so they didn't have to stand.

"Thank you for this. I had a real rush this morning. I'm hoping it'll be quiet now. There's only so many times I can mop a floor."

"Are you closing early?" Zoe asked. She took the top panini and handed the other two to Jada and Belle.

"Yeah. The ferry is booked for six, and we're hoping to leave the harbour by three." Belle took a bite of the panini and hummed in appreciation.

"I can't believe you're taking Nick home for Christmas," Zoe said.

"You're taking Jada to your parents," Belle pointed out.

"Yeah, but at least mine live in this country."

"Is he excited?" Jada asked.

"I think so. He's worried about me because I haven't seen my dad or Estelle since summer."

Zoe nodded. "How do you feel about it?"

"I'm nervous, but I feel as though I've done enough work with my therapist to not get too caught up in everything again."

"I think you'll be fine. You're a lot stronger

than you were last summer, Belle. We're proud of you. Your confidence has grown, and I saw you lend Tegen a fiver at the pub on Friday when she was short of money. Only a truly decent person could bring themselves to do that." Jada raised an eyebrow.

"Oh, I have your Christmas presents here." Belle pulled two perfectly wrapped boxes from behind the counter. "They're the same, so open them together."

"Can we open them now?" asked Zoe, her face lit up.

Belle chuckled. "Of course."

The women ripped open the boxes and burst out laughing at the contents.

"They're friendship bracelets," Belle said between laughs. She rolled up her sleeve to show them the matching one she had on her wrist. The bright pink bracelet was woven together with string to create a zigzag pattern, similar to the ones Jada and Zoe had in front of them.

"I love it," Zoe squealed and immediately put hers on.

"Thank you, Belle." Jada smiled as she tied hers around her wrist.

"There's something else underneath the tissue paper," Belle told them.

Zoe had a small peacock brooch and Jada an amber hairpin that she'd admired a few weeks ago but had decided against it saying she spent too long in a hairnet to spend money on hair accessories.

"Thank you." Both women came around the

counter to envelop Belle in a hug.

"Merry Christmas," Nick said from the doorway. Belle's head snapped up in time to see him step onto her floor in muddy trainers.

"Nick," she shouted, but it was too late. There was already a trail of footprints across her shop.

"I'll mop it in a minute," he promised and greeted her with a kiss. Pearl stretched and trotted over to him to be picked up.

"Now Nick's here, we can tell you about your Christmas present," Jada said and handed the fourth coffee to Nick.

"What's going on?" Belle narrowed her eyes.

"I'm going to repaint the front of the shop in summer. I thought we'd go with the powder blue," he explained.

"And once it's painted, I'm going to do the sign writing," Zoe chipped in.

Belle's jaw dropped. "That's too much. I can't ask that of you."

"Belle, your sign has given me enough work to keep me going for the next five years. It's the least I can do."

"And I can't contribute anything to this, so I've got you a Christmas cake. Homemade by yours truly." Jada handed Belle a tin with the cake inside. Belle laughed and blinked away the tears of happiness.

"Thank you for everything," she said as she glanced around. They might not be blood-related, but this was her family, and they'd supported her unconditionally over the last six months.

"Right, we should head off. Zoe's family is expecting us soon. See you in the new year. Are you going to Tamsyn's party?"

"We are. Nick's parents are having Pearl."

They said their goodbyes and left.

"Thank you for my Christmas present," Belle whispered as she stepped back and leaned against Nick.

"Don't worry, I've still got you something to open on Christmas Day."

"We should start shutting up," Belle said, glancing around at the shop. The sky outside had grown darker, and the harbour looked empty. There wouldn't be any more customers today.

"I need to get my suitcase from my flat. Shall I meet you at your car? I'll take Pearl with me to give her a quick walk before we leave." Nick asked, already heading towards the door. "I'm so glad you got rid of that old car."

"So am I. We can enjoy the heated seats on the way to the ferry."

"See you in a bit," Nick said before he disappeared, with Pearl still curled up in his arms.

"Wait, what about my floor?" she called, but he'd already left with a chuckle.

Belle rolled her eyes but laughed. She couldn't wait to spend their first Christmas together while she showed him around her hometown in France.

I hope you enjoyed your visit to Padstow-on-Sea.

I would be incredibly grateful if you could leave a review on Amazon or Goodreads - just the star rating is fine if you don't want to write anything.

Follow me on Amazon or one of the below social medias
Twitter (X) EHollandAuthor
Instagram e.holland.author

Sign up for my newsletter at
www.elizabethhollandauthor.com

**Have you read The Cornish Vintage Dress Shop?
Continue on for the first chapter...**

Other books...

THE CORNISH VINTAGE SERIES

THE CORNISH VINTAGE DRESS SHOP

THE CORNISH VINTAGE JEWELLERY SHOP

THE PEACE, JOY AND LOVE SERIES

A MERRY CHRISTMAS AT THE CASTLE

A SPRING FLING AT HOTEL MAYFAIR

The Cornish Vintage Dress Shop

Chapter One

Rosie unlocked the door to The Cornish Vintage Dress Shop after popping out to grab a sandwich for lunch. It was like stepping into the arms of a loved one. Rosie immediately felt her body relax as she breathed in the familiar scent of roses. The smell transported her back to her grandmother's bedroom. Granny Maeve's perfume bottle was always on the dressing table and when Rosie was little, she would sneak in and cover herself with the delicious scent. Rosie unwound the scarf from her neck and hung it on the hook in the backroom. She pulled out her sandwich from her pocket and took a bite.

"Hello? Rosemary, are you there?"

Rosie jumped at the interruption. She hadn't heard the bell as the front door opened. She placed her cheese and chutney sandwich back on the counter. The voice was familiar. It was Wendy from the charity shop up the road. The old post office had closed down a few years ago and so Wendy had converted the building into a treasure trove filled with household items. Thankfully, Wendy didn't sell clothes. There was no competition between Ives-On-Sea's Bits "N" Bobs and Rosie's Cornish Vintage Dress Shop.

"Coming!" she called back. Rosie flicked the few crumbs from her jumper and walked towards the voice. Standing in the middle of her shop was the older lady with three black bin bags at her feet.

"There you are. I have to be quick as I've turned the sign on the door to 'closed'. These just came in with a house clearance. I'll see you soon, bye!"

"Thanks Wendy!" Rosie called after her, but it was too late. The door had already shut behind her. Wendy often dropped off clothes that came in with a house clearance, and in return, Rosie would give her any unexpected household items that appeared in her auction purchases. They supported each other.

All thoughts of her lunch disappeared as Rosie's eyes settled on the bags in front of her, each one filled to the brim with strangers' treasures. She was itching to dive in and look at them. Without pause for thought, Rosie emptied the contents of the first bag onto the floor and gasped. It was beautiful. She ran her fingers over the pile of clothes and sighed in contentment as she picked up a beautiful 1920s beaded dress. It was in exquisite condition, given its age. The blush pink beads sparkled in the overhead light and they let out a soft jingle as they brushed against each other. A handful of them showed signs of wear, but Rosie loved that. It showed that the dress had lived a life. It saddened Rosie to think she would never know the history behind it. Who had worn it? What parties had it been worn to? Rosie forced herself to put the dress back down and return her attention to the other items of clothing. Each piece was special in its own way; the black leather driving gloves to the fur stole. Although Rosie could appreciate the beauty of vintage furs, she refused to sell them in her shop. She would contact her buyer and they would collect them shortly.

After moving the bags of clothes to the storeroom, Rosie picked up the rest of her sandwich and took it onto the shop floor with her, sitting behind the till to eat. Her mind was still thinking about the clothes in the bags. Some items would need altering, others needed mending, and they all needed steaming before she could put them out for sale. Rosie finished her sandwich and took the empty plate back out to the kitchen area. As she walked past the mirror, she caught a glance of herself. She was smiling. Her red curly hair framed her face in a wild mess from the sea breeze, and her freckles were proudly speckled across her face. This Rosie was worlds apart from the woman she was only six months ago, but she was finally feeling happy and confident again. She was free, and there was nobody telling her how she should live her life. Rosie intended to keep it that way. At least she did until her phone bleeped.

There was a message from her mum asking her

how the shop was going and if they could come up in a few weeks. A message from her friend in London saying she missed her and asked when she was coming home from her little quarter-life crisis. Rosie chuckled darkly at the message. Her friends all thought she would soon come running to London. The last message sent a chill down Rosie's spine as she saw who it was from. It was Oliver. Her hands shook as she opened it.

I got a letter from my solicitor today. Do you really want me to sign the papers? I've bought a little flat. It will always be your home, too. I love you and miss you. Your Oli xxx.

Rosie felt her heart constrict as she read the words over and over. He could be so charming. When Rosie had met Oliver at a University dance, she had thought she was the luckiest girl in the world. They loved each other dearly, and they worked hard to create their perfect life together. Their friends all aspired to relationships like theirs. How silly they had been to think things were perfect. How silly Rosie had been to think everything had been perfect. She stuffed her phone into the drawer underneath the till and forced herself to concentrate on the shop.

It was early afternoon and she would soon have a few stray tourists peering through the window and wandering into her treasure trove of history. The welcoming warmth of Rosie's shop drew in lots people, and few left without purchasing a piece of history. The brass bell above the door chimed as a few stragglers walked in. They rubbed their hands, warming themselves up. Rosie watched as they took in the interior; their eyes lit up. The Cornish Vintage Dress Shop was a feast for the senses.

"Good afternoon!" Rosie called, greeting them with a big smile. The two women smiled back at her and wandered over to the display of jewellery that was scattered over the up-cycled sideboard. The jewellery ranged from costume earrings to antique diamond rings, some of which were on loan to the shop, as Rosie couldn't afford to purchase them. Many of the locals had donated items to help Rosie launch. They knew the shop would benefit their little seaside village and wanted to do everything they could to support it. Their generosity and good nature had overwhelmed Rosie.

Rosie's heart swelled with pride. She had poured her heart, her soul, and her life savings into this venture. Rosie had spent hours painstakingly deliberating over every inch of the shop. Her past life as an interior designer meant she knew just how to make the shop into the welcoming time capsule that made her heart soar every time she stepped inside. There was the herringbone floor, finished with a walnut stain, which was complimented by the dark wallpaper adorning the walls, covered with floral blooms in muted pinks, blues, yellows, oranges, and whites. It was dramatic - the perfect backdrop to selling snippets of people's lives. Velvet pink lampshades with tassels hanging from the ceiling flooded the shop with light. Rosie had displayed the vintage clothes, jewellery, shoes, bags, and accessories in several ways. From shelves made of driftwood, an up-cycled antique sideboard, and brass clothes rails. Each allowed the items to take centre stage. The up-cycled furniture had come from a lovely workshop in North Wales. Rosie had bonded with the owner, Alexis, over their love for vintage items. Alexis had helped Rosie find the perfect pieces for both practicality and prettiness.

"How much is this?" The woman dressed in a beautiful fur coat held up a costume brooch in the shape of a flower and scattered with faux pearls. Rosie checked her price list and informed the woman, who immediately decided she had to have it.

As Rosie took the brooch from the woman so she could wrap in some tissue paper, she glanced at the paper tag which was tied to it with a dusky pink ribbon. Each piece in the shop had a note attached detailing as much of its history as possible. Rosie had bought this brooch at an auction in London. There was a little number in the corner showing that there was an accompanying photograph. Rosie pulled out the leather book from below the till.

"Are you here on holiday?" Rosie made small talk as she flicked through the book, looking for the corresponding photograph.

"Yes, we are. Cornwall is so beautiful but we hate the crowds in summer, so we prefer coming in the winter. Ives-On-Sea is stunning all year round and the friendly welcome from the villagers makes up for the bitter cold." Rosie recognised the smile on the woman's face. It mirrored how she felt about the place she now called home.

"Here it is." Photograph number eighty was of a young woman, wrapped in a black coat with the brooch pinned to the front of it. Rosie remembered the story behind this piece. She had been lucky enough to meet a family member at the auction. The picture dated back to 1939 and showed the woman waving her husband off to war. The woman's great-granddaughter had told her that the brooch had been a present from her husband before he left for war. Tragically, he had died and never returned. The poignancy of the photo never failed to bring tears to Rosie's eyes.

"What a heartbreaking story," the woman commented. "Thank you. It means a lot to know the history behind it." The woman was ecstatic with her purchase and promised to return whenever she was holidaying in the area.

As the door shut, Rosie wiped a stray tear that was slowly making its way down her cheek. She knew all too well the sadness of losing a husband. The feeling of having your heart torn out and trampled upon. Rosie swallowed hard to stop the memories from overcoming her. All the pain and heartbreak had been worth it. Without it, she wouldn't be here. Now she had her own little slice of heaven on the Cornish coast.

354

ACKNOWLEDGEMENT

This book was an absolute joy to write. I've visited Padstow a few times now and I love the stunning landscape, the foodie scene, and the quaintness. Immediately, I knew I had to set a book there. The Cornish Vintage Jewellery Shop was a chance to indulge in the area's beauty while also exploring vintage jewellery.

There are several people I'd like to thank for their input on this book. Without them, The Cornish Vintage Jewellery Shop wouldn't be the escape I envisioned. Thank you Deborah Klée, Rosemary Millican, John Wheatley, Chris Towndrow, and Rebecca Chase.

A big thank you to my partner and dog for putting up with the click-clack of my keyboard at all hours, accepting that I live in my head most of the time, and supporting me through it all.

And finally, thank you to you for reading my book.

Printed in Great Britain
by Amazon

44129217R00209